KILLER CUTS

**Center Point
Large Print**

**This Large Print Book carries the
Seal of Approval of N.A.V.H.**

KILLER CUTS

A DEAD-END JOB MYSTERY

Elaine Viets

CENTER POINT PUBLISHING
THORNDIKE, MAINE

ACKNOWLEDGMENTS

Special thanks to Mario, Gracie Cuervo, James, and the other stylists and staff at the salon. I enjoyed watching artists at work. Gracie has an amazing ability to squeeze extra hours into the day for scheduling appointments.

Many other people helped me with this book, including Detective R. C. White, Fort Lauderdale Police Department (retired), and Rick McMahan, ATF Special Agent.

Special thanks to Valerie Cannata, Colby Cox, Jinny Gender, Karen Grace, Kay Gordy, Jack Klobnak, Bob Levine and Janet Smith. Thanks also to Carole Wantz, who could sell burnt matches. There are also some who I cannot publicly acknowledge. I appreciate their help all the same.

Thanks once more to the librarians at the St. Louis Public Library and Broward County Library. Anyone who believes the Internet made libraries obsolete has never needed a serious search.

Thanks to my editor, Kara Cesare, who thoughtfully critiques my manuscripts when many editors are too busy to do that. Thanks also to Lindsay Nouis, who always has time to help, to publicist Megan Swartz, and the staff at the Penguin Group. To my agent, David Hendin, who is still the best (sorry, he's not taking any more clients) and to

Patti Nunn and the staff at Breakthrough Promotions (she is taking more clients). And to my husband, Don Crinklaw, who is my friend, lover and first editor.

Thanks also to my sister bloggers on the Lipstick Chronicles for their advice and encouragement—Nancy Martin, Michele Martinez, Harley Jane Kozak, Sarah Strohmeyer, Lisa Daily, Kathy Sweeney, and Margie. You can read us at thelipstickchronicles.typepad.com.

I'm also grateful to the many booksellers who hand-sell my work.

Is the six-toed Thumbs a real cat? He belongs to librarian Anne Watts. She gave me the literary loan of her cat. Thumbs has six toes on each paw, like the famous Hemingway cats in Key West. Check out Thumbs' photo at www.elaineviets.com.

Chapter 1

Two tiny women in their sixties stood outside the door to Miguel Angel's salon on Las Olas. They were both about five feet tall and wore pantsuits, one pink and the other blue. Their hair was short and gray. They looked like little round twins.

Helen Hawthorne towered over them as she opened the salon door. "May I help you?" she asked.

"Is this where Miguel Angel works?" Ms. Pink asked. She pronounced his name "Mig-well" and said *Angel* with a flat Midwestern accent.

"*The* Miguel Angel," said Ms. Blue.

"Yes, he's the owner," Helen said.

"Wow, you're tall," Ms. Pink said, looking up at Helen.

"Six feet," Helen said.

"Are you a model?" Ms. Blue asked.

"I'm only a gopher," Helen said. "I go for drinks and magazines for the clients, fetch lunches and run errands for Miguel Angel. I'm too old to model."

"You don't look old," said Ms. Pink. "Your dark hair is pretty."

"Thanks," Helen said. "Getting my hair done by Miguel Angel is the best perk of this job."

"We saw the *People* magazine article about how he changed LaDonna and gave her a new look. It saved her acting career," Ms. Pink said.

"'From street to elite,'" Ms. Blue said. "We'd love to meet him. He's a real artist."

"He's here," Helen said. "Come on in."

"Can we actually come inside?" Ms. Pink asked.

"Sure, why not?"

"Because we're fat," Ms. Blue said. She said the F-word as if being slightly chubby was shameful.

"We like fat," Helen said. She didn't add that the salon really liked fat wallets.

The two women entered cautiously, as if they expected a supermodel with a flaming sword to banish them. They surveyed the sculpted black-and-chrome client chairs, the chic black dryers, the outrageous bouquets of flowers. Billie Holiday was crooning "Stormy Weather."

The salon's softly lit mirrors were designed to flatter. The floor sparkled as if sprinkled with diamond dust.

"Oh, my," Ms. Pink said.

"It's beautiful," Ms. Blue said.

"Everyone here is beautiful," Ms. Pink said.

Black-clad stylists were working on two models in the sculpted chairs. Paolo was doing the blonde's color: Her head was crowned with tinfoil for highlights. Richard was adding extensions to the glossy hair of a brunette. You could have built condos on their jutting cheekbones.

Ms. Blue ran her hands over the leather scrapbooks on the salon's rosewood center table.

"Those are Miguel Angel's credits," Helen said.

Ms. Pink opened one book. "Look at that. Miguel Angel has been in *Vogue*, *W*, *Glamour*, *Vanity Fair* and *People*. He did the MTV awards show. He's worked with so many celebrities."

"May we have his autograph to take back to Pittsburgh?" Ms. Pink asked. "Our friends won't believe we actually had the nerve to walk in here."

"Let me see if he's busy," Helen said. "Would you like some water or tea?"

"Oh, no, we can't afford to stay," Ms. Blue said. "We just wanted to say hello. Everyone talks about his work. He's famous."

"And handsome," Ms. Pink said. "Even if he won't be interested in us."

They giggled. Helen wondered if they knew Miguel was gay, or if they were talking about their cute, frumpy figures.

"What would it cost us to get our hair done here?" Ms. Blue asked.

"Three hundred for a color and cut," Helen said. The price tripped off her tongue as if everyone paid that much for hair care.

"Oh, dear," Ms. Blue said. "I don't think I can manage that. I'm still paying off my Saturn."

"Besides, we don't have much hair to work with," Ms. Pink said.

"Never underestimate Miguel Angel," Helen said. "Let me ask if he's seeing visitors."

Miguel Angel worked in his own alcove at the back of the salon. He was blow-drying the tawny-haired Kim Hammond, this season's top model. Miguel looked dangerous in his trademark black leather pants and black shirt with the collar turned up.

He wore his two enormous blow-dryers in black leather holsters, like six-guns. Why not? The man produced killer hair.

"Two nice women from Pittsburgh want to meet you," Helen said. "They admire your work. They want your autograph."

"That's sweet," Miguel Angel said. He was an international celebrity stylist, in a class with the hunky Oribe, and Frédéric Fekkai. Cuban-born Miguel Angel specialized in making aging beauties look glamorous. Actresses swore his touch could revive their flagging careers, and flew into his Fort Lauderdale salon from around the country. Ordinary women paid big bucks for his remakes.

Miguel asked Kim, "Do you mind if the ladies come back to meet me?"

"Really, Miguel. Are you giving tours now?" the model said in a bored voice.

"It's good for business," Miguel Angel said.

"But Pittsburgh?" Kim said with a sneer.

"There's money everywhere in America," he said.

"Then bring them back," Kim said. "Give the little people a thrill."

What a snob, Helen thought. In a few years, she'll be begging Miguel Angel for a new look.

Helen gave Ms. Pink and Ms. Blue the good news. "Is Angel his last name?" Ms. Pink asked.

"No, it's part of his first name," Helen said. "Cubans, especially the men, are partial to double names. They prefer combos like Marco Antonio, Juan Carlos and Miguel Angel."

"Sort of like my Southern cousins," Ms. Blue said. "I have a Billy Bob and a Larry Joe."

"Yes," Helen said. "Let's go back and meet him before his next appointment."

Helen took off across the salon with her long, loping stride. The two women struggled to keep up. "Stop! I mean, slower, please," Ms. Pink said. "Our legs aren't as long as yours."

Helen slowed. Mss. Pink and Blue stopped when they saw Miguel Angel brushing Kim's long mane.

"Look at her hair," Ms. Pink said, in an awed voice. "It's like a silk curtain."

"You do such beautiful work," Ms. Blue said, handing Miguel Angel an old-fashioned autograph book. "Would you sign this?"

"I'd be delighted." When Helen had first started working at the shop last month, she'd expected Miguel Angel to sneer like Kim, but he was surprisingly kind.

"Did anyone ever tell you that you look like a young Elvis?" Ms. Pink said, handing him a sheet of hotel stationery.

"Thank you," he said as he signed it.

Ana Luisa, the salon receptionist, came back.

"Excuse me, Miguel Angel. Honey is here for her final appointment before the wedding."

"We'd better leave," Ms. Pink and Ms. Blue said. "Thank you," they chorused, then toddled toward the door, trailing girlish giggles.

"Just a warning," Miguel Angel whispered to Helen. "Honey is six months pregnant. She may say something. Act like you already know she's having a baby."

"Miguel, I wouldn't say anything rude. This isn't 1950."

"I know, but Honey used to be a nurse and she is very frank. You don't have a poker face. Your eyebrow went up when I said she was pregnant."

"I was just surprised," Helen said. "You never gossip about your clients. I've been trying to get the dirt on LaDonna since I started here, and all you'll say is she's nice."

"There is no dirt on LaDonna," Miguel Angel said. "I leave the gossip to my clients. Be careful what you say around Honey."

"Why?" Helen asked.

"Her fiancé is Kingman 'King' Oden. He writes the Stardust gossip blog and hosts the TV show *Stardust at Night*."

"Yuck. He's King Odious, right?" Helen asked.

"That's his nickname, but we never use it in this salon."

"But he is nasty," she said. "The man makes fun of older celebrities who put on weight and young ones who are too skinny. He enjoys revealing who is in rehab. Didn't he out a couple of women actresses as lesbians?"

"That's him," Miguel Angel said. "King is mean. Lots of people hate him. But even more read his blog and watch his show. Two weeks ago, someone gave King a photo of Bianca Phillips without her makeup, and he posted it on his blog. Poor Bianca looked a hundred years old. She nearly lost a movie deal because of King."

"Did Honey take the Bianca photo here?"

"I don't know," Miguel Angel said. "But if there's a rumor King got that photo at my salon, it could ruin my business. Go help her."

Helen handed Honey Miguel Angel's signature black silk robe embroidered with his name. Honey took the robe and a hanger into the changing room. She was a honey blonde, like her name, with a pale oval face and small, delicate features. Her heels were high and skinny, and her legs were long and encased in designer denim. She was wearing a gauzy top. Now that Helen knew Honey was pregnant, she thought she saw the outline of what King and his ilk called a baby bump.

Honey carried a large, flat white box. She presented it to Miguel Angel as if it held the crown jewels. "That's my bridal veil. It's silk illusion. That's very soft tulle."

Miguel had done enough weddings to recognize illusion of all types. He opened the box and gently lifted out the veil. "It's long," he said.

"It's a ninety-inch circle veil with silk-edged stitching." Honey handed him a smaller white box. "This is my tiara. It's crystal stars, in King's honor—for Stardust, you know. We're also getting Swarovski crystal stars for the dinner guests' place settings. We got a good deal on them—only seventy dollars a star."

"How many guests?" Helen asked.

"Two hundred," Honey said.

Helen did the math. Honey was spending fourteen thousand dollars on wedding favors. She'd already spent nearly every cent of her savings to be one of Miguel's Angels. He'd transformed her from a practical nurse with thick-soled shoes into the spike-heeled consort of King Oden.

"We'd better get started," Miguel said. "The wedding is Saturday, and we still haven't decided on a hairstyle."

"I'd like to try my hair up this time, in a French twist," Honey said. "Sort of Grace Kelly-ish. King will like that. Very classy."

"Phoebe," Miguel Angel commanded his assistant, "wash Honey's hair."

"But I washed it this morning," Honey said.

"It will look better after my treatment," he said.

Many customers thought they'd save time or money by washing their own hair. But they didn't get out all the soap, and their hair looked flat and lifeless when it was styled.

"I use something special that will brighten the color," Miguel said. "You don't need your roots done yet."

Phoebe tucked a towel around Honey's neckline and washed her hair. The two women chatted like old friends. Phoebe usually didn't get along well with the women customers, but she knew how to flatter and flirt with the older men.

The hair washing, from soaping to a mini scalp massage, took almost ten minutes. When a wet-haired Honey was installed in Miguel Angel's chair, Helen asked, "May I bring you a drink? How about a magazine?"

"Just water," Honey said.

Helen went back to the prep room and poured ice and cold water into a crystal glass, added a thin lemon slice, then wrapped the glass with a paper napkin so the bride's delicate fingers wouldn't be chilled.

When she returned, Miguel Angel was blowing Honey's hair dry. In half an hour, he had it up on her head in a golden twist.

"Now the veil," he said. "Stand up."

Honey stood. Miguel carefully draped the veil over her hair, pinned it in place, and added the tiara. The crystals caught the light and gave Honey an angelic halo.

"Beautiful," he said.

"This is how I want to look," Honey said. "Now will you brush out my hair? I want King to be surprised on Saturday."

Miguel Angel unpinned the veil, and Helen carefully folded it and packed it away. The tiara went back in its smaller box. When Miguel finished brushing out Honey's shoulder-length hair, the bride-to-be gave Ana Luisa her credit card, added a substantial tip for Miguel Angel, handed Helen five bucks and gave Phoebe a thick wad of money.

But still she didn't leave. "I'm worried about Saturday," Honey said. "All of King's celebrity friends will be there. What if something goes wrong?"

"What can go wrong?" Miguel Angel said. "We're supposed to have beautiful weather, and you're a beautiful bride."

"What if I lose the baby?" Honey asked. "He wants a son more than he wants me."

"That's not true," Miguel Angel soothed. "He loved you before you were pregnant."

"But he's only marrying me because I said I'd abort the kid unless he walked me down the aisle without a prenup. I had Daddy Dearest by the short and curlies. The deal was, no son if I had to sign a prenup."

Helen quickly turned away, afraid Honey would see the shock on her face.

"I really wanted a girl," Honey said. "But King

said it had to be a boy or else. He wanted proof. I had to show him the baby's ultrasound."

"King will adore the mother of his only son," Miguel Angel said. "Do you love him?"

"Of course," Honey said. "King's first marriage was a mistake. He'd knocked up Posie, and they had to hurry and get married by a judge at city hall. Posie was so desperate she signed the worst prenup agreement ever. But we're doing this marriage right. King wants a traditional white wedding with all his friends there and a real honeymoon. He loves me. He tells me so all the time. And I love him to death. I mean, till death parts us."

"You're just having a case of bridal nerves," Miguel Angel said. "The weather will be beautiful, and so will you. What could go wrong?"

"I guess we'll find out on Saturday," the bride said, and kissed him lightly on the cheek.

Chapter 2

The round bed was made for orgies. Surrounded by four white Roman columns, it had a mound of what looked like whipped cream in the center.

Honey, the bride who would spend tonight in that bed, lovingly stroked the creamy pile of taffeta on the white spread.

"What do you think of my wedding dress?" she asked.

"It's lovely," Helen said.

"It's just like the dress Sarah Jessica Parker wore in *Sex and the City*," Honey said.

Not quite, Helen thought. The dressmaker had skillfully added another poufed tier to hide Honey's pregnancy.

"My wedding dress and veil cost twenty thousand dollars, not counting the diamonds," Honey said. She wasn't shy about mentioning prices. She'd gambled her savings to snag King.

Helen wondered how many other women had been on this round bed. King was a notorious womanizer. Gossip said King might forget a scandalous story if a woman was willing, but that was never reported in his blog. King had a taste for tarts, and not the kind from the bakery.

Society was amazed when King announced his engagement. His bride was a cut above the bosomy tramps he usually dated. Honey's pregnancy had stayed out of the gossip columns—so far.

"King said nothing but the best for me," Honey said, as she stroked her fabulous dress.

That's what she was getting, if you measured everything by money. Honey's wedding-day makeup and hair would cost about three thousand dollars. Her Dior heels were another eight hundred. Helen, who used to work at a bridal salon, estimated the cost of the wedding and lavish dinner at King's waterfront palace on Hendin Island at close to a million dollars.

"Where are you going on your honeymoon?" Helen asked, to be polite.

"We're spending tonight here," Honey said, patting the bed. "Tomorrow, we're flying to Paradise Island in King's private jet. He got a good deal at Atlantis: an ocean-view suite for only eight hundred a day."

"Is that all?" Helen asked, trying to keep out the sarcasm. That one-day room rate was almost what she made in a month.

"Well, that's not bad, considering," Honey said, as if she'd made her living carrying silver trays instead of bedpans. She checked her diamond watch. "It's one thirty. Almost time for the photos before the wedding. Will you help me into my dress?"

Helen carefully lifted the creamy cloud of taffeta off the bed. Miguel Angel ducked out onto the bedroom balcony for a quick cigarette as Honey tossed her white lace peignoir over the dressing table chair. Her long strapless slip was embroidered with lace. Helen thought it was pretty enough to serve as a wedding dress, except that it didn't hide King Junior.

Honey stepped into her wedding dress. Helen zipped it up and fastened the dozens of tiny hook-and-eye catches, then helped Honey arrange the poufed skirt. The expensive taffeta made a delicious rustling sound.

Honey handed her a distinctive Tiffany box. "Would you help with my necklace, please?"

21

"Very pretty," Helen said.

"It's a gift from King—double-drop diamonds in platinum."

Helen figured the diamonds cost even more than the dress. She fastened the safety catch on the clasp and called, "We're ready."

Miguel Angel returned, trailing tobacco smoke like a fallen angel. Once again, Helen was startled by his good looks. He had thick, shiny black hair with a slight curl and dark eyes. His long lashes were the envy of his female clients. He was strong and slender, except for a belly that came and went, depending on his craving for Cuban sandwiches.

"Miguel, those cigarettes will kill you," Honey said.

"Nobody gets out of this world alive," he said. "And you are not a nurse anymore."

"Will you put on my veil, Miguel Angel?" Honey asked.

He draped the bride's smooth shoulders with his satin styling cape and began pinning the long tulle veil into her honey-colored hair. Miguel Angel's black makeup case was open on the dressing table. Helen stood nearby, handing him hair brushes and pins, like an operating room nurse assisting a surgeon. Once the veil was in place, he added the crystal crown.

"Look, there's Phoebe," Honey said, pointing out the window.

Miguel Angel's assistant was flirting with a

silver-haired gentleman. He was gazing deep into Phoebe's cleavage, and he had lots to see. Phoebe wore a peacock blue dress with a plunging neckline. Even from this distance, Phoebe's dress looked expensive. Helen wondered how she could afford it.

"Her blue dress looks like my bridesmaid dresses," Honey said.

Miguel made a sound that was almost a growl.

"I hope you didn't mind that I invited your assistant as a guest, Miguel," Honey said. "I have so few gal pals."

"I do not need her," Miguel Angel said.

Helen thought she heard a flicker of malice in his statement. Helen suspected Phoebe might be trolling for a sugar daddy here. If she failed to find a rich man, and the ambitious Phoebe could last with Miguel Angel for a year, she'd be welcome at almost any salon.

Helen had no such ambitions and no cosmetology license. She survived on tips, minimum wage, and running the errands that Phoebe avoided. Helen was going to be a June bride, too. But Helen's wedding to Phil, Helen's private eye fiancé, would be nothing like this extravaganza.

Honey studied her face in the mirror with obvious satisfaction, then frowned. "I think my skin looks a little puffy underneath my right eye. Can you fix that?"

Miguel Angel touched the area with a soft camel-hair brush. Helen was sure there was no makeup on the brush, but the small gesture satisfied Honey.

"That's better," she said. "Let's see. I have something new, my wedding dress. Something borrowed, a lace handkerchief from my sister, Melody. My garter is blue. Now all I need is something old."

"There's the groom," Miguel Angel whispered in Helen's ear, as he reached for more hairpins.

His words seemed to conjure up the man. King appeared in the bedroom doorway. He was definitely old—every inch of him. King was naked as a newborn, and not nearly as cute. His breasts were bigger than his bride's, and his sagging chest was covered with a thatch of gray hair. It didn't match the spiky black hair on his head. His manhood dangled under a white, waxy gut. It was definitely not king-sized. Helen wondered how much his rivals would pay to know King was hung like a hamster.

Helen winced and wished she hadn't seen so much of the man. Sixty-one wasn't old for some people, but King looked every year.

"Honey, you're beautiful," King said. His smile lit up the room. "Stand up, so I can see you."

Miguel whipped off the cape and Honey obediently rose and did a pirouette.

"She's got a great body," King said. "She could have worked at my old strip club."

Helen was appalled. King talked about Honey as

24

if she were livestock. But the bride blushed prettily, as if the groom had given her a charming compliment.

"That's how I started, you know," King said. "I used to own my own strip club with a partner, Wyllis Drifford. Then I noticed how many celebrities hung around the strippers, and I tipped off a New York gossip columnist. Wyllis went apeshit and bought me out. He barred me from the club. I took the money and decided, Why go for peanuts when I can make big bucks with gossip?

"I parked my car down the street and watched the club. Three nights later, Ramona showed up drunk. She walked out at two in the morning kissing Amber, the club's hottest stripper. Had her tongue down Amber's throat. I snapped their photo, and my career was made. Amber got fired. She was supposed to be a babe, not a dyke. Nearly ruined Wyllis' business. A few more scoops and I started a blog and got my own cable TV show. Now I have six million readers—and probably six million enemies."

He seemed proud of that.

The naked King wandered into the master bath, left the door open, and sat down on the toilet. The bathroom was mirrored. Helen turned her head away in disgust.

Miguel Angel threw down the thick roll brush he'd been holding. "No!" he shouted. "I do not have to put up with this. That man is a pig! He does not have enough manners to close the door. I am leaving."

"It's my house," King said as he flushed the toilet. "I can do what I want."

"So can I," Miguel Angel said. "Good-bye."

"No!" The bride grabbed Miguel Angel's arm. "Please stay. I'll double your fee."

"It is not worth the money. Honey, you are beautiful. You are sweet. You do not have to marry this man."

"But I do, Miguel Angel. I'm not getting any younger. I'm thirty-eight and I'm pregnant. This is my last chance. You don't understand King. He's a diamond in the rough. Please do it for me."

Honey looked so sad, Miguel Angel agreed. "But only if he puts on some clothes," the stylist said.

Honey kissed King's cheek. "Sweetheart, you have to get dressed for the ceremony," she said. "Why not do it now?"

King went into his dressing room to change.

A cheerful Latina in black pants, sensible shoes and a white blouse stood in the bedroom doorway. She held a video camera. "Are you ready for your pictures?" she asked. "My name is Mireya. I am photographer Marco Antonio's assistant. I'd like to start with you preparing for your wedding. Do you want your maid of honor in the photo?"

"That's my sister, Melody," Honey said. "She's outside. I'll call her cell phone. Do you need to get your camera?"

"No, this takes still shots and video." Mireya started shooting the bride at her dressing table. Helen stepped out into the hall so her reflection wouldn't show in the mirror.

"She's a great-looking girl, isn't she?" a man said. King had crept up behind Mireya. He was wearing the ugliest tux Helen had seen since her high school prom. It was black with brown lapels. The cut seemed expensive. He wore a brown bow tie and shiny brown shoes. He was drinking straight from a bourbon bottle like an aging rock star.

"I own all this, and that yacht out there," King said. He made a sweeping gesture to include the spectacular view of the water outside the hall windows—and the huge swimming pool. Below them was a living room covered with acres of white carpet. It had a mirrored fireplace, a black lacquer television cabinet trimmed with gold, black leather couches flanked by gold-and-black end tables, and a pool table.

"I live on Hendin Island, the richest real estate in Fort Lauderdale," he said.

"That's nice," Helen said.

"With my TV show and gossip blog, I'm raking in the money."

"Good for you," Helen said.

"It will mean more when I have a son. Don't get me wrong, I love my daughter. Cassie's a great kid. But sons are special." He took a big gulp of bourbon. "Do me a favor and get your boss, will you? I have to ask him something."

"Sure," Helen said, eager to escape.

In Honey's dressing room, a blonde in a peacock blue dress was fluffing the bride's veil. That must be the maid of honor, Helen thought. Melody looked like her sister, only older and tougher. Her dress was almost a duplicate of Phoebe's.

The Latina photographer snapped pictures and issued instructions: "Turn your head this way. Melody, please lower your arm. You're blocking my view of the bride."

"Miguel Angel, the hair at the back of my neck won't stay in place," Honey said. Mireya stopped taking pictures.

"It's okay," Honey told her. "Take his picture. Miguel is an important part of my wedding."

Miguel Angel trimmed a millimeter off one lock. He had his long scissors in his right hand when Helen said, "The groom would like to speak with you."

"Go talk to him, please," Honey said, patting Miguel Angel's arm. "I'm sure King wants to apologize."

Miguel Angel reluctantly left the room. "You wish to see me?" he asked King.

"Yeah, sorry I blew up at you in there, buddy." King slapped him on the back. "Nerves, I guess."

Nerves? Helen wondered. She made no effort to

hide that she was listening. So were Honey, Melody and Mireya.

"I wanted to make deal with you," King said. "You get the big celebrities in your salon. You give me a little information, and I'll make it worth your while."

"No," Miguel Angel said. "I've told you this before. I don't need your money."

"Everyone needs money," King said.

"If my clients do not feel safe, they will go somewhere else." Miguel Angel's eyes narrowed and his voice was a hissing whisper. He was about to explode. "I kept Honey's secret. I didn't tell your competitors that King Junior is a bastard, like his father. The boy's problem is an accident of birth. You are a self-made man."

King's beefy arm reached out and grabbed the stylist by the throat. "Listen, you Cuban cocksucker. I've got friends in the city and state government. I can have that salon of yours closed down for so many violations, your dyed head will spin. Got it?"

Miguel Angel nodded, then shook off King's arm and whipped the scissor points into the man's neck. The stylist's arms were ropes of muscle from years of wielding heavy dryers and wrestling with unruly hair. "And I can kill you, you fat, lazy American. No one will care."

"Stop!" the bride ran out and forced her way between the two men. "This is my wedding day.

Behave. Both of you." Tears brimmed in her eyes.

Miguel Angel and King backed off. Helen saw a small dot of blood where Miguel's scissors had pierced King's neck. Mireya still had her camera running.

"Honey, I apologize for what I said about your baby," Miguel Angel said. "I lost my temper. No child is to blame for his father."

"Uh!" Honey said. She was whiter than her dress.

"What's the matter?" King was suddenly frightened.

"The baby kicked me," Honey said. "I think we've upset your son with our fighting."

"Sit down, sweetheart," King said, and led her to a chair. "What can I get you?"

"Just let me sit for a minute," Honey said. Tears leaked down her face.

King dropped to his knees and threw his arms around her. "Oh, baby, I don't want anything to happen to you."

Helen wasn't sure if he was talking to his bride or his son.

King kissed Honey gently. "I love you. What can I do?"

"Please see to our guests while Mireya finishes the pictures up here," Honey said.

The groom picked up the bourbon bottle and lurched downstairs. Melody carried in a glass of water. "Drink this, sis," she said. "Everyone gets on edge at a wedding. It doesn't mean a thing."

Helen and Miguel Angel slipped out to the balcony, where the stylist fired up another cigarette. "Why is Honey marrying that man?" Helen asked. "Nurses make a decent living."

"Not enough to live on Hendin Island," Miguel Angel said. "She wants a baby, and she's nearly forty. King is supposed to be worth ninety million dollars. She likes money so much she's willing to put up with that drunken druggie."

"He's using drugs?" Helen asked.

"That's not powdered sugar on his nose."

"But he's drinking heavily," Helen said. "And he just had a heart attack."

"Maybe she thinks he won't live long," Miguel Angel said. "I hope so, for her sake."

Chapter 3

The afternoon sun gilded the bride's taffeta wedding gown and turned her nose into an oil slick.

"My nose is shiny," Honey wailed. "I can feel it."

Miguel Angel patted it with a sponge to keep Honey's complexion photo ready.

"Why don't you use powder?" Honey asked.

"It makes your face look dry and old," Miguel said. "Brides are supposed to look dewy."

Honey shut up at the mention of the O-word. The bride showed no trace of her recent tears, no sign that her future husband had threatened to kill her hairstylist, or that her baby had been kicking up a storm. Hollywood has lost a great actress, Helen thought.

She guarded the makeup case and tried not to look bored. She was stuck doing Phoebe's job. Again. Worse, she had to watch Honey's "gal pal" flirt outrageously with a man who looked like a dissipated grandfather. Helen thought he might be a former TV host who'd had DUI problems.

"You're funny," Phoebe said, and giggled. The white-haired man puffed out his scrawny chest and put his hand on Phoebe's nearly bare shoulder. It inched toward her breast.

Mireya, the photographer's assistant, crawled along the pink pavers on the terrace, moving pots of pink impatiens away from the bride's skirt. Her brown curls shone in the sun.

"Look this way, Honey," the photographer, Marco Antonio, said. "Tilt your chin up."

Honey tilted.

An inhuman screech rent the air. Mireya nearly dropped a pot of flowers.

"It's okay," Honey said, chin still tilted at an unnatural angle. "It's one of King's peacocks. It's mating season."

The gaudy bird strutted in front of the bride and fanned its fabulous tail, screeching again, hoping to impress a dun-colored peahen six feet away.

"Beautiful," the photographer said. "Hold still.

Nobody move." Marco Antonio dropped to his knees as if he were worshiping the bride and the bird, and clicked his camera.

Helen thought of her mother's favorite saying: "The most beautiful things in the world are the most useless, peacocks and lilies." Later, Helen learned that quote was from John Ruskin. She never thought beauty was useless. Honey's good looks got her this peacock palace—and her ugly groom.

Honey waited until the photographer finished, then said, "King loves those peacocks. He read somewhere that the old-time estates had them. He bought three peacocks and three peahens. The hens are drab and dowdy. Peacocks are noisy, bad-tempered birds, and they wake me up every morning during mating season."

Helen could see the groom lurking by a pink stucco arch near the terrace. King was taking swigs of bourbon and practically drooling over Mireya's rounded rear end. Mating season, indeed. The man was getting married shortly, and he was mentally undressing the photographer's assistant. Helen wondered whether Honey knew about his antics and turned a blind eye. Was she that desperate to marry money?

The peacock folded its tail and strutted away. "You'll lose those tail feathers come August, mister," Honey said to the departing bird. "Then you'll have nothing to crow about.

"I hate their screeching call," she told Helen. "But King says it's the sound of money. That's why I had my attendants wear peacock blue."

A woman in a peacock blue dress marched down the aisle on the terrace and took a seat in a white folding chair on the groom's side. Her blond hair was longer than her short, tight skirt. Her face was deeply tanned. Dark lipstick crept into the cracks on her lips.

"Is she a bridesmaid?" Helen asked.

Honey laughed, her voice rich with contempt. "Her? That's King's old girlfriend, Tiffany. She's a stripper. Tiffany expected King to marry her, but he chose me instead." Her voice was smug with satisfaction.

"Tiffany is very bitter," Honey said. "But King insisted she be invited to our wedding—and she had the nerve to show up."

Tiffany had a lean, muscular body with over-sized breasts. Helen wondered if she'd worn the skimpy dress to show King—and everyone else—what he was missing.

"There's my bridesmaid, Cassie, standing by the palm tree. She is King's daughter."

Helen expected Cassie to be as gross as her father. But the young woman was small and slender with shiny gold hair. She wore only a little pink lipstick. Her peacock blue dress hugged her curves without being too tight. How did the disgusting King spawn this elegant creature?

The older woman beside Cassie was a classic Boca babe. Even from a distance, Helen could see her forehead was smoothly paralyzed by Botox. Her eyes had an Asian slant from too many surgeries. Her bee-stung lips bulged with collagen. Her dress was almost the same style as Cassie's, but it didn't look as good on her.

"The older one is King's ex-wife, Posie," Honey whispered. "She's furious that he divorced her to marry me."

"King invited her, too?" Helen asked.

"Yes, it's awkward, but I'm making the best of it," Honey said. "King invited a lot of sex-industry workers, too. I'm not friends with them, but it's good for his business. King pays strippers and hookers to find information for his blog and TV show. That's what keeps this house going."

Helen surveyed the huge pink Spanish-style mansion, the long green lawns and bright gardens. The house that sleaze built, one dirty little act at a time.

"Are your friends from the hospital here?" Helen asked.

"Uh, no," Honey said. She hesitated, then added quickly, "They were busy."

Or you were busy, Helen thought, dropping the people you knew before you climbed your way to riches.

"We had room for only two hundred guests," the bride said. "I'm so glad we have good weather and didn't have to cram the tables inside. We don't have a backyard because of the Olympic-sized pool."

The pool looked like something in a resort hotel, with a swim-up bar and a waterfall. Pool toys bobbed in the water, including a floating chaise with a drink holder.

"You can see the problem," Honey said.

Nice problem, Helen thought.

"King bought the house next door and had it torn down so we could have the terrace and the fountain," Honey said. "We needed to spread out a little."

More not-so-subtle bragging. Waterfront houses on Hendin Island started at four million dollars. The land was so valuable it should have been sold by the inch.

A florist struggled to carry an overwrought bouquet of blue and purple flowers to a bridal arch covered with purple orchids and peacock feathers.

"That's a beautiful bridal arch," Helen said.

"Thirty thousand dollars, and it will be dead tomorrow," the bride said. Conspicuous consumption made her glow. A breeze rustled her skirt, and Honey's sister, Melody, held it to keep it from blowing into the fountain. Helen grabbed the long veil as the wind caught it.

"Do we have time for more pictures?" Honey asked.

"Less than fifteen minutes until the wedding,"

the photographer said, checking his watch. "You might want to freshen up."

Honey gathered her skirts and hurried toward the house, her sister trailing behind her. Miguel Angel followed with his sponge. As Helen closed the makeup case, she heard the sound of a sharp slap. An angry young woman said, "Get your hands off me. You bought my pictures, not me."

A red-faced Mireya charged out from under the stucco arches along the side of the house, her dark curls bobbing. King strolled off in the other direction, a red handprint on his cheek. Helen wondered if it would fade before the ceremony.

King chugged more bourbon and surveyed his kingdom. The rows of white chairs set up on the thick green grass were nearly filled.

Helen wondered which guests were in the so-called sex industry. She decided the men in the shiny suits were in the business. Some were lean, some were fat, but they all had a hungry, feral look, as if all the sex they could buy wouldn't satisfy them. Many looked vaguely familiar, but Helen couldn't put names with the faces. She assumed they were celebrities King had promoted or ruined—or both.

Peacock blue was the color this season for the women. There were so many dresses in that shade, Helen couldn't keep the women apart. All had dyed blond hair. Many had leathery, tanned faces, lean bodies, and a slightly dirty look to their skin.

Helen decided they were strippers or hookers.

The Latino photographer and his pretty assistant wandered everywhere with their cameras, taking pictures of the flowers, the food, the musicians and the wedding party. Many of the men gave young Mireya hungry looks, as if they were predators at a watering hole instead of guests at a wedding.

Phoebe was still giggling with the older gentleman guest.

"Helen," Miguel Angel called from a window, "I need you here."

Helen hurried upstairs. I hope that worthless Phoebe marries the scrawny old guy with his skinny arms and flabby bottom, Helen thought, as she lugged the heavy case. Serves her right. She'll work for that man's money a lot harder than she works at the salon.

"Hurry, Miguel Angel," the bride said. "The ceremony is starting soon. We don't want to keep King waiting."

"He might grab someone else," Helen said.

Miguel Angel frowned at her. He must have noticed the groom's wandering hands.

"Are you feeling better?" Helen asked Honey.

"Oh yes. My boy has a kick like a soccer star. That's what I tell his daddy." Honey paused, then said, "King didn't mean any harm. He can be a little moody."

Moody? Threatening to ruin a man was moody?

"He shouldn't have been walking around without

his clothes," Honey said. "He's so comfortable with me, he forgets sometimes. I'm a nurse, so I don't count."

"I understand," Helen said. I understand that you will put up with anything for his money, she thought.

"Look!" Honey pointed out the window at a portly man in black robes. "There's the judge who is marrying us."

Helen remembered the groom's threat that he knew people in government who could ruin Miguel Angel. King had at least one judge in his pocket.

"He's a circuit court judge. King doesn't associate with criminal judges." Honey made it sound as if the judges were criminals.

"There's Jonathan, the governor's assistant." Honey pointed to a pale young man sweating in a gray suit. "See that woman in the coral dress? She's a city commissioner. The man in the Armani tux with the pretty gray hair is King's lawyer, Harris. He's giving me away."

"Not your father?" Helen asked.

"My father's dead," Honey said.

"I'm sorry," Helen said.

"It was a long time ago," Honey said, and shrugged. "The short man in the shiny black suit with the red tie is King's old partner from the strip club, Wyllis Drifford. He's suing King."

"And he came to the wedding?" Helen said.

"King says keep your friends close and your enemies closer."

Helen looked at the colorful panorama spread out below them—the women in jewel tones, the men in drab suits—and wondered how many were King's enemies.

The musicians began "Air on the G String." Helen thought that choice was appropriate, considering the groom's interest in strippers and strip clubs.

The bride got a panicked look, like Cinderella as the clock struck midnight. For one instant, she looked like she might run away.

"That's the processional," Honey said. "I have to be downstairs."

Miguel Angel gave Honey's face one last dab with the sponge and touched up her lipstick. Then he gave her a light kiss on the cheek. Honey squared her shoulders and picked up her white rose bouquet. Melody helped her sister down the carpeted stairs, holding the poufy skirt.

"Be careful you don't catch your heel," Melody said. "Those shoes are high."

She tottered downstairs on equally high heels. In the living room, the florist handed Melody a star-shaped bouquet of blue flowers.

The wedding party lined up. The groomsmen waited by the pink stucco arch. The aisle was white satin, flanked by candles and swags of greenery.

King's daughter walked down the aisle first, to murmurs of approval from the wedding guests. "Cassie has class, even if her father doesn't," Helen said to Miguel Angel.

Melody was next. She clutched her bouquet as if it might save her from drowning.

Handel's "Arrival of the Queen of Sheba" announced the bride's entrance. Helen thought it fit Honey's newly exalted opinion of herself. The groom dropped his bourbon bottle in a potted palm and walked out to meet his bride. The bottle seemed nearly empty, but he didn't stagger.

The bride promised to love King until death parted them.

"She doesn't deserve this," Miguel Angel said. "She's too good for him."

"But not too good for his money," Helen said.

Miguel glared at her.

"I now pronounce you man and wife," the judge said. "May I present the new Mr. and Mrs. Kingman Oden?"

The wedding guests applauded. Someone yelled, "Long live the King!"

The musicians struck up Handel's *Royal Fireworks* "Overture." Helen wondered if the royal theme was deliberate. She guessed it was better than "Pomp and Circumstance."

The triumphant Honey towed her red-faced, sweating groom down the aisle. Helen could see the relief on the bride's face.

"Does she know that man is no prize?" Helen asked.

"Poor Honey," Miguel Angel said. "Her troubles are just starting."

Miguel Angel had delivered a prophesy on the marriage.

Chapter 4

S oon you'll be the bride in your own receiving line," Miguel Angel said to Helen. "I could fix your hair like Honey's."

"Not unless you can give me her chin," Helen said. "My chin disappears when you pile my hair up on my head."

She waited for Miguel to disagree. Instead he said, "Maybe it's better to wear your hair long and loose. But I can do your hair and makeup so you'll be the most beautiful bride in Fort Lauderdale. It will be my gift."

"I'll take it," Helen said. "But my wedding won't be like Honey's. It will be in Margery's backyard, with tiki torches, box wine, hors d'oeuvres from Publix, and naked chairs."

"Naked chairs?" Miguel Angel looked puzzled.

"All the chairs at this wedding dinner have rented covers," Helen said.

"Then I will sit naked," Miguel Angel said.

Melody, the maid of honor, widened her eyes at Miguel's remark.

"Uh, that lost something in the translation," Helen said to Melody, and pasted on a smile.

They moved quickly past the maid of honor and smiled vaguely at the young bridesmaid, Cassie. King's daughter looked sulky. At last they stood before the bride, a shining princess in white taffeta.

Miguel Angel kissed Honey and said, "I know you'll be very happy." Then he patted her nose with the makeup sponge again.

"You look lovely, Honey," Helen said. At least that was the truth.

"Please get yourselves a drink and some hors d'oeuvres," Honey said. "And save room for dinner. You're sitting at table twenty-nine, near the flower urns."

"That's very kind of you," Helen said. Most brides made the hairstylists and makeup artists eat in the kitchen—if they got to eat at all.

The groom wrung Helen's hand like a dishrag. His hand was damp and he'd sweated through his tux. King was so drunk he could hardly stand.

"Do you think he's intoxicated by love?" she whispered to Miguel Angel.

"Love doesn't smell like a distillery," he said, and wrinkled his nose.

A white-gloved server passed a tray of champagne glasses. Helen snagged one, then headed for the appetizer bar. She piled a small plate with spicy shrimp, smoked salmon, and blue cheese canapés with candied pecans. She added a carrot stick, which made her feel virtuous.

"Are you going to be able to fit into your wedding dress?" Miguel Angel asked.

"Don't have one," Helen said. "I've been through the white-wedding routine. Never again. Phil knows he's not getting a virgin."

"You still need a wedding dress," Miguel Angel said. "I can advance you the money, if you want. Men are romantics, Helen. What Phil knows in his mind is different from what he feels in his heart. He should see you in a special dress."

"Thanks, Miguel. That's good advice." Helen piled four mini quiches on her already overloaded plate.

"But you are not going to take it, are you?" he said. "You are stubborn."

"Right now, I'm hungry," Helen said. "Look at that wedding cake. It's like a water slide."

The towering cake had seven layers, with auxiliary layers branching off on four sides. The calories in the sugar roses would equal the national debt.

On a nearby table was a chocolate fountain surrounded by heaping bowls of fresh strawberries, bananas, oranges, nuts and whipped cream.

Helen heard someone tapping on a glass, and the guests quieted. King's best man stood at a microphone near the wedding cake, holding a champagne glass. The man leaned as if he were charging into a high wind. Helen suspected he was a sex-industry worker. His face was acne-scarred and flushed with alcohol. His bow tie was undone, and his wrinkled shirt bulged over a purple paisley cummerbund.

"Hi." He breathed into the microphone, and there was earsplitting feedback. "Oops."

He adjusted the mic. "I'm Barry, the best man. And ladies"—he waggled his eyebrows—"there's no better man here tonight, now that King is taken. I want to toast the bride and goon—I mean, groom."

Helen groaned at the corny joke.

"Honey met King in bed, which is how King met most of his ladies, but he didn't have to pay this one." Helen could see wedding guests squirming in embarrassment.

"Put your eyebrows down, folks," Barry said. "The new Mrs. Oden was a nurse, and she met King when he was in the hospital. She looks a lot prettier today, holding roses. When I met her, she'd just stuck a needle in King's hairy ass."

There was a shocked silence. Honey was pale with fury. She didn't enjoy this memory.

"I can say this because I'm King's oldest friend." Barry stifled a belch. "Speaking of hairy asses, the bride has seen her share—in the line of duty, of course. But those days are over. Now all she has to do is put up with King. That's not easy, either. I should know. I'm his TV show producer. Now a toast. To King and his Honey."

The guests raised their glasses and said, "To King and Honey."

King reached for his abandoned bourbon bottle and finished it.

"Now, everybody, grab a table," Barry said. "Eat and drink up. King's paying the bill, and it's lobster and prime rib."

The bride looked relieved that the toasting was over. She was regaining her color. Helen wondered how many sly humiliations she'd had to endure from King and his low-rent friends.

"But wait, folks. One more thing." Barry was back at the mic, a drunken grin on his face. The mortified bride clutched her bouquet. Helen thought the bouquet hid her shaking hands.

"Let me give you one more toast, the one my daddy used to say." Barry paused dramatically: "May you live forever, and may I never die."

Some guests raised their glasses again. Others looked confused. The toast made Helen shiver. Before Barry could say more, the musicians started playing Handel's *Water Music*.

Helen had no idea who gave the signal to start the music, but she was glad Barry was drowned out by it.

The slightly unsteady groom led his drooping bride to the head table. The wedding party followed, two by two. Barry gave maid of honor Melody a lopsided grin and a sneaky grope as she settled into her seat. She inched her chair away from him. Cassie sulked, ignoring her escort, an older man with thin hair and an underslung jaw. She had a small camera near her bouquet, and kept snapping pictures of her father when Honey's head was turned.

Helen and Miguel Angel found table twenty-nine. It was as overdressed as the bride. The table had a peacock underskirt, a white linen overskirt, and a centerpiece of peacock feathers and blue carnations. Each place setting was marked with a crystal star. Each chair was covered in white fabric and tied with a blue bow.

"These are the rented chair covers?" Miguel Angel whispered.

"Yes," Helen said. "Get a good look. You won't see them at my wedding."

Phoebe sat on Miguel Angel's right. "Hi," she said.

He ignored her.

Across from Helen was the older man Phoebe had been flirting with. He sat next to a full-figured brunette in a daring red dress. The gentleman kissed the brunette's manicured fingers. Phoebe smiled at him and said hello. He looked right past her. Two snubs in less than a minute.

A white-gloved server brought pasta in a cream sauce for the appetizer.

"Ew, fattening," Phoebe said, and pushed hers away. Helen and Miguel Angel dug in.

The second course was Caesar salad.

"It's delicious," Helen said. "The chef used real anchovies."

"More fat," Phoebe said with disgust.

"Shut up," Miguel Angel said through gritted teeth. "One more word out of you, and you're fired."

"You can't fire me. I'm not working for you today. I am a guest, and I can do what I want." Phoebe got up without excusing herself and disappeared.

"I'm going to find the men's room," Miguel Angel said. He didn't come back for his lobster and prime rib. Helen finished hers and eyed his plate, but resisted eating her boss's food.

The dinner plates were removed, and some guests were heading toward the dessert table. Helen heard cries of "Ooh, chocolate" as they approached the fragrant fountain and mounds of cut fruit.

The musicians packed up their instruments. In a corner of the dance floor, a DJ said, "I'm E.J., your electric DJ. Let's have the new Mr. and Mrs. King Oden cut the cake."

His voice was dislikable, boomy and sneery at the same time. His Hawaiian shirt was as loud as he was. Helen saw the bride flinch, then look around. King's seat was empty. Did he wander off for a quick snort? Was he passed out drunk? Groping a wedding guest for his first official act of adultery?

"Where's King?" E.J. the DJ said. "Come on, man, this is no time to be shy."

The bride whispered something to her sister. Melody nodded and scurried toward the tennis courts. Cassie got up and hurried off in another direction. Helen wondered if they were looking for the groom, too.

"Oh, Kingy," the DJ said in a singsong voice. "Come out, come out, wherever you are."

No sign of King. Now there were murmurs among the guests. The bride looked frantic. She stood up, her bouquet abandoned by her plate. Honey gathered her skirts and managed an odd, hobbling run.

"I think she's looking for King," Helen said, but Miguel Angel still hadn't returned. Phoebe was missing, too. Where did they go?

"Usually, the groom disappears *before* the ceremony," the DJ tried to joke.

No one laughed.

"Okay, while we're waiting for the groom to return, let's play a golden oldie," the DJ said.

He hit a button, and the Turtles began wailing "Happy Together." The Turtles were old men now. Their young voices sounded eerie as they sang about investing a dime to call the woman they loved. When was the last time a pay phone call cost a dime?

The old song went on, the verses empty and endless, while the bride searched for her groom. Helen could hear her stiletto heels clattering on the terrace's pink pavers, and her voice calling, "King!

49

Where are you, King?" It sounded as if she was looking for a lost dog.

And where was Miguel Angel? Helen felt uneasy. The bride's cries grew louder and more frantic as the Turtles sang that they were so happy together.

Helen saw the bride running toward the back of the mansion. Was she checking King's yacht? Had he escaped by boat?

Then Helen heard a shrill scream.

"King, no! King!" the bride shrieked.

"I think she's in the backyard," Helen said to no one.

The other guests sat in stunned silence. Helen ran. She wasn't hindered by high heels or wedding finery in her salon uniform of black shirt and pants. The wedding photographer followed, video camera hoisted on his shoulder. Mireya, his assistant, was nowhere in sight.

Helen got to the pool deck. The bride was standing by the vast turquoise pool, screaming, "No, no, no!" over and over. The front of her dress was drenched with water, the creamy poufs deflated like melting ice cream. Honey pointed at the pool.

Helen wondered why there was a giant inflatable toy on the bottom of the deep end. The new addition was black with pink rubber flippers.

Then Helen realized that wasn't a toy.

The groom was facedown on the bottom of the pool, wearing that dreadful tux.

Chapter 5

"Help! Save him," the bride said. "Get him out of the water. I can't lift King. He's too big."

Jonathan, the sweaty young governor's assistant, was the first to rip off his suit jacket and tie. He kicked off his wing tips, stripped to his blue boxers, and dove into the pool, still wearing his black executive-length socks. Helen was impressed by his quick reaction, and wondered if his job taught him to react in a crisis.

He was followed by the E.J. the DJ, who tore off his Hawaiian shirt, scattering buttons across the deck. He stripped off his tennis shoes but kept on his khaki shorts. He had about forty pounds of belly fat.

The young assistant had long, lean muscles and looked fit. The flabby DJ seemed to add to the confusion. The two men struggled to raise King's body out of the water, but only managed to flip him over. Now King looked like he was waving with his fat flipper paws.

Honey screamed in horror.

Someone shouted, "Call nine-one-one." Helen saw the glint of the sun on a squadron of cell phones and BlackBerries.

Barry, the drunken best man, tore off his jacket and pants, tried to step out of his cummerbund, and fell headfirst into the water with a geyserlike splash. He wore his cummerbund like a deflated inner tube.

A dark-skinned waiter shoved his tray on a table, knocking water glasses to the ground. He pulled off his white gloves and black vest, and joined the rescue attempt. Helen thought he might be helpful. He was muscular and younger than the best man.

There were now four men flailing in the water. The governor's assistant tried to organize them. "Okay," Jonathan said to Barry the best man and E.J. the DJ. "You two take King's shoulders. I'll take the lower right side and you, sir, take the left side. We'll try to push him up and onto the deck."

It didn't work. King was too heavy. His wet, slippery body fell back into the pool. Honey cried louder, "Please save him."

After much coughing and sputtering, the young assistant said, "Let's each take a limb and tow him to the shallow end."

The four half-dressed men formed a strange cortege as they carried King through the pool water.

The bride wept and wrung her hands. Wedding guests gathered to watch the spectacle, nearly pushing the front-row gawkers into the water. "Back up, people," someone said, "before we have another pool accident."

At last, the makeshift rescue team reached the shallow end. They dragged King onto the concrete pool deck. If he survives, Helen thought, he's going to have major concrete burns.

"Watch his head. Watch his head," Honey cried.

Water streamed from King's wedding suit in small rivers and ran down his smooth scalp.

A woman screamed, "There's a dead rat in the pool."

More shrieks, until another guest figured out the dark object waving in the drain was King's toupee.

"Stand back," someone else cried. "Give him air."

Even Helen could tell the groom needed more than air. His chest wasn't moving and his body looked like wax and rubber. Helen wondered why the bride's gown was soaking wet. Had Honey tried to pull her husband out of the pool before she called for help? Or had she pushed him in?

"I know mouth-to-mouth resuscitation," Honey said.

"I just bet you do," snarled King's ex-wife, Posie. She had a wineglass in her hand and a mean look on her face.

"Daddy!" cried their daughter, Cassie. She ran surprisingly fast for someone in high heels. She pushed her mother aside. Cassie seemed terribly young as she dropped down on the pool deck and tried to hug her father. She looked like a golden water sprite. The small camera dangled like a bracelet on her right arm. She started taking pictures of Honey trying to revive King.

King's lawyer gently guided Cassie away from her father's body toward an umbrella table. "You'll help him more if you stay out of the way," Harris said. His impeccable Armani was wrinkled and his bow tie was crooked.

"At least let me get him a pillow so he's comfortable," Cassie said. "He's lying on concrete."

"I think he's supposed to be on a hard, flat surface," Harris said. "It's the best way to save him. Honey knows what she's doing. She's a nurse."

The bride had bunched her shimmering skirts to form a pad so she could kneel on the wet pool deck. Honey loosened King's brown bow tie, opened his soggy jacket, and pulled the studs out of his pleated shirt. Honey's long, sheer veil trailed over his face. She tore it off and flung it behind her. It floated on the pool surface like an exotic sea creature.

Honey ran her fingers around the inside of King's mouth.

"Why is she poking around in his mouth?" the drunken ex-wife, Posie, said. "Is she trying to steal his gold fillings?"

"She's checking to make sure the airway is clear. I had CPR training," said a man in a navy blue suit.

Honey tilted King's head back slightly, then pulled open his jaw.

"She's trying to break his neck," Posie said.

"No, she's doing it the right way," the self-proclaimed CPR expert said.

Honey ignored her critics and her defenders. She pinched King's nose closed, put her mouth tightly over his, and gave two quick breaths. Then she stopped and studied her husband.

"What are you doing?" Posie demanded. "Why are you pinching his nose? Why did you stop? Do you want to kill him?"

Honey said nothing. The CPR expert said, "She needs to make a tight seal if she's going to get him breathing. She stopped to see if his chest was moving. That's standard procedure."

"Right," Posie said. Her sarcasm was like acid. "And if she screws up, she's a very rich widow."

"Let's let Honey work without interruption, please," King's lawyer said. "We don't want to slow her down. She's a trained professional. If she does something wrong, there are plenty of witnesses."

"And you can sue," shouted someone from the crowd.

Honey put her mouth over her husband's and blew two more breaths. Then she stopped and studied his chest.

"No sign yet that he's breathing," Honey said. "I'm going to keep trying until help arrives."

Cassie started crying. "He's dead. He's dead. My daddy's dead."

A man who looked like one of King's creepy sex-industry friends came up behind Cassie. "Come with your uncle Max, sweetie." His hand moved across her shoulder like a hairy spider. Cassie flinched at his touch, but Uncle Max didn't notice.

"Honey is a good nurse," he said. "She'll help him." Uncle Max tried to lead the dazed young woman through the crowd.

"You better do the right thing," Cassie screamed at Honey. "You better save my daddy. I've got pictures."

Cassie's wail blended with the approaching sirens. Many of the guests by the pool looked relieved at the sound. Helen thought the trouble was just beginning. How long had King been underwater? Even if the paramedics saved his life, would he be brain-dead? And where were Miguel Angel and Phoebe? Mireya, the photographer's assistant, was also missing. But her employer, Marco Antonio, was dutifully videoing the drama.

Four sturdy paramedics rushed in through the garden gate with a stretcher and a bright orange bag. They expertly lifted King onto the stretcher. One put a mask over his mouth and nose. King didn't move. The paramedics brought out a portable resuscitator to help him breathe. Then they practically hurled the stretcher through the crowd.

The bride tried to follow. "That's my husband," she said. "I have to ride in the ambulance."

"There's no room for you in that big dress, ma'am," the paramedic said.

Honey started to rip off the ruined skirt, but Harris stopped her. "I'll take her," he said.

The doors shut and the ambulance roared off, lights flashing and sirens shrieking. Helen wondered if the lawyer was naturally thoughtful or if he realized he'd just acquired a rich new client. "I'll be right back, Honey," the lawyer told her. "I have to get my car from the valet. We'll follow King to the hospital." The elegant lawyer would have been shocked to realize he really was an ambulance chaser.

The bride threw herself into a garden chair and sobbed. Honey's pregnancy was clearly visible in her water-soaked dress.

Posie, the ex-wife, walked up to the weeping bride and said, "If he'd stayed with me, he'd still be alive. You killed him for his money, and now you don't even have to sleep with him."

"But I did," Honey said.

"We can all see you slept with him," the angry ex said.

"Why would I kill my own husband?" Honey asked.

"The same reason I divorced the bastard," Posie said. Her face—cruel and expensively made-up— was a mask of hate. "King was crude and nasty. This way, you get his money without having to put up with him. You stole millions from my daughter, Cassie."

"That's not true," Honey said. "King created a trust for his daughter."

"But you and your new brat will get the lion's share, won't you?" Posie said. "King didn't even make you sign a prenup, the way he did me."

At that point, Helen realized the police were pouring through the garden gate in a blue wave. They'd had time to hear the whole ugly conversation between Posie and Honey.

Helen glanced at her watch. It was four thirty.

Honey had been married an hour and a half. If King was really dead—and really worth ninety million dollars—his bride had earned a million dollars for each minute of her marriage.

Chapter 6

King's wedding guests scrambled for the exits like scalded roaches. Honey's dream wedding had turned into a nightmare. It was a well-dressed riot.

A blonde in a nearly sheer dress slipped through the ficus hedge. The sharp twigs tore her expensive clothes and scratched her face. The blonde pushed her way through to freedom and emerged on the other side, badly scratched and nearly naked in her leopard-print thong underwear. Helen watched the blonde rip off her shredded dress, sling it over her shoulder, and lope across the lawn in high heels.

The blonde wasn't the least bit self-conscious about her nakedness, and Helen wondered if she was a stripper or an actress.

A man in a hideous plaid tux nearly ran over a delicate grandmother in lavender chiffon. The plaid guy bulled his way through the fleeing crowd to the main door.

The bride was gone. The lawyer had led a bedraggled Honey to his Lexus and driven away. More guests tried to follow. Helen saw tuxedoed men in the driveway, waving money and promising huge tips if the valets got their cars *now*.

A thin old man with a black cane was nearly trampled by a linebacker in a gray suit. The linebacker rudely knocked the old man against a pillar and ran for the back door. The old man was trembling so badly he could hardly stand.

Women screamed. Men cursed and shouted. Peacocks screeched. Glasses and china crashed to the ground, and Helen could hear furniture breaking. Someone overturned the chocolate fountain table, and the Sterno ignited the tablecloth. Little flames started licking the covered chairs, and suddenly the flowers were roasting and the blue silk ribbons went up in an orange blaze. The flames fell upon the wedding feast like hungry guests, devouring tablecloths, napkins and filmy swathes of tulle.

More guests screamed and tried to push their way out. Some looked vaguely famous, and Helen wondered if she'd seen their faces on magazines in the supermarket checkout line. The mad escape stopped when two police cars blocked the narrow drive, the only way out. Six uniformed officers, holstered weapons plainly visible, informed the valets that they were not to fetch any more cars without police permission.

Helen heard a police officer arguing with the wedding videographer. "I can give you the original tape," Marco Antonio said. "But it's a mini DV format. Do you have a player for one? I didn't think so."

"But I think I can lock you up for obstruction of justice," the officer said. "Now, take a deep breath and ask yourself how much trouble you want to be in."

The videographer waited a beat, then apologized. "I am sorry, officer. I wasn't thinking. I have to protect my clients. Mr. Oden's competitors would pay a lot of money for this wedding video, and I had to sign an agreement that I would not sell it."

"You're not selling it," the officer said. "We need it for evidence."

Now the photographer was all smiles. "Of course you can have the tape. Please let me make sure it's stored properly, so we don't lose anything. I can check it in my van."

The officer followed the photographer outside. Ten minutes later, the officer was back with a small tape. He bagged it. The photographer gave the cop his card and waved good-bye.

Helen was nearly knocked over by a leathery-skinned woman with unnaturally red hair. "Sorry, sweetie," Ms. Red said as she sprinted past.

Now Helen could smell smoke, and she saw a raging fire had developed in the dining area. So far, it hadn't reached the house, but she couldn't stand around watching the guests run away. She had to get out of there.

There were more sirens, and Helen wondered if someone had called the fire department, police reinforcements, or both. She thought many of the frantic escapees were sex-industry workers. Those people wouldn't welcome any contact with the police, she thought.

Oh, hell, who I am kidding? I don't want another close encounter with the cops, either. Not so soon after I was accused of murdering my ex-husband, Rob.

There was also the problem with the court in St. Louis. That had sent Helen on a zigzag course through the country before she wound up in South Florida with a new name and a new life.

No, Helen didn't want a smart cop, or even a dumb one, looking into her past. She ducked inside the French doors and found herself facing the kitchen, an oddly angled room overlooking the pool. There was a tiny bathroom on the right. Next to it was a door leading to the pool deck.

Helen heard footsteps. She ducked into the bathroom and locked the door. A narrow window over the toilet was covered with a pink shade. Helen estimated the size of the window and wondered if she could slide through it. She decided it would be tight, maybe a matter of millimeters. She wished she hadn't piled her appetizer plate quite so high.

Helen took off her shoes and black pants, stepped up on the toilet seat, raised the shade and opened the window. She threw her pants and shoes outside. They landed on the pool deck with a thud. Then she boosted herself onto the toilet tank, knocking over a scented candle and shattering a jar of potpourri. She pulled herself through the window up to her hips.

Damn. She was stuck.

Helen wiggled and squirmed. It felt like she was scraping off a layer of skin. No, two layers. I'm going to look fabulous on my wedding night, she thought. I'll be bruised from waist to knees.

She twisted and turned, and finally she was free. Helen fell headfirst onto a padded wicker couch. It wobbled, but didn't fall over. Thank heavens King only bought the best.

Helen stood up gingerly and realized she'd lost her underpants in the frantic struggle through the window. No way she was going back in there. Helen slipped on her black pants and shoes. She threaded her way around the pool furniture, past the umbrella tables, and found a gate by a small waterfall. Helen peered through the fence and saw no one. She still smelled smoke.

She made a run for the back exit. She was out!

She counted at least three fire trucks in the street, along with a herd of police vehicles. Helen dodged her way through them and was nearly to the street when she was stopped by a police officer. He had buzz-cut red hair, pale skin and a zit on his chin.

"We're asking the staff and wedding guests to stay while we ask them a few questions," Officer Buzz said.

"But there's a fire," Helen said.

"The blaze has been contained," Officer Buzz said. "For safety's sake, guests may wait in the empty house across the street. It's for sale, and there's an open house today. The Realtor gave us permission to use it to question guests, since potential buyers can't get down the street with all the activity."

"Why do you need to talk to us?" Helen asked.

"It's routine in a suspicious death," the officer said.

"Is King dead?" Helen asked.

"He was pronounced DOA at the hospital," the officer said.

"But King drowned," Helen said.

"We don't know how he got into the water, ma'am."

Another officer with STEVENS on his name tag walked Helen across the street to a mansion slightly smaller than King's. They crossed a vast empty parquet floor and climbed a curved staircase to a small bedroom.

"Wait here," Officer Stevens said. "We'll be back shortly. Do you have a cell phone?"

"No," Helen said.

"May I check your purse?"

The officer looked through her purse, then left, closing the door. Helen sat down on a blue quilted spread and waited. She picked up the phone by the bed to call Phil, her fiancé. The line was dead.

Helen paced back and forth until she was sure she'd worn a path in the pale rug. It was nearly five o'clock when Officer Stevens returned and led her to a nearly empty kitchen with stainless steel appliances. A man in a dark suit was sitting at the oak kitchen table.

"Sit down," he told Helen. "I'm Detective Richard McNally, and I'm in the Crimes Against Persons Unit."

McNally was her worst nightmare. His white hair said he was a veteran. His steel blue eyes said he was smart. His questions started out mild. Helen tried to be as honest as possible.

Was she a guest at the wedding?

No, she was here to assist the bride's hairstylist, Miguel Angel.

Where was he?

Helen didn't know.

When was the last time she'd seen him?

He'd excused himself to go to the bathroom just before the main course was served.

No, she had no idea what time Miguel Angel had left the table.

Helen was worried and tried not to say so. Would the police see the stylist's disappearance as a sign of guilt? Did they know about his fight with King? Miguel Angel had a hot temper, and he'd threatened to kill the groom. But his anger passed quickly. Helen was sure Miguel would never hurt anyone.

Where was Helen at the time the groom went into the pool?

She didn't know the exact time, but she'd sat at table twenty-nine during the whole dinner.

Anyone else with her at the table?

Yes, Phoebe, Miguel Angel's assistant, who was there as a guest of the bride. Also an older gentleman with a woman in a red dress. They'd never introduced themselves.

Where was the bride during this?

At the head table, until the DJ announced it was time to cut the wedding cake. Then Honey went to look for the missing groom. So did Cassie, King's daughter, and Melody, the maid of honor.

Did Helen know the groom?

She'd never seen him before today.

Did anyone have a reason to kill King?

Helen said she didn't know. She remembered the bride saying King liked to keep his friends close and his enemies closer, but she didn't say that. King's ex-wife and former girlfriend must have hated his guts. King had groped a young staffer. His former business partner was suing him. How close did King's enemies get—close enough to kill him?

How did the deceased behave? Detective McNally asked. When was he last known to be okay?

"He stopped by to see the bride about an hour before the ceremony," Helen said. "I think he was drunk. Just before the bride marched down the aisle, I saw him take a drink out of a bourbon bottle and then stash it in a potted palm."

Helen didn't mention drugs. She hadn't seen King using those. The police didn't seem to know about the fight with Miguel Angel, so she didn't mention that, either. She gave McNally the name she'd used since fleeing St. Louis, plus the salon information, her current address and her landlady's phone number. Helen didn't have a phone in her name. She wanted to stay hard to find.

It was six o'clock before Helen was allowed to leave. Across the street, she could see that the fire trucks were gone. A faint odor of smoke lingered. Trampled flowers littered the pavement, and shattered crystal stars glittered in the waning light. King's velvet lawn was scarred with brown tire ruts.

The wedding guests' cars had been valet parked along the street. Some vehicles were still there.

Helen saw no sign of Miguel Angel or his ride. He'd driven her to the wedding.

Well, it wasn't that bad a walk. She started hoofing it home when Miguel Angel's Jeep drove up. A woman leaned out of the driver's side and asked, "Want a ride?" It was Miguel Angel, with long blond hair and a blue dress.

Chapter 7

"Miguel Angel, is that really you?" Helen said. "You're beautiful."

"I had the best stylist in Fort Lauderdale," he said.

Helen laughed. "Meaning yourself."

"It's true," he said. "I cannot lie."

The evening sun gleamed on his blond hair. His complexion was smooth and creamy, and his makeup was perfect.

"If it's the truth, then it's not bragging," Helen said. "I've seen the photos of your Halloween costumes at the salon, especially that one of you dressed as a cheerleader. You can perform miracles."

"Daily," Miguel said, without a trace of modesty.

If Miguel Angel could give ordinary women the illusion of beauty, he could easily transform himself into an attractive female. It helped that Miguel was slender, round-faced, and looked younger than his forty years. His makeup case was crammed with wigs and extensions. Miguel Angel's blond hair had to be a wig.

"Where did you get the peacock blue dress?" Helen asked.

"Out of the bride's closet. We're the same size."

Not quite, Helen thought. The dress was tight around his waist. The top had to be padded.

"I slipped into King's bathroom and shaved my face and legs with his razor," Miguel Angel said.

And probably your chest, Helen thought. That neckline dipped pretty low.

"Then I did my makeup," Miguel Angel said. "I had to leave my black traveling case behind."

"You heard that King is dead?" Helen asked climbing into the passenger seat of Miguel Angel's Jeep.

"How could I not hear? The screams, the sirens, the fire. I watched it from the upstairs window like a TV show. When the police arrived, I had to disappear, so I borrowed Honey's dress and high heels."

"Borrowed?" Helen watched the sweat stains spread on the peacock blue silk. "Do you think she'll want that dress back? Or those shoes?"

His feet were stretching out high-heeled sandals several sizes too small for him. They were ruined.

Miguel Angel shrugged. "Honey won't miss them. She can afford more."

"Why didn't you just run when you saw the fire?" Helen asked.

"Because the TV crews were outside, photographing the guests. I could be here as a stylist, but if someone thought I was feeding King gossip, my business would be dead. So I put on a dress and ran outside. Even if I was on TV, my clients wouldn't recognize me."

"Why would anyone think you betrayed them to King?" Helen asked.

"Because I believe his last two scoops originated at my salon," Miguel Angel said. "Remember when he reported that Fernanda was drinking again, after a month in rehab? She turned up drunk for her appointment, carrying a champagne bottle. Her photograph was on King's gossip blog the next day. She was wearing the same outfit she had on at my salon. And Richelle's baby bump? She told me she was pregnant but was keeping it quiet until her wedding next Saturday. Two days later, the news was on King's TV show."

"But if she told you, she probably told other people," Helen said. "And Fernanda walked down Las Olas at noon, drinking champagne."

"She was drunk, but I took the bottle away from Fernanda before she left my salon," Miguel Angel said. "I made sure she was escorted to her limo. That photo was taken at my salon. But the real gossip—Honey's baby—has never been reported. You know why not? Because Phoebe is feeding information to her good friend Honey. And Honey is paying her."

"Are you sure?" Helen asked.

"How could Phoebe afford that expensive blue dress for the wedding? It had to be at least three thousand dollars. Why was she an honored guest—because she's such a good friend? Something is wrong. I am watching her. Phoebe will be gone soon. Then she will have big problems, because King's gossip empire is dead."

"Do you think Honey killed King?" Helen asked.

"No!" Miguel almost shouted. "She's not like that."

"But she would marry King for his money."

"That is the way of the world," Miguel Angel said. "Do you really believe in happily ever after?"

"I did once," Helen said. "Then I quit believing any marriage could be happy. Now with Phil, I'm beginning to hope again."

"Your ex-husband must have really hurt you."

"He did," Helen said. "But I survived. If Phil betrays me, I'll survive that, too."

"But he won't," Miguel Angel said. "Phil loves you."

"Right now he does. Forever is another issue."

Helen still remembered the warm afternoon when her faith in forever was destroyed. She'd come home from work early and found Rob naked with their next-door neighbor, Sandy. Those two had been so busy rocking the chaise longue on the new back deck, they didn't notice Helen. She was frozen in the doorway, her mind refusing to believe what her eyes saw.

The couple didn't realize Helen was there and that she had picked up the crowbar Rob had used to work on the deck. Until Sandy peeked over Rob's shoulder and screamed.

Rob had dismounted with record speed and left his buck-naked lover to fend for herself. He sprinted for the safety of his Toyota Land Cruiser—the SUV his wronged wife had bought for him.

Helen, in a red rage, beat the vehicle into dented metal, busted glass and broken plastic. She'd totaled the SUV and still regretted it. Her life would have been simpler if she'd destroyed Rob instead. She would have only served seven years or so for his murder. Instead, she'd killed the car and let her unfaithful husband live. Now she was facing a life sentence with Rob. Helen discovered ex-husbands were like cockroaches; you never quite got rid of them.

A frantic Sandy had called the police. The cops had stopped Helen from beating the SUV—and laughed themselves silly at the naked Rob cowering inside the ruin.

Rob and Sandy had declined to press charges against Helen, but Rob had the last laugh. When Helen filed for divorce, his lawyer used the photos of the smashed SUV to show that Helen had an uncontrollable temper. He claimed that Rob had been a steadying influence who kept her successful career on course. Helen told the court the man hadn't worked in seven years, unless you counted jumping other women's bones. Helen's lawyer sat there like a cardboard cutout.

The divorce judge had awarded Rob half of Helen's six-figure income, plus half the house she'd bought with her money. Her ex had earned himself hundreds of thousands of dollars.

Helen swore that Rob would never see another nickel of her income. She fled St. Louis, crossing the country in grief-crazed zigzags to keep Rob from finding her. Her car died in Fort Lauderdale and she started her new life, taking dead-end jobs for cash under the table and trying to stay off Rob's radar. She'd succeeded until earlier this year, when he'd tracked her down.

"So who killed King?" Helen asked, steering the conversation to a safer topic.

"Who knows?" Miguel Angel said. "Maybe one of his strippers. Or his hookers. Or his ex-wife. Or some celebrity he ruined by his gossip. Even his old business partner wanted him dead. I heard the lawyers' fees were eating Wyllis alive. Everyone hated King."

"Even you?" Helen teased.

"Especially me," Miguel said, tossing his long hair. "Not enough to kill him, though. But I was afraid the police would hear about the fight, so I thought I'd better get away."

"You were lucky to avoid the cops," Helen said.

"I didn't avoid them. Not totally. An officer

caught me leaving the house. He looked so young, I thought he was a Boy Scout in the wrong uniform. I said, 'No spik English' over and over and cried like a hysterical woman. I did the whole Cuban-drama routine. They thought I was the bride's crazy auntie. I gave them a fake name and address in Miami, and left."

"Miguel Angel, the police will get you for that," Helen said, conveniently forgetting her own fake name.

"They'll get me, anyway," Miguel Angel said. "I hated that man. I had a fight with him. I begged his wife not to marry him. I'm gay and I'm Cuban."

"You're an American citizen," Helen said.

"Not to the police. I'm still Cuban, no matter how many citizenship tests I pass. If they have to choose between arresting a Cuban nobody and a pretty American, you know who they'll throw in jail."

"They're not like that," Helen said. But she wondered if that was true. She was a middle-class American and lived in a different world. Besides, she'd had her own troubles with the law.

"I still wish you'd talked to the police," she said.

"I wish this had never happened," Miguel Angel said. "But it did."

It was six thirty when Miguel Angel pulled up in front of the Coronado Tropic Apartments. Helen waved good-bye and walked up the path to the backyard. The waning light was kind to the old Art Moderne building, tinting the Coronado's elegant curves a soft bluish-white. The palm trees rustled like taffeta petticoats in the gathering dusk.

Helen's landlady, Margery Flax, was stretched out on a chaise longue by the turquoise pool. Margery was seventy-six. Tonight she wore a long, summery lavender dress slit high enough to reveal purple gladiator sandals. Margery loved purple. Her gray hair was bobbed, and her tanned face creased with wrinkles. Cigarette smoke wreathed her hair.

When Helen saw Phil, her heart beat faster. Her man looked impossibly handsome with his long white hair in a ponytail. He was wearing her favorite shirt—medium blue—and blue jeans that matched his eyes. His nose was slightly crooked. When he smiled, he had sexy eye crinkles.

Phil was drinking a beer and eating spicy chips. He put down his bottle and got up to kiss Helen. His slightly beer-flavored kiss had that special zing. Damn, she was lucky to find him.

"Are you okay?" Phil asked. "You look tired."

"I am tired," Helen said. "It's been an awful day. The groom is dead."

"At the wedding?" Margery asked. She poured Helen a glass of white wine out of the box. Phil handed over his chips.

Helen took a deep gulp of cold wine and said, "Died right after the ceremony. The police suspect

74

he was murdered, but nobody knows for sure. The bride tried to save him." Helen told them about the wedding, the fire and her police interrogation.

"It's so sad," Helen said. "It was a fairy-tale wedding. A little overdone, maybe, but beautiful."

"Did you get any tips for our wedding?" Phil asked.

"Yes, your ex-wife is not invited," Helen said. "And you're not wearing a tux with brown lapels."

"Uh, I wasn't planning to." Phil looked puzzled.

Helen kissed him on the forehead. "I don't understand why King bothered to get married in the first place. He could have all the women he wanted."

"All the hookers," Phil said. "There's a difference."

"Honey is no hooker," Helen said. "Though I think she married him for his money."

"The other problem was his profession," Margery said, and blew more smoke into the soft night. "His gossip empire embarrassed King's daughter, Cassie. Some of the women at his former strip club were selling so-called special services, and King was arrested for pimping. His lawyers claimed that King wasn't responsible for the after-hours activities of his employees, and he had no idea they were engaged in prostitution.

"No one bought that argument except the jurors. King was acquitted. But his daughter suffered for his sins. He'd sent Cassie to an expensive private school. The students were merciless about her father's arrest. They taunted her with how the man made his money. They hung strings of king-sized sausages on her locker door, left sex toys in her backpack and condoms in her textbooks."

Helen felt a pang of sympathy for Cassie. The young woman had been sulky at the wedding, but she'd loved her father—or so it seemed. "Kids can be cruel," Helen said. "Didn't the school step in and stop the harassment?"

Margery snorted. "Are you kidding? Not when every other daddy and mommy is a lawyer. The headmaster claimed he'd cracked down on the troublemakers, but very little was done. The parents complained that King's daughter couldn't take a joke, their kids didn't mean any harm and, besides, a child with her background did not belong in their fancy school.

"King wanted to sue the school, or yank out his daughter and send her somewhere else, but his advisors told him it was time to tone down his act. King actually listened, for once. Next thing you know, he announced he was marrying Honey, and he started donating millions to charity."

Helen didn't ask where her landlady got this information. Margery always knew the local gossip.

"And that solved the problem?" Helen asked.

"Let's just say the kids stopped harassing Cassie once their parents had to go to King, begging for their favorite causes. Society managed to hold its nose and accept his dirty money. Cassie was never popular, but her life was better when her daddy changed his ways."

"Did he really change?"

"Not all that much," Phil said. "King has attracted some very nasty stories. They say he uses sex workers to help gather his gossip. Hookers know who's unfaithful, who's kinky and who's back on drink and drugs."

"While we're on the subject of change," Margery said, "I have two new tenants for apartment 2C."

Helen and Phil groaned.

"Who did you rent to this time?" Helen asked. "A bank robber? A grave robber? A cradle robber? Or someone who fleeces widows and orphans?"

"Are their pictures in the post office?" Phil asked.

"That's enough," Margery said. "I do not have crooks in 2C this time."

"That's a first," Phil said. "You've rented to con artists, embezzlers, a fortune-teller who advertises on late-night TV, and assorted thieves. You've never had an honest tenant in there since I've lived at the Coronado."

"These two young men are different," Margery said. "Josh and Jason are in the construction business. They have special senior discounts. Jason is from Maryland. Josh is from the Midwest, where people still have a work ethic."

"Like my ex-husband, Rob?" Helen asked. "He was from St. Louis, Missouri. A drop of that man's work sweat was so rare, it would cure cancer."

"Go ahead and laugh," Margery said. "You'll see."

Chapter 8

The woman sitting in Miguel Angel's chair looked tired. She had dark circles under her eyes and her jawline had a slight sag. Her hair was frizzy and shapeless.

"Miguel Angel, I don't know what's wrong. I look old. I guess I am old—I'm fifty-five. But my husband is complaining that I don't look good."

"Cecilia, you've had a stroke and brain surgery," Miguel Angel said. "You've lost your hair, but it's growing back."

"Not fast enough. I exercise and eat healthy, and it still doesn't do any good."

"You've been very sick," Miguel Angel said. "It takes time. Six months ago, you thought you were going to die. Look at you now. Up and walking."

"And partly bald," Cecilia said.

"Hair grows back," he said. "But you do not rise from the dead. You're a fighter."

A tear slid down her ravaged cheek. "I'm tired of fighting. I'm thinking about getting a face-lift."

"No!" Miguel Angel said. "You don't want a face-lift, Cecilia. You'll look like everyone else.

It's hard to style hair around the face-lift scars. And those Chinese eyes!" He slanted his own eyes with his fingers. "Your face has character. Don't ruin it."

"I'm tired of listening to my husband complain about my looks. The world is full of pretty young women on the prowl."

"And your husband, is he asking his barber for a makeover?"

"No," Cecilia said. "It's different for a man."

"It's not different," Miguel Angel said. "We let men get by with more. We tell them they are distinguished when they're really old."

"I used to be a knockout before I got sick," Cecilia said.

"And now you are well," Miguel Angel said. "Anything plastic surgeons can do with a knife, I can do with a brush. I will give you a face-lift using makeup. It's the best kind—no infection, no pain, no swelling, no scars. If you don't like the new look, you can wash it off."

"A washable face-lift," Cecilia said. "I like that idea."

"Let's start by washing your hair. Then I'll show you some makeup tricks. Phoebe!" Miguel Angel called. There was no response.

He stalked over to Ana Luisa's reception desk. "Where is that worthless woman? Find her. Get her on the phone," he said. "I will wash Cecilia's hair myself."

Cecilia picked up her cane and limped to the washing sinks. Helen carried the woman's briefcase. Cecilia was a teacher. She never rested at the salon. She packed a case full of papers and education magazines to read, as well as healthy snacks and herbal tea.

Miguel Angel washed and rinsed Cecilia's hair, then wrapped her head in a towel. When she was back in his chair, he combed out her damp hair.

"What are we going to do about my hair?" Cecilia asked. "It's so thin."

"We will fix that, too," he said. "But let's start with the makeup first. Helen, bring my case, please."

Helen hauled the heavy salon case out of the cabinet in the prep room. Miguel Angel opened it and took out his salon makeup brushes. They were packed in a black container that reminded Helen of the holder for her grandmother's good silverware. It was like a giant leather envelope, with a slot for each size makeup brush. Some brushes had only a few hairs. Others were thick and fat, and one was a feathery fan.

Miguel Angel took a wedge sponge and began patting foundation on Cecilia. He took three times as long as Helen would have to cover Cecilia's face from jaw to hairline. He made sure there was foundation in the creases around her nose and chin, on her forehead, even under and around her eyes.

Then he picked up a dark brown "studio touch-up stick" and drew lines under Cecilia's cheekbones, along her jaw, and two lines down her nose. With the clean side of the makeup sponge, he carefully blended the dark lines, creating shadows under her cheekbones and drawing attention away from her slightly sagging jaw.

"Brilliant," Cecilia said. "I have cheekbones like a model."

Miguel Angel took a fat brush, dipped it in a rose powder blush, and brushed the tops of her real cheekbones with color.

"Are you going to put concealer under my eyes?" Cecilia said.

"No, that gives you shiny white rings." Instead, he blended a tiny amount of concealer at the edge of her eyes, then brushed wheat-colored powder on her eyelids. He lined her lids with dark blue powder. The lines slanted upward, giving her an eye lift.

Miguel Angel spent what Helen thought was an ungodly amount of time putting mascara on Cecilia's lashes, constantly instructing her to look up while he seemed to paint each lash individually. Sometime during the mascara, Phoebe materialized by the chair.

Miguel glared at her but said nothing. He lined Cecilia's lips with a neutral lip pencil and painted them a soft rose.

"I like that lip color," she said. "The lip gloss tastes like raspberries."

Miguel Angel removed one of his huge blow-dryers from its holster and dried Cecilia's hair, pulling on it until it was longer and straighter. Older women's hair tends to get thin and frizzy, but Miguel knew how to give them the thick, glossy hair of their youth.

"How do you do that?" Helen said. "My wrists would hurt."

"Practice," Miguel Angel said. "You need strong hands for this job."

Cecilia's hair color was a rich brown, and thanks to Miguel's shampoo and styling potions, it was shiny. Helen noticed that Cecilia's hair was thick on the right side, but so thin on the left that her ear showed. Miguel Angel opened a drawer and brought out a fall of brown human hair. He held it against Cecilia's own hair.

"Too dark."

Miguel Angel rummaged in the drawer for a lighter shade and held it up again.

"Perfect match," Cecilia said.

"Still not right," Miguel Angel said, though the hair looked okay to Helen.

He pulled out a third fall. "Perfect."

He used the combs in the fall to hold it in place, then accepted the hairpins Phoebe handed him. She passed them gingerly, as if Miguel might bite.

Miguel brushed some of Cecilia's own hair over the fall, fluffed and sprayed it, then said, "There. What do you think?"

"I look ten years younger." Cecilia smiled for the first time since she'd entered the salon.

Helen handed Cecilia her blouse on a hanger, and she changed in the dressing room. Ana Luisa gave Cecilia the bill. Helen noticed that Miguel Angel had given her a price break on the makeup lesson and the fall. Cecilia tipped him fifty dollars.

Cecilia left the salon, wearing her black blouse and jeans. Her limp disappeared. Her walk was a confident strut, and she turned heads up and down Las Olas.

"Bravo," Helen said. "But you shaved some money off her bill."

"She really can't afford to come here, but she is a nice person," Miguel Angel said. "I cried when I thought she was going to die."

"You old softie," Helen said. There it was again: Despite the salon's hard, chic exterior, Miguel Angel could be unexpectedly kind. He closed his salon case and handed it to Helen to put away.

"Not everything is about money," Miguel Angel said. "I can afford to indulge myself sometimes."

"So you're a fairy godmother?" Helen asked.

"Let's not talk about sex, please," he said, and laughed.

"Is Cecilia's husband as big a jerk as he sounds?"

"No. He's a good man, but he doesn't understand how he hurts her when he talks about her appearance. Cecilia is getting older, and she's trying to look good for him, but it's hard."

Helen heard Ana Luisa shout, "Miguel! Quick! The wedding murder is on the noon news."

Helen and Miguel had carefully avoided the subject all day, as if talking about King's death would make the cops materialize in the salon. Now Helen, Miguel Angel and Phoebe crowded into the back prep area, where there was a tiny television. The story was headlined A KING IS DEAD.

Helen saw shots of King's palace, a clip from the wedding video, and footage of the hospital where he was pronounced dead. There was also an interview with a police spokesman who said King's death was murder.

"The autopsy shows that the victim was alive when he went into the water," the police spokesman said, "and injuries indicate that he struggled to get out of the pool. The victim was a strong individual, but he was in an intoxicated state, which impaired his ability to fight for his life. The victim drowned in his pool. The coroner has ruled Mr. King Oden's death a homicide."

A reporter interviewed a woman identified as DEATH WEDDING GUEST. "I saw the groom—the dead King—arguing with a woman in a blue dress by the pool. The woman wore high-heeled sandals and had blond hair."

Helen groaned. "Miguel Angel, why did you pick blue? Didn't the bride have any black dresses?"

"Blue is a better color for me," he said.

"They'll never find the killer now," Helen said. "Every other woman at that wedding wore a blue dress."

"But I'm the one who ran," Miguel Angel said.

Helen noticed that Phoebe was hanging on to their words. Miguel Angel noticed that, too.

"Back to work, everyone," he said. "We've wasted enough time today. Helen, sweep the floor around my chair, will you?"

"Sure." Helen picked up a broom.

"Carolina is here," Ana Luisa said. "And after her, there's Ursula."

Carolina wanted color, a cut and a blow-dry. Her skeletal arms were freckled with liver spots. Helen figured the woman was close to seventy, but Carolina had convinced herself that she looked forty. She wore her blond hair draped over one eye, like a forties movie star.

Phoebe handed Miguel Angel squares of foil while he painted highlights into Carolina's thinning hair. When he finished, Phoebe plugged in a color-processing dryer, which had two heated wings, like a mechanical butterfly. The heat sped up the color process. Miguel Angel set the timer, and promised to be back in twenty minutes.

Meanwhile, he turned his attention to Ursula, a large woman with shoe-polish-black hair.

Miguel Angel mixed her color and covered the skunk stripe of white roots with a brush. Ursula

85

insisted that her hair be dyed flat black. Miguel Angel tactfully suggested that she lighten her hair or add some highlights, but Ursula refused.

"I was born with raven hair and that's the color I'll keep," she said, shutting down all discussion. No one told her the raven had long ago turned into a common crow.

Ursula and Miguel Angel debated the merits of trimming her bangs.

The timer dinged. That was Phoebe's signal to wash Carolina's hair. She led the woman to a sink and carefully pulled out the foils. Then Phoebe held up a peach bottle and said, "We have a special shampoo for thin, older hair."

The woman twitched as if she'd been stung. Helen thought Carolina was angry, and Phoebe was so clueless she didn't know she'd insulted a customer.

Phoebe wrapped a dark towel around the neck of Carolina's cape and adjusted the height of the sink. She gently rinsed Carolina's hair. "Is that water too hot?" she asked.

"No, I like it hot," Carolina said.

"Do the Hustle," an ancient disco tune, played on the sound track. The woman tapped her foot.

"Is this the music you liked when you were young?" Phoebe asked.

Carolina shot straight up. "When I was what?" She tore off her cape, threw the towel on the floor and marched over to Miguel Angel. "That idiot insulted me. I'm not paying three hundred dollars to be told I'm old."

"Carolina, please wait," Miguel Angel said.

"Why? So you can insult me again? Do I look stupid enough to have danced to disco?"

Carolina marched out of the salon, wet head held high.

"Do you know what happened?" he asked Helen.

"Yes," she said, and told him what Phoebe had said.

"That moron," Miguel Angel said. "I've wanted Phoebe out of here. Now I will get my wish."

He took Phoebe aside and fired her. She ran for the door, weeping.

"You've ruined my life. I'll make you sorry," Phoebe cried. "I'll make you both regret this."

Chapter 9

Phoebe flounced out, slamming the salon door behind her. "Do the Hustle," the disco tune that got Miguel Angel's useless assistant fired, faded away in a flurry of silly squeaks.

Helen and Ana Luisa stared at each other. The silence was deafening, but the two women didn't dare break it. Ana Luisa raised one perfectly waxed eyebrow.

"I should have fired her weeks ago," Miguel Angel said. "God knows how much business she's cost me with her stupid remarks."

Helen was relieved that Phoebe was gone, but she was worried by her threat. Now the bitter assistant knew that Miguel Angel had escaped the police by dressing as a woman—wearing the same outfit as the last person seen talking to King before his death.

"Miguel, do you have Honey's dress in your apartment?" Helen asked.

"No," he said. "I threw it away."

"Where?" she said.

"In the Dumpster in back of the salon."

Fear gripped Helen's heart. "Phoebe heard us talking about that dress. What if she tells the police?"

"She won't," Miguel Angel said. "She can't go to the police because of her boyfriend, Ramon. He's a drug dealer."

"The skanky guy with the brown hair and bad skin?"

"That's him."

"He looks like a rough-trade Fabio. His hair is dirty. You'd think Phoebe would at least wash it for him. Doesn't he make deliveries for the shops around here? I wondered what she saw in him."

"A lot of white powder," Miguel Angel said. "He delivers more than Cuban sandwiches. Besides, she was wearing a blue dress at the wedding, too."

"But—" Helen said.

"I am not going to worry. She has as much to

lose as I do. Drug dealers' whores do not go to the police. I'm safe."

Before Helen could say anything more, Ana Luisa softly interrupted. "Virginia is here," the curvy blond receptionist said. "She's scheduled for color, a cut and blow-dry."

"Just what I needed today," Miguel Angel said. "Well, I will deal with it—and her."

Virginia's clothes dripped designer labels. She was a gym-toned woman in that gray no-man's land between fifty and sixty. And it was gray. Her roots were nearly an inch long, but she'd combed her hair to hide as much gray as possible. Some women thought they saved money by delaying their touch-ups. Instead, it cost them more. Their color grew dull, and Miguel had to give them new highlights plus color, instead of a less expensive touch-up.

Miguel Angel commandeered the darkly handsome Carlos, the assistant to Paolo and Richard, the other two stylists, to wash Virginia's hair. Helen brought a Diet Coke for her and a thick Cuban coffee for Miguel Angel. The demitasse cup was so small, there was barely room for all the sugar cubes he used.

"Dear," Virginia said in a syrupy voice, as Helen started to walk away. "Hey, you!" she shouted.

Helen stopped. "Are you speaking to me?"

"Yes. I think my parking meter has expired. Would you put some money in it?" She handed

Helen two dollar bills. "I drive an eighty-six Jaguar. It's the black XJ6 in the lot behind Las Olas. I drive one of the real Jaguars, before they became Fords. You can't miss it in the first row."

Ana Luisa helped Helen exchange the two dollars for eight quarters. Then Helen walked four blocks in the sweltering June heat and dutifully dropped coins into the almost-expired meter.

Two hours later, Virginia's hair was a glorious red-gold. She paid her bill, then handed out three envelopes. "This is for you," she said, giving Helen the thinnest envelope. Carlos got a slightly thicker one. Miguel Angel got the third, and fattest, envelope.

Helen opened her envelope and her eyes widened in surprise and disgust. "A McDonald's coupon," she said. "I hiked in the heat to her stupid car, and she tipped me with a McDonald's coupon."

"You got one," Carlos said. "I got two. She is a cheap bitch." With his Latino accent, it sounded like *chip beech,* which made the insult somehow endearing.

"Did you get money?" Helen asked Miguel Angel.

"I got coupons, too," he said. "But because I did such brilliant work, I got five."

"And they are worth what? One one-hundredth of a cent?" Helen said.

"They are worth nothing. And she is worth millions. She has a mansion on Hendin Island, and she inherited a share in her father's auto-parts business."

A standard tip for a salon like Miguel Angel's was twenty percent for the stylist, which meant he should have had at least sixty dollars—more than the average woman paid for a haircut. Carlos should have had at least a ten spot, and Helen should have had a fiver for running an outside errand.

"How can people be so cheap?" Helen asked.

"Because they have no shame," Miguel Angel said. "When I am tired of her, I will dye her hair orange, and she will torment someone else."

Helen was amazed by the cheapness of the superrich. It was almost a sickness the way they clung to their money until it hurt them personally and professionally. Virginia needed Miguel Angel to maintain the illusion of youth that was so important in her circle. Few stylists could match his skill with color. Yet she'd insulted him with a worthless tip.

Helen crumpled her coupon and took a small, spiteful glee in tossing it in the trash.

She went back to dusting the salon counters, using her anger to attack the hair that drifted over everything. Humans shed like dogs. When Helen wasn't sweeping up the cut ends, she was wiping hair off counters, picking it off shampoo jugs and shaking it out of glossy magazines. It was a battle she and a daily cleaning crew could never win.

As she worked, Helen pondered King and Honey's fatal marriage and wondered if it was an omen for her own wedding day.

No, that was ridiculous. King had lived a dreadful life and paid the price. She wondered who'd killed him and why. Was it his bride, Honey? One of his many ex-girlfriends? His former wife? Some employee he'd groped? His humiliated daughter? A celebrity whose career he'd ruined? King's gossip blog could be unbelievably cruel. He'd ridiculed Valencia, a runway model, for being fat. When word got out that Valencia had breast cancer and was taking medication that made her gain weight, he never apologized.

If ever a man deserved killing, it was King. Helen didn't envy the police this investigation. She'd wandered into a few murders by accident, but she wanted to stay away from this one. She was going to be married soon.

Helen sighed happily at that thought. She imagined herself and Phil saying their vows before a minister in the soft twilight at the Coronado Tropic Apartments. Her wedding would be simple and sweet. The only guests would be their friends and her sister, Kathy. After the backyard reception, she and Phil would leave for a honeymoon in the Keys and live happily ever after.

These bridal daydreams were interrupted when a woman of about eighty tottered into the salon.

"Bernice is here," Ana Luisa announced.

The client held herself like a grande dame and wore a flattering shade of lavender, which made her big eyes seem bluer. Her bones said Bernice had been a beauty once, but too many years and too many face-lifts had taken their toll. Now her trim body sagged and her long hair was stringy.

Helen handed Bernice a robe and a hanger, and the woman went into the dressing room to change. When she came out, Helen settled her into Miguel Angel's chair, brought her a magazine and iced tea. She saw an old square-cut diamond ring on the woman's finger and felt a small pang of sadness. Bernice had been a young bride once. Now Helen could see pink scalp shining through Bernice's carefully arranged hair.

"Miguel Angel, I want my hair to be longer and fuller," Bernice said. "And don't tell me to get a wig. They're too hot in June."

"I will do my best," Miguel Angel said.

Back in the prep area, he mixed products while Helen dusted the shelves.

"I am forty years too late to help her," he said. "And she is a nice lady."

Ana Luisa glided into the room, a fearful look on her face. She stood there, not saying a word.

"Yes?" Miguel Angel said.

"Phoebe called and asked if she could get her tote bag from the staff storage area. She says she was too upset to get it when she was . . . uh, let go."

"She can get it," Miguel Angel said. "But she'd better not come near me. She's lucky I didn't throw it away."

"She'll be here in ten minutes." Ana Luisa looked relieved. She click-clacked away on her stylish black heels.

Miguel Angel was working on Bernice's hair when Phoebe crept into the salon. He ignored her. The other two stylists, Paolo and Richard, were suddenly busy at their stations, cleaning drawers and examining brushes. Phoebe went to the prep area, where the staff kept their belongings.

Two minutes later, Ana Luisa was back again, wringing her hands. "We have a problem," she said. "Tassie is here and she's two hours early. She says she drove in from Palm Beach and couldn't judge the time because of the traffic. I suggested she shop until her appointment, but she says she can't wait."

"Then Carlos can wash her hair and blow-dry it," Miguel Angel said. "If that's okay with him."

"I'd love to." Carlos smiled happily. He looked for every opportunity to work on customers' hair.

"Carlos has a gift," Miguel Angel said to Helen. "You can tell by how he handles hair. The man is an artist with a brush." He meant a *hairbrush*.

Phoebe walked by Miguel Angel's chair, her face bright red with suppressed anger, her nose in the air. Her tote was slung over her shoulder. She didn't say a word.

"Good riddance," Miguel Angel said under his breath, as she closed the door.

Carlos was back at Miguel Angel's chair, looking hurt. "Tassie said she doesn't want me to touch her. She says she's paying for you, not some assistant."

"If she wants me, then she shows up at *my* time. I will talk to her."

Miguel Angel marched over to Tassie. Helen couldn't hear what he said, but there seemed to be angry words and furious hand waving. Tassie ripped off her cape and marched out. She was the second customer who left the shop angry that day. Hairstyling was an emotional business.

Miguel Angel stormed off to the prep room and fixed himself another Cuban coffee. Helen thought he had to be wired like NASA after all that caffeine.

"Hah! She says she'll never come here again," Miguel Angel said. "I try to be nice. I try to be cute. But there are times when I can't. I know what this is really about. Phoebe did this.

"The last time Tassie was here she told me, 'I want my hair my natural color.' Her hair was so neglected I couldn't figure out what her color was. I was trying to guess when Phoebe said, 'But your natural color is gray.' Tassie was insulted, but it was the truth. She just didn't want to hear it. Now she rejects Carlos, who is too good for her. I should have asked you to get the pills out of her cheap, fake designer purse and give one to me. Because whatever she's on, I need it today."

Miguel Angel drank his coffee in one gulp and went back to Bernice and her thinning hair. When he finished with her, Helen thought Bernice's hair looked amazing for her age. But the woman wasn't happy.

"It's not what I expected," Bernice said.

"I'm sorry," Miguel Angel said. "It's the weather."

Bernice paid her bill with a smile, tipped generously and left. When she was gone, Helen said, "The *weather?*"

"Life is a hurricane," Miguel Angel said. "She's been hit hard."

"You're a genius if you can get someone to swallow that excuse," Helen said.

"Yes, I am," Miguel Angel said, without a trace of shame.

The salon door opened, and a uniformed police officer came in with a man in a navy blue suit. Helen's heart sank. It was Detective Richard McNally—and he wasn't there to get his gray hair colored.

"Miguel Angel?" Detective McNally said.

"*Sí?*" Miguel Angel said.

"Don't *sí* us, Mr. No Spik English. Your English is fine, except when you're talking to the police. But we have an interpreter this time. Officer Gomez speaks fluent Spanish. We have a warrant to search your salon and your apartment."

"What for?" Miguel Angel said.

Helen noticed that his accent, which was usually only a trace, had thickened so much she could hardly understand him.

"A blue dress, among other things," Detective McNally said.

"What blue dress?" Miguel Angel said.

"The one you wore when you killed King Oden."

Chapter 10

Miguel Angel sat at his workstation, like a toddler in time-out. He gripped the chair arms with shaking hands. Helen couldn't tell if he was afraid, angry or too wired by the Cuban coffee to stop shaking. He'd been ordered to sit down by Detective Richard McNally.

"I don't know what you're talking about," Miguel Angel said.

"If you can't keep quiet, I'll have to detain you," McNally said.

"But—" Helen said.

McNally interrupted her before she could finish her sentence. "You be quiet, too," he said. "Take that chair over there."

Helen sat in the client chair on the far side of the room. That gave her the best seat in the salon for watching the drama. Ana Luisa sat, in tense silence, across from Helen. Once again, she raised that expressive eyebrow. Her creamy skin was flushed, her lips compressed. One lock of blond hair straggled down her forehead. Helen knew that Miguel Angel would be itching to fix it. He couldn't stand a hair out of place on his staff.

A half-dozen uniformed officers were searching the shop. Helen could hear drawers, cabinets and closet doors slamming. There was a crash of glass, and Helen wondered which product jar had been broken. Some of the hair compounds sold for two hundred dollars or more.

One officer pawed through Ana Luisa's desk, heaping papers, pens and notepads on the desktop. When he pulled out a box of supersized tampons and poured the contents on the desk, Ana Luisa went rigid with anger and embarrassment.

A pudgy younger officer was going through Miguel Angel's station drawers, ignoring Miguel's glare. A brown-haired officer, who looked like an anteater, carried in the stylist's salon makeup case from the prep area.

"Sir, there's a hypodermic needle in among these bigger brushes," Officer Brown reported.

"Bag it," Detective McNally said.

Miguel Angel twitched and moved uneasily, but said nothing.

"Sir, there's a suspicious white substance in one of these makeup wells," Officer Brown said.

Miguel Angel could keep quiet no longer. "It's eye shadow," he said.

"It's not in cake form, like the rest of the makeup," Officer Brown said.

"Then we need to field test it," Detective McNally said. "Do you have a field-test kit?"

"Yes, sir. And I'm trained to use it," Officer Brown said.

Helen watched him open a small box printed with NIK PUBLIC SAFETY, INC. and take out an even smaller packet and something labeled LOADING DEVICE. He took a tiny amount of the "suspicious substance" for testing.

"It's tested positive for heroin and opium alkaloids," Officer Brown said.

Helen could tell by the stunned look on Miguel Angel's face that he had no idea there was heroin or a needle in his case.

"No!" Miguel Angel said. "I no use drugs or needles." His English deteriorated as his fear grew.

Helen figured there was only a small amount of heroin in the makeup well. How much trouble could her boss be in?

Detective McNally seemed to read her mind. "There's probably less than ten grams of heroin," he said. "But you don't need much. Heroin is sold on the street in bags of about fifty milligrams, or five-hundredths of a gram. Ten grams of heroin would make up about two hundred bags."

"No, please!" Miguel Angel said. "I don't need to sell drugs. I make enough money at my salon."

"Really?" McNally said. "This is quite an

expensive operation you've got here. When times get rough, even the rich are short of money. They can go to Supercuts and save a couple hundred a month. But a junkie can always find money for a fix. They'll lie, cheat and steal purses for the cash."

Miguel Angel had been in America long enough to know his salon could be seized if he was convicted of selling drugs. "Check my hair," he begged. "That will prove I don't use drugs. Hair keeps a record that does not lie. You will know I've not used drugs for ninety days. I will give you my hair without asking for a lawyer."

The detective read Miguel Angel his Miranda rights, then clipped a sample of the stylist's hair as close to the scalp as possible. Miguel winced at the inexpert cut. The tiny hair bundle was about as big around as a shoelace tip. McNally dropped the hair in an evidence bag and labeled it.

"We should have the results from the lab two to three business days after they get this hair sample," Detective McNally said. "I'm overnighting it this afternoon."

"There's something you should know," Helen said.

McNally cut off any further conversation with a curt, "I'll find out when I talk with you, miss, after the search is conducted."

Miss. Well, that is better than ma'am, she thought, then was disgusted with herself. Great.

You're about to get hauled off to jail, and you're worried about whether you look young. Orange jumpsuits are so flattering.

The salon door opened and a dark-skinned officer stood in the doorway. Helen could see sweat dripping off his shaved head and dark sweat circles under his armpits. "I found these in the Dumpster behind the store." He held up a wrinkled peacock blue dress and one black high-heeled sandal.

"Are those your clothes?" Detective McNally asked the stylist.

"No, it is not my dress," Miguel Angel said.

That was the truth, but not the whole truth.

Please don't lie, Helen prayed silently. The police will figure it out and then you'll really be in trouble.

"I can have it tested for DNA—your DNA," Detective McNally said.

"Okay, I wore it," Miguel Angel said.

"Then it's your dress," McNally said.

"It's Honey's dress. I borrowed it the day of the wedding."

"Oh, were you a bridesmaid?" Detective McNally's sarcasm could have curled hair.

"No, I had to leave in a hurry," Miguel Angel said.

"Most people ran out the door," McNally said. "They didn't take the time to cross-dress. Especially when the house was on fire."

"I am not a cross-dresser," Miguel Angel said.

"Then what were you doing in a dress?" the detective said.

"It was the easiest way to leave," Miguel Angel said.

The detective held up the heel. "This doesn't look easy to walk in. You're wearing black cowboy boots right now, pardner. Much easier to run in those."

"I am famous. I am a celebrity stylist," Miguel Angel said. "There were television cameras all around, King's rivals in the gossip business. My reputation would be ruined if I was seen there. My top clients would think I gave him information. I needed to disguise myself."

"So you stole the bride's dress?"

"She won't miss it," Miguel Angel said. "She has a closet full of dresses."

"Not if she has many friends like you," the detective said. "Why did you run?"

"I am not from this country," Miguel Angel said. "I didn't think the police would believe me."

"We don't believe liars, no matter what their country of origin," Detective McNally said. "I've got a bit of advice for you. Don't leave town until the hair test results come back. Otherwise, I will hunt you down. You can go now."

Miguel Angel grabbed his already-searched satchel from the bottom drawer at his station, and left without another word. Detective McNally pushed Ana Luisa's desk chair over to Helen and sat down. Helen felt sick with fear. This man was smart. He frightened her.

"Let's talk," he said. "What were you dying to tell me earlier?"

"I think Miguel Angel was set up by an employee," Helen said. "Her name is Phoebe, and she was pretty useless."

Out of the corner of her eye, Helen could see Ana Luisa nodding in agreement.

"Her boyfriend, Ramon, is a drug dealer," Helen said.

"And how do you know that?" McNally said. "Ever see him sell an illegal substance?"

"No, not really. I just heard that's what he was." From Miguel Angel, she remembered. Helen's voice withered and died, strangling her next words. "It was gossip."

"And you hear a lot of gossip in this place," McNally said.

"Yes," Helen said. "But I could see Phoebe was furious at Miguel when he told her to leave. She set him up. She forgot her tote bag and had to come back. She was alone in the back prep area for several minutes. I think she planted drugs that she got from her boyfriend and put the needle in Miguel Angel's salon case."

"Why would she set up her employer?" the detective asked.

"Because Miguel Angel fired her."

"So she framed him?" McNally said. "I don't think so. People get fired every day."

"But not from Miguel Angel's salon," Helen said. "That was a big deal. If she'd worked here a year, she could have gone anywhere. An Angel-trained stylist makes big bucks. He ruined her chances when he threw her out."

McNally abruptly switched the topic by pulling out a photo of someone in a blue dress arguing with King Oden in his ugly tux. The two were in profile, facing each other, but the face of the person in the blue dress was hidden by long blond hair. She—or he—was shorter than the beefy Oden.

"Do you recognize the man in this photo?" McNally asked.

"That's the dead groom, King Oden," Helen said.

"Who's wearing the blue dress?"

"I have no idea," Helen said. "I didn't know most of the wedding guests. I was there to work."

"You should recognize your own employer."

"Miguel Angel has never worn a blue dress to work," Helen said. "He wears black pants and a black shirt with the sleeves rolled."

"Cute," McNally said. He sounded disgusted. He produced a second photo. This one was blurry and seemed to have been taken from a distance. "Why is Miguel Angel paying this man?"

He showed Helen a photo of Phoebe's stringy-haired boyfriend, Ramon. Miguel Angel seemed to be handing him cash. Ramon was giving Miguel a fat, white paper bag.

Helen's heart seized. Was Miguel Angel really buying drugs? No, that wasn't possible. It couldn't be. She looked around the salon wildly, as if the answer was written on the walls.

"Uh." Helen took a deep breath, and hoped her voice was steady. "Miguel Angel likes Cuban sandwiches. Aren't those grease spots on that bag?"

She pointed to some gray splotches that could have been grease or shadows. It was hard to tell. "That must be an old photo," Helen said. "Miguel hasn't bought anything from Ramon recently. He's been on a diet. There's no such thing as diet Cuban food."

"Yeah, right," Detective McNally said. She could tell he didn't believe her.

Chapter 11

Helen felt like Detective McNally had removed her brain and pumped her skull full of air. She probably had the IQ of a carrot after his inquisition. She just wanted to sit and veg in the cool evening.

Helen couldn't wait to get home to the Coronado Tropic Apartments, her peaceful haven. Night was falling. Her fiancé, Phil, would be out by the pool with a sundown beer and spicy chips. She missed him. She hadn't seen him since breakfast, and he'd been ridiculously cheerful this morning, singing at six a.m. She'd snapped at him.

Helen owed him an apology. What the heck was the matter with her lately? Well, she'd make it up to him.

Her plans were dashed as soon as she walked in the backyard. To get to Phil, she'd have to pass her landlady, Margery, talking to two shirtless twenty-somethings. Damn. She was in no mood for polite conversation.

"Helen!" Margery said. "I want you to meet your new neighbors in 2C—Josh and Jason."

Both were bare-chested, broad-shouldered, and tanned a tempting light brown. Josh had a goatee. Unless it was Jason. Their features were so bland, Helen couldn't tell them apart. Both were sucking Coors from bottles, and Helen wondered how long they'd keep those flat bellies flat. The lads grunted greetings.

"I hear you have a special rate for senior citizens with your construction business," Helen said. "That's very nice."

"Lotta geezers here," Josh said. Unless it was Jason. The two vanished upstairs.

"So what do you think?" Margery asked, as she handed Helen a glass of white wine fresh from the box. Helen took a sip and then a long gulp.

"They're okay, if you like dumb guys," Helen said.

"But you don't like them?" Margery said.

"How can I? They communicate in grunts. I'd get more conversation out of a chimp."

"Well, at least they won't cause problems in 2C," Margery said.

"That remains to be seen," Helen said. "So far, that apartment has been a den of thieves."

"It's hard to find good renters," Margery said.

"Your record for finding bad ones for 2C is unblemished," Helen said.

"Don't be cruel to a poor old woman," Margery said.

The landlady looked anything but old and helpless. Margery's gauzy purple top fluttered in the evening breeze. Purple flip-flops with trimmed lavender crystals showed off her tangerine-painted toes. She was smoking a Marlboro. Margery surveyed Helen with her shrewd, old eyes. "I've got some things to do. I'll leave you lovebirds alone."

"Good," Helen said, then realized that was rude. "Bye," she added as she fell into Phil's arms. He smelled like sandalwood soap with a slight hint of beer.

"I missed you, my Silver Fox," she said, kissing his neck and face.

"Your what?" Phil said.

"That's what the gossip magazines call a mature man who lets himself age naturally," she said, ruffling his thick, silver-white hair.

"Thanks, I think," Phil said.

"It means you don't need Botox to cover the lines in your forehead or the laugh lines," she said, kissing a laugh line.

"This just gets better and better," Phil said.

"I'm sorry I barked at you this morning," Helen said. "I'm not a morning person."

"I sort of figured that out," Phil said as he kissed her back. "Rough day?"

"You wouldn't believe," she said, nipping his ear. "You have cute ears. They're covered with light fuzz, like summer peaches."

"I don't think my ears caused your problem today, though you can keep nibbling them if you want. I like how you apologize. What happened that has you so upset?"

"Detective McNally came to the salon and all but accused Miguel Angel of dealing drugs and killing King Oden. It was horrible."

She kissed Phil lightly along the neck to his jawline.

"Did they arrest him yet?" Phil asked.

"No, but the police did a field test on some suspicious substance they found in his makeup case. Turned out to be heroin."

"Ouch," Phil said.

"Did I hurt you?" Helen asked.

"Not yet," Phil said. "I was referring to the suspicious substance."

"Miguel Angel doesn't use drugs," Helen said.

"Are you sure, Helen? Did you ever go to a party with the man?"

"No, we travel in different circles, as you well know. But he's never used them around me. I think he was set up by Phoebe, his worthless assistant. She has a drug dealer boyfriend. Miguel Angel begged the police to test his hair for drugs."

"That's smart," Phil said. "Hair will show drug use for about ninety days."

"The cops are waiting for the test results. They should have them back in two or three days."

"Mmm. You say the sweetest things." Phil rubbed her taut neck. "Let's finish this at my place." He unbuttoned the top button on her blouse.

"I'd love to," Helen said. "But let's discuss how to make this legal first."

"We're consenting adults," Phil said. "It is legal."

"I meant our wedding plans," Helen said, prying Phil's hands off her.

"Why don't you sit down with your wine, so I can think straight?" he said. "Do we really need to talk about the wedding again? I've already said whatever you want is fine with me."

"But it's not my wedding," Helen said. "It's our wedding. I bet you can't tell me a single detail."

"Sure, I can," Phil said. "We're not having a big church wedding. It's going to be here at the Coronado. By the pool, right?"

"Close," Helen said. "After Honey's wedding day, I'd rather you didn't stand too near the water."

That memory made her queasy, and she took a comforting sip of wine. Then she took a gulp. "I'd like our wedding to be in Margery's garden, under the palm trees, with box wine"—she patted the box next to her—"and party food. If that's okay with you," she added quickly.

"Can we have beer and spicy Doritos?" Phil said.

"Yes, and champagne for the toast, and some real wine with a cork in it, along with the box wine. And a wedding cake. What do you think of chocolate cake with white icing and sugar roses?"

"I like carrot cake," Phil said.

"We can have that, too. I'll get a caterer for the hors d'oeuvres. I'd like Peggy and my sister, Kathy, to be bridesmaids. My little niece Allison is probably too young to be a flower girl, and at ten—or is he eleven?—my nephew Tommy Junior is probably too old to be a ring bearer."

"Boys that age don't like hanging around weddings, wearing good clothes, anyway," Phil said.

"Who do you want to be your best man?" Helen asked.

"I don't know," Phil said. "Maybe I could get a vice cop."

"Nice touch," Helen said.

"I gather you're being sarcastic. What about Cal the Canadian? He's in town, isn't he?"

Helen thought that could be awkward. Cal lived at the Coronado, when he wasn't in Canada so he could qualify for his national health insurance. He was notoriously cheap. Helen had dated him briefly, long before Phil, and he'd stiffed her for his share of the restaurant tabs.

"Maybe he'll give me my share of those expensive dinners for a wedding present," she said.

"The man lives on boiled Brussels sprouts and baked potatoes," Phil said. "I doubt you'll ever see your money."

"Maybe having Cal in the wedding party is a way to mend fences," she said, without much enthusiasm.

"Have we decided where we're going to live?" Phil asked. "Your place or mine?"

"Both," Helen said. "We only have a total of four rooms together."

"Including two kitchens," Phil said.

"We could make my kitchen into a sitting room—or a closet. I rarely use it except for making coffee," Helen said. "What if we keep both apartments for now and run back and forth to them? They're right next door, anyway. It will give our marriage a nice illicit feel until we get used to holy wedlock. When we tire of commuting, we can move in together. But we've been single for a long time. I think we still need the safety of separate retreats."

"Where will Thumbs sleep?" Phil asked.

"Wherever he wants," Helen said. "Probably with you, since you bribe my cat with shrimp."

"Who's going to marry us?" Phil asked. "You don't want a religious ceremony. How about a judge?"

Oh no, Helen thought. How could I forget that major detail? "No judge," she said. "A judge caused too much trouble when I divorced Rob. Maybe Margery knows a minister. I'll ask her."

Helen set down her wineglass and ran across the damp grass to knock on Margery's jalousie door. Her landlady came out holding a homemade screwdriver in a tall glass. She trailed cigarette smoke and fluttering gauze.

"Come join us," Helen said. "We're planning our wedding." She gave Margery the details.

"You want your wedding here in my yard?" Margery asked.

"I hope that's okay. I've always wanted a garden wedding," Helen said.

"*Garden* is a grand term for a bougainvillea and a couple of palm trees. How many people are invited?"

"Peggy and her date, of course. And Pete."

"Her parrot is invited to the wedding?" Margery asked.

"She's had him longer than Daniel," Helen said. "Elsie. Anyone Phil works with. The stylists at Miguel Angel's salon. I'm thinking fifty people, max."

"Where are they going to sit? On the ground?"

"I'll rent chairs and a bridal arch."

"Who's doing the food?"

"I thought I'd have a caterer for the hors d'oeuvres."

"That's expensive, Helen," Margery said. "Spend the money on your honeymoon. What if we all brought some food? Peggy can make her Thai chicken salad. I'll bake brownies. Cal will drag out those same two tomatoes he brings to every party. You can provide a few other snacks and the cake, plus the wine, beer and soft drinks."

"But won't that be a lot of work for all of you, making so much food?" Helen asked.

Margery shrugged. "Cal never even bothers to slice the tomatoes. He plops them on a plate. I can make the brownies ahead of time and freeze them. I'll have to mow the lawn. That's it."

"I can mow the yard," Phil said. "I'll set up the chairs, put up the arch and put out some tables."

"See, it's not a big deal," Margery said. "I'm in charge of the bachelorette party, too."

"Let's not have it the night before the wedding," Helen said. "I don't want to walk down the aisle hungover."

"The bachelorette party will be the Sunday before the wedding. You'll have time to recover."

"Sunday? How will we party on a Sunday?"

"Wait and see," Margery said. "Who's giving you away?"

"I'm old enough to walk down the aisle by myself," Helen said.

"What about music?"

"I could hire a DJ, or we could just get a boom box and some tapes."

"I'd like a boom box," Phil said. "We can play Clapton CDs. I'll make up the playlist. Any particular songs?"

"Whatever you want," Helen said. "We do have one problem, Margery. We need someone to marry us."

"I will, if you want," Margery said. "I am an ordained minister."

Helen nearly dropped her wine. "You are?" She'd never seen her landlady darken a church door.

"Universal Life Church," Margery said. "I'm just as legal as any reverend or JP. I'd be honored. I have a purple robe and white dog collar."

"Where did you find a purple robe?" Helen asked.

"On eBay. I think it was from a Baptist choir, so at least part of my getup has been in a church. Now it's my turn for a question: Helen, are you going to invite your family?"

"My sister, Kathy, certainly, and her husband, Tom, and their two kids."

"And your mother?"

"No way. She says I'm still married in the eyes of God. She never accepted my divorce from Rob."

"But Rob married Marcella," Margery said.

"You couldn't remarry him if you wanted."

"*Maybe* they were married," Helen said. "The records and the witnesses for that ceremony have disappeared. So has the groom. Marcella, the Black Widow, claims she has no idea where Rob is, but she gave him lots of money to go away. Rob runs through money the way you go through Kleenex when you have a cold. If Rob and Marcella never married, my ex can come after me for the money that stupid judge says I owe him. Mom will turn me in, for sure."

"I can't believe that," Margery said.

"You've never met Mom. That woman is more Catholic than the pope."

"Why don't you get an annulment? Wouldn't that make her happy?"

"Only Catholics with a lot of money qualify for annulments. Maybe if I was a Kennedy, I could get one, but not as some nobody who works in a hair salon."

"That's a little cynical," Margery said.

"The church has cracked down on the rules for annulments. They felt Catholics were using them like divorces. Rob and I were married seventeen years and we were both adults. It's hard to claim that marriage never took place. Anyway, Mom is so weird on the subject of religion, I'm not sure she'd accept an annulment."

"Helen, my fee for this wedding is that you invite your mother," Margery said. "If she doesn't want to come, that's her business. But it's time you grew up and ended those old feuds. Don't start your new life with old baggage."

"Margery, if I invite my mother to the wedding, we'll both regret it."

Chapter 12

"You're lucky you're an orphan, Phil," Helen said, pulling herself out of the comfortable chaise longue.

"Ouch. That's a rotten thing to say. Mom was a nice woman. You'd have liked her. Besides, my ex-wife, Kendra, more than makes up for any lack of relatives on my side."

"Sorry." Helen gave Phil a conciliatory kiss. "I've been snapping at you a lot lately."

"Yes, you have," Phil said. "Should I put it down to bridal nerves?"

"That's a good reason," Helen said. "But I don't know what excuse I'll have after we're married. How about, 'That was an ugly thing to say and I'm sorry'?"

"Apology accepted," Phil said.

She filled her wineglass with more liquid courage and trudged toward her apartment. Phil followed, clutching his spicy chips and beer.

"You can use my phone if you want," Phil said when they reached her door. He opened his apartment, and Helen sat on his couch.

He massaged her neck. "Your shoulders are tight."

"Just thinking about talking to my mother makes me tense," Helen said. "Mom's not only in another time zone, she's on another planet. I'll call Kathy first. I can deal with my sister."

Helen still didn't have a phone. She kept a cell phone she hoped was hard to trace when she had to talk to her family. Kathy was the only person she trusted to know how to reach her. She had Margery's phone number. Helen checked her watch. It was seven thirty in St. Louis—not so late her call would alarm Kathy. Helen's sister lived in the near-perfect suburb of Webster Groves. She and Tom had a big, old house that needed paint and new plumbing. Tom didn't make much money teaching. Kathy worked part-time as a checker at Target. She rarely mentioned their money worries.

Helen took a deep breath and dialed.

"Helen?" Kathy said, as soon as she heard her sister's voice. "What's wrong?"

"Nothing," Helen said. "I'm calling with good news. I'm getting married. This time, I've found the right man. I met him at the Coronado. His name is Phil, and he's terrific."

She smiled at Phil. He smiled back and squeezed her hand.

"That's wonderful," Kathy said. "And about time." She'd never liked Rob. "When do I meet this paragon?"

"Soon, I hope. This is kind of last-minute, but we're getting married a week from Saturday, and I wondered if you could be here?"

"I'd be delighted." Kathy sounded like she meant it.

"Can Tom and the kids come, too?" Helen asked.

"Yes," Kathy said. "He's teaching summer school, but Tom can call in sick if he has to."

"Good," Helen said. "I'll send money for gas."

"Helen! We're not that bad off."

"You can stay in my apartment. There's a nice pool for the kids to play in." That would save Kathy and Tom the cost of a hotel.

"Deal!" Kathy said. "What about Mom? Is she invited?"

"I'll call her after I talk to you. She'll go ballistic. She's still trying to get me back with Rob."

"I can break the news to Mom and invite her to your wedding," Kathy said. "She can ride down to Florida with us."

"No!" Helen said. "Don't shut her in a car with poor Tom. He'll go crazy."

"Okay, she can fly. But I'll tell her for you. That will be my present."

"I'd like that better than a cut-glass candy dish," Helen said. "I have one more favor to ask. Will you be my maid of honor?"

"Are you going to make me wear powder-blue chiffon with ruffles and daisies, like you did last time?"

Helen winced. Did she really do that to her sister? She'd wiped most of the details of her first wedding from her mind. "Nope. This time you can choose your own dress—any style you like, any color you want."

"Short or long?" Kathy asked.

"It's a backyard wedding. Short is fine."

"Good. I'll get more wear out of it."

"That's what all bridesmaids say," Helen said. "I bet you never wore that dress again."

"Oh, I did," Kathy said. "We had an ugly-bridesmaid-dress party. We wore our worst dresses, got drunk on margaritas, then changed into shorts and burned the dresses in the barbecue grill. The neighbors called the police." She sounded proud.

"Well, at least that dress provided a hot time. But you should have burned the groom," Helen said.

"Instead, he burned you," Kathy said. There was a long pause. "Sorry. I didn't mean to stir up bad memories."

"This wedding will have good memories," Helen said. "Please be part of them. I can't wait to see my niece and nephew."

They said their good-byes. Helen hung up, weak with relief. Kathy really had given her a gift. She'd escaped the confrontation with her mother.

"Dodged that bullet," she said to Phil. "Kathy's going to call Mom for me."

"Coward," Phil said, unbuttoning her blouse. "I have just the thing to relax you."

119

"What about the cat?" Helen said.

"What cat?" Phil said.

"Your shrimp-eating buddy, Thumbs, hasn't had dinner yet."

"He can wait a little longer," Phil said. "And speaking of longer . . ."

Helen was awakened by howls in the dark room. She stumbled out of Phil's bed and tripped over her shoes.

Phil sat up and switched on the light. "What's going on?" His silver-white hair was tousled with sleep.

"It's Thumbs," Helen said. "He's screaming for dinner so loud I can hear him here in your apartment. What time is it? We fell asleep."

"Ten thirty," Phil said.

Helen slipped on her jeans and shirt, grabbed her purse and house keys, and ran barefoot to her apartment. Phil threw on his pants, picked up her shoes, and followed.

They were met at her door by an angry Thumbs. The big gray-and-white cat lashed his long tail, his yellow-green eyes burning with anger.

"If he weighed eight hundred pounds, he'd eat us," Phil said.

Thumbs' metal water bowl was flipped upside down to demonstrate his displeasure.

"All right, all right," Helen said to the irate cat.

"I'll feed you. But you don't look like you're starving."

She filled his bowl with dry food, mopped up the spilled water and gave him fresh. The cat pushed Helen aside with his huge six-toed front paw and gobbled his chow.

"Are you hungry, Phil?" Helen said. "I can scramble some eggs."

"Sounds good. I'll make toast and have a bed-time beer."

Helen poked around in her fridge and found a green onion past its prime, added some cheddar cheese and a slightly wrinkled green pepper. She didn't trust the ham. It was nearly as green as the pepper.

Helen beat six eggs, folded in the cheese, chopped the pepper and onion, fried the mixture, then plunked half on Phil's plate.

"Yum," Phil said. "A Denver omelet."

That was a grand name for scrambled leftovers, but Helen didn't correct him. She ate the other half.

Phil opened a cold beer, gave Helen a slice of toast and put a jar of strawberry jam on the table. He poured hot sauce on his omelet. They ate in companionable silence while Thumbs twined around Phil's leg.

"No shrimp for you, greedy guts," Helen said to the cat.

Phil finished his omelet, carried his dishes to the

kitchen sink and filled the dishpan with hot water and soap.

"Don't bother with that, Phil," Helen said. "I can wash those later." She tried to suppress a yawn. "I hate to throw you out, but I have to work tomorrow. Unlike some people, I can't sit around all day."

"I'm on hiatus until after the honeymoon," Phil said. "How can I help with the wedding?"

"Just round up a best man—or a good one, anyway," Helen said. "And would you buy the booze?"

"Finally, a job I'm qualified for," Phil said. "Want to sleep over at my place tonight?"

"Thanks, but I really need to go to bed—and sleep for a change." Helen pushed Phil toward the door. They had a last, lingering kiss in the doorway.

"I can't wait until we're married," Helen said.

"Me, either," Phil said. "Good night."

Helen fell asleep wondering how Kathy's conversation with their mother went. If anyone could get through to Dolores, it was Helen's patient, nearly perfect sister.

Helen's alarm went off at seven thirty-eight the next morning. She tried to roll over for a few more minutes of sleep, but Thumbs jumped on the bed and yowled for breakfast.

"Hang on," Helen said. "Let me find my head."

She wandered into her tiny bathroom, looked in

the mirror and winced. Sleep wrinkles creased her face. Her brown hair looked like an uprooted plant.

"Ugh." Helen showered and washed her hair, then put on coffee and fed Thumbs. She drank her coffee while she blow-dried her hair. The hair seemed to take forever, but she thought it looked good. Maybe some of Miguel Angel's genius was rubbing off on her.

Helen believed that all the way to the salon. The June morning was so humid, it was almost like wading through a swimming pool. She reveled in the blast of cool air as she opened the salon door. How did people live in Florida before air-conditioning?

"Good morning," Helen said. Ana Luisa was talking on the phone, and waved at Helen.

Miguel Angel was at his station, putting his things back to rights. Helen didn't think the cops had done any damage except for the broken jar in the back room, but Miguel Angel had a discerning eye.

"Sit in my chair," he said. "Let me fix your hair."

"I fixed it myself," she said.

"I can see. What have you done to your bangs?"

Helen sat. Her hair had never looked so good since she'd had this job.

"If you don't look good, you make me look bad." Miguel Angel removed his hair-dryer from its hol-

123

ster and brushed out her long hair, pulling it taut with his strong wrists. Soon Helen's hair was as dark and silky as a shampoo ad.

"I need a new assistant," he told Helen. "I have to replace Phoebe. Are you sure you don't want to get your license?"

"Thanks, but I don't have the talent to work with hair," Helen said.

"You'd be better than Phoebe," he said.

"My cat would be better," Helen said.

"Then Carlos will assist me," Miguel Angel said. "He has a little trouble with English, but that's not a real problem."

"Mrs. Crane is here for her appointment," Ana Luisa announced.

Helen didn't know the woman's first name. The crabby, charmless Mrs. Crane wore her pale hair in a helmet style forty years out of date. Helen wondered why she paid Miguel Angel's prices when she could get the same style at a neighborhood salon. Mrs. Crane favored frumpy shirtwaists, stockings and low heels.

She plopped in Miguel Angel's chair, demanded coffee with cream and sugar from Helen and said, "I have an important charity board meeting this afternoon."

Carlos stood by, smiling happily. He was clearly thrilled with his new promotion. Miguel Angel gave his assistant instructions in Spanish. Helen could translate about every third word, but she knew Miguel Angel was telling Carlos what color to mix.

Mrs. Crane grew increasingly irritated, twisting in her seat. Finally, she erupted angrily, "We're in America. The least you can do is speak American."

Carlos looked hurt. Helen blushed for the woman's boorish behavior. Why did rude people insist everyone "speak American"? Were they proud of knowing only one language?

"We were speaking Spanish," Miguel Angel said in a cold voice, "which is the major language of the Americas. I did not want Carlos to make a mistake. But if you wish, I will speak English. Or Helen can translate for you."

"Never mind," Mrs. Crane said. "I can't wait to get back to Wisconsin, where people still speak English."

Miguel Angel painted the woman's roots. Carlos put her under a color-processing dryer, carefully setting the timer.

Mrs. Crane tipped Miguel Angel a measly five dollars for her hair and gave Carlos a dollar. Both were elaborately polite in their thanks. No one asked her to return.

"I'm sorry," Carlos said, after she left.

"Why?" Miguel Angel said.

"I should have spoken English."

"Your English is better than mine," Helen said.

"Quick!" Ana Luisa interrupted. "King's death is on TV."

Helen, Miguel Angel and Carlos joined her in the prep area.

"There have been no arrests in the murder of gossip mogul King Oden," the reporter said. "This evening, Channel Fifteen will show King being threatened with death moments before his murder. Tune in for this exclusive at—"

"Turn it off," Miguel Angel said.

"But we want—" Ana Luisa said.

"I don't care what you want," Miguel Angel said, turning off the television. "It's my TV and my salon and I don't want to know."

But Helen did. She wondered why Miguel Angel was so anxious to avoid the subject, and who was in that video.

Chapter 13

"Miguel Angel, I want to look like Lindsay Lohan," said the woman sitting in his sculpted chair. She tossed her long hair flirtatiously, an odd gesture for a sturdy brunette in her forties. She had pale, unlined skin and long fingers.

Helen guessed the woman was about six feet tall and weighed close to two hundred pounds. She seemed too smart to admire an airhead actress.

"Uh, how would you like to look like her?" Miguel Angel asked.

Helen had to force herself to keep from applauding his amazing tact.

"My bangs," the woman said, and draped her dark locks across her right eye.

"I can cut you some bangs," Miguel Angel said. "I can also add layers for volume."

"Would you like some water?" Helen asked her.

"Tea would be better," the future Lindsay look-alike said. "Hot tea, herbal, no sugar."

"Coming up." Helen headed toward the prep area to make tea. Miguel Angel joined her to mix the Lindsay look-alike's color.

"I want to look like Paris Hilton," Helen said.

"Shut up," Miguel Angel said. "I can do it."

He could, too. Like a wizard in a folktale, he could transform Helen into the sheep-faced heiress—without the money.

Helen said nothing more. She suspected Miguel Angel was reaching the end of his patience, and she didn't want to push him further. His temper explosion over the TV news show was unlike him. He was no tyrant at the shop and rarely yelled at his staff.

Helen poured hot water into a cup, added a chamomile tea bag and slid three thin slices of lemon on a saucer.

Why did Miguel Angel become so angry? Who was in that video? Why did Miguel Angel insist on turning off the television? Was the story too painful? Was he afraid the police had found something damning? Worst of all, did he murder King?

Helen couldn't ask him, and he wouldn't tell her.

The subject weighed on her mind all afternoon. She went through the motions, handing clients drinks, fetching magazines, dusting and sweeping up the eternal hair. She wished the day was over.

At two thirty, Ana Luisa reminded Miguel Angel that Sandra would be in at three. Miguel swore softly in Spanish.

"What's wrong with Sandra?" Helen asked, as she dusted a nearby counter.

"Wait and see," Ana Luisa whispered back.

Sandra was a flirtatious divorcée in her midforties who dressed like a teenager in tight white jeans and a belly-baring top. She carried a small, silly pink purse. Her breasts and hair were artful fakes, and she moved in a choking cloud of perfume.

"Miguel Angel, I have a new man. I need to look perfect tonight," Sandra said. "Work your magic on me, so I can work my magic on him. He's a rich one."

Soon Sandra was wearing silver highlight foils that looked like a crown of leaves. Each hair section had been painstakingly painted by Miguel Angel.

After twenty minutes, he checked the color, then told Carlos to remove the foil and wash Sandra's hair. Then she was back in Miguel Angel's chair, draped in a styling cape. He dried her hair, pulling the frizzy curls into the straight, sophisticated style currently favored by network news anchors—and nearly impossible to attain in the Florida humidity.

"Nice," Sandra said.

Ana Luisa presented her with a bill Helen thought could have been the down payment on a car, and Sandra paid it without blinking. Then she reached into the tiny pink purse and pulled out a wad of bills.

Miguel Angel reacted quickly. "Carlos!" he ordered his assistant. "Go clean up the prep room."

Carlos hesitated.

"Now," Miguel Angel commanded.

Carlos looked startled, but obediently walked toward the back room.

Sandra handed Helen a five-dollar bill, then took a fat roll of cash and shoved it in the change pocket of Miguel Angel's jeans, running her hand suggestively along his crotch. The stylist flinched.

"And there's more for little Carlos," she said in a husky voice, stuffing more money in the other pocket and running her hand along Miguel Angel's zipper.

Eeuww, Helen thought. A stripper tipper. She'd heard of these women. They tended to be over forty. Some were seventy or more. They copped a feel when they tipped the stylist, as if they were at a Chippendales show.

Sandra left the salon, swinging her jeans-clad rear end seductively.

"Yuck," Helen said. "That was nasty. Is that why you sent Carlos to the back?"

"Yes," Miguel Angel said. "He doesn't need to be molested by that woman."

"Does she know you're . . . uh . . ." Helen stopped, unable to think of a tactful way to continue.

"She doesn't care if I'm gay," Miguel Angel finished. "Or she thinks her so-called beauty will overcome my nature. She acts like I'm some sort of pet and have no feelings. I hate being touched by people I don't like. Hate it."

Anger flashed in his eyes. "Let me give Carlos his money," Miguel Angel said. "At least he didn't have to go through that."

Helen had no doubt that he disliked the humiliating way Sandra had pawed him in his own salon. And the murdered King did more than touch Miguel Angel—he'd threatened the stylist and his livelihood. Did Miguel Angel kill the gossip columnist for that?

Half an hour later, a young model named Tara rushed in, out of breath. Yards of taffy-colored hair trailed behind her. A tiny scrap of fabric clung to her breasts. Her jeans were so tight, Helen wondered how she could walk.

"Help, Miguel Angel!" Tara cried.

"Do you have an appointment?" Ana Luisa said, barring her way.

"This is an emergency," Tara said.

"And what is this emergency?" Miguel Angel said, sounding amused. "Should I call an ambulance?"

"You can see my roots," she wailed, pointing to her nearly perfect hair.

Only with a microscope, Helen thought.

"You have to save me," Tara said, as if Miguel Angel was armed with six-guns instead of hairdryers. "I have a shoot with *Gold Coast* magazine tomorrow on South Beach."

"Well, let's see what we can do," Miguel Angel said. "Sit down."

Helen brought Tara bottled water and the latest issue of *Vogue*, then swept the floor one more time. Miguel Angel gave her a nod that she could go, and Helen left gratefully at five thirty.

She stepped out into the sweltering Florida sun. Even late in the day, the heat took her breath away. Sweat ran down her face, neck and back as she walked home toward the Coronado. Her blouse clung to her damp body.

Phil was waiting for her at the back gate. "Hurry," he said, not even stopping to kiss her.

Margery called from her door, "Get in here quick, both of you. You don't have time to canoodle."

"Canoodle?" Helen said.

"Your boss is about to be featured in a special news report on the six o'clock news," Margery said. "It doesn't look good."

Helen and Phil raced toward Margery's apartment. Helen could hear a woman announcer saying ". . . an important clue in the murder of Kingman

'King' Oden. Channel Fifteen has obtained an exclusive video of a death threat to the late gossip king. We'll have more for you after our commercial break."

"Sit down," Margery said.

"I don't want to ruin your living room furniture," Helen said. "I'm dripping sweat."

Margery plunked a kitchen chair in front of the TV, then brought Helen a towel and a tall, cold glass of water.

"Is water okay?" she asked. "Or do you want something stronger?"

"Perfect," Helen said. "I like being waited on. I've been fetching drinks and magazines at the salon all day."

"You poor thing," Margery said. Helen didn't know if she was being sarcastic.

"Sh!" Phil said, perching on the arm of Margery's purple recliner. "Here comes the story."

A harried-looking woman reporter stood in front of King's slightly smoked mansion. She was sweating, too. Yellow crime-scene tape fluttered in the hot breeze. One pink stucco wall was blackened by the fire, and Helen thought she heard a power saw in the background.

"Police say they have no leads in the murder of King Oden, who drowned in a swimming pool at his palatial Fort Lauderdale mansion on his wedding day," the reporter said. "A fire started at the mansion as his guests fled the scene.

"There has been no progress in the murder investigation. Now Channel Fifteen has obtained a groundbreaking video. It shows King being threatened with death minutes before his murder."

The reporter said the last three words with a dramatic flourish.

Helen felt her heart pound. This was it. The TV station was going to ruin Miguel Angel. The scene switched to a video from a camera so shaky, it was like looking in a fun house mirror.

Helen could see an enraged, bare-chested King screaming at Miguel Angel. "Listen, you Cuban *bleep*," King said, as spit flew from his angry lips. "I've got friends in the city and state government. I can have that salon of yours closed down for so many violations, your dyed head will spin. Got it?"

He punched a sausagelike finger in Miguel Angel's face.

Helen watched in horror as Miguel Angel shook off King's hand, then pressed his long, sharp scissors so the points were stuck in King's neck. "And I can kill you, you fat, lazy American," Miguel Angel said. "No one will care."

The video showed a shell-shocked Honey pushing her way between the furious men. "Stop!" she pleaded. "This is my wedding day. Behave. Both of you."

There was a close-up on the drop of blood the scissors left on King's neck, then the video faded to black.

The story was back to the reporter in front of King's mansion. "The man in the black shirt has been identified as society hairstylist Miguel Angel"—she mispronounced it "Migwel Angel." Even the pros couldn't get his name right—"the person responsible for the career-saving makeover on superstar LaDonna. We talked with the police about this incriminating video. They are still refusing to arrest anyone."

Detective Richard McNally was on camera now, looking older and heavier than he did in person. "We need evidence to make an arrest," he said. "All we have here is a video showing two men arguing. We don't know if the man in question acted on his threat."

The story ended with a shot of the reporter standing on the sidewalk in front of Miguel Angel's salon. Helen thought the woman could have used a good haircut. The reporter said, "Many famous names have passed through these doors for makeovers by Miguel Angel. No one doubts his talent. The only question is, Does Miguel Angel do killer hair?"

Helen groaned. "This is horrible," she said.

"They were reaching for that pun," Phil said.

"No, I mean what the reporter said about Miguel Angel. She practically called him a killer right in front of his salon. And he looked crazy-mad in that video."

"Was it doctored?" Phil asked.

"No, I was there. That's what happened. But it's not fair to run it on TV. Miguel Angel has worked so hard. This story could ruin his salon."

"How?" Phil said. "Who is going to care what's on a nowhere local news show?"

"Everyone," Margery said. "Helen is right. King's gossip blog and TV show were national. The networks will pick this up so quick, Miguel Angel won't know what hit him. Too bad. I kind of like Miguel Angel. He's a hard worker. I hate to see him ruined by a lowlife like King Oden."

"I think I'll have that drink now," Helen said.

Chapter 14

Helen woke up with the sun streaming in her bedroom window. Too bad the sunny weather didn't match her mood. Helen had that uneasy, stomach-full-of-snakes feeling she got when things were going wrong. It had nothing to do with her upcoming marriage. That couldn't be better, once Margery had agreed to perform the ceremony.

Helen was worried about Miguel Angel. The Cuban stylist could lose his salon. He'd worked many long, hard years to get where he was. He didn't deserve that. She didn't, either. If the salon closed, Helen would be out of work, and for a dead-end job, this one was cushy.

Helen mentally ticked off the advantages: She

spent her working day in a pleasant salon. The heaviest lifting was picking up the fall fashion issue of *Vogue*. Mostly, she fetched cold water and hot tea and swept up hair clippings. She'd had worse jobs.

Telemarketing won the booby prize for worst verbal abuse. Cleaning hotel rooms was a job that still made her back ache. And talk about lifting. As a hotel maid, she'd hauled heavy vacuums and piles of unspeakable laundry, and pushed a cleaning cart that weighed as much as a minivan.

Working for Miguel Angel was easy in comparison. Thanks to his quest for perfection, her hair almost always looked good. He couldn't resist correcting her homemade attempts at styling. Helen had one of South Florida's most expensive hairdressers itching to style her hair. For free.

If you have such a terrific job, you'd better get there, Helen told herself. She gave her hair one last brush, and knew that was a waste of time. Miguel Angel would restyle it the moment she walked into the salon.

She finished her coffee, grabbed a bottle of water, and started the short walk to work.

Even at nine in the morning, the June humidity was like a thick, damp pillow over her face. She could hardly catch her breath. She could feel her hair frizzing as she moved.

Helen had barely rounded the corner onto Las

Olas Boulevard when she saw the throng of TV vans parked by the salon door.

Uh-oh. Media ambush.

They were after Miguel Angel. She could see the CLOSED sign was still on the door. The shades were drawn. Was the salon going to open today?

Helen ran back to the Coronado and knocked on Phil's door. He wasn't home. She used her key, unlocked his door, and called the salon from Phil's phone.

The answering machine clicked on, and Ana Luisa's voice asked her to leave a message.

"Ana Luisa, is the salon open today?" Helen asked. "I saw the TV vans. Should I come into work or not? Is Miguel Angel okay? Is—"

Ana Luisa herself picked up the phone. "Miguel Angel is avoiding the TV cameras," she said in a whisper. "The press is camped out in front and in back. He called me. He's parked his Jeep in the metered lot off Las Olas. He's sitting there while we find a way to sneak him into work."

"I have an idea," Helen said. "Tell him to wait for me. I'll be at the lot in fifteen minutes."

Helen ran home and searched her closet. She found a soft blue blouse in a matronly style. She rarely wore it, except when she went to job interviews. She threw her makeup into a small plastic bag, added a brush and hair spray, a pair of gold clip-on earrings, a plastic disposable razor, a hotel toiletry bottle of hand lotion, and crammed them all into a big green tote.

Then she knocked on Margery's door. Her landlady was still wearing her purple robe. She looked bleary-eyed.

"Do you have to break the door down?" Margery asked. "What time is it?"

"Nine twenty," Helen said. "What's wrong?"

"I slept late for a change," Margery said. "What's your problem? Tell me you didn't break up with Phil."

"No, we're fine. I have an emergency. The press is after Miguel Angel and I have to help him. Do you still have that wig you wore at Halloween?"

"The black curly one?" Margery said. "I looked like an Omaha church lady."

"I don't know," Helen said. "I've met some stylish women from Nebraska."

"I'm trying to say it's an awful wig," Margery said.

"That's why I want it," Helen said.

"Well, hold on and let me find it. Maybe I'll find my head while I'm at it." Margery really did look her age for once. Helen had always seen her landlady as indestructible, but this morning she looked frail, and yes, old. Helen felt a small flash of fear. What would she do without Margery? Her landlady was one of the pillars of her world.

Helen followed Margery into her bedroom. "Can I fix you some breakfast?" Helen asked.

"You? Cook? Then I'd really be sick."

Ah, that was better, Helen thought. Margery sounded like her surly self. The landlady got down on her knees to look in the lower dresser drawer, and Helen heard her joints pop and crack.

"I could buy you a muffin or pick up something at the bakery," Helen said.

"I can light my own cigarette and turn on the coffeepot. And I will, as soon as you leave," Margery said. She rooted around in her lower dresser drawer and pulled out something black and hairy. She handed it to Helen.

"It's either road kill or your curly black wig," Helen said.

"Are you going to insult it or take it?" Margery said. "I want a cigarette and my coffee. I'm in no mood for your wisecracks."

Helen stuffed the wig into the tote before Margery changed her mind. "One more thing," she said.

"Yes, Columbo?" Margery said.

"May I borrow that purple throw on your living room chair?" Helen asked.

"Take it, take it," Margery said, waving her toward the door. "Just bring it back. And don't slam the door."

Helen stuffed the purple throw into the tote and closed the door so softly the jalousie glass didn't even rattle. She ran the three blocks in the other direction, and arrived out of breath at the steaming parking lot.

She spotted Miguel Angel in his black Jeep. He beeped his horn in greeting.

"Ana Luisa said you were on the way," he said.

"I'm here to sneak you into the salon," she said. "I brought some makeup and a wig."

"The wig is ugly." Miguel Angel made a face.

"It's supposed to be. You're a tourist. Put it on."

Miguel Angel fussed with the fake hair. Then he put on the matronly blouse.

"I brought the razor and hand lotion so you can shave your beard," Helen said.

He made some quick swipes, then put on Helen's makeup.

"This lipstick is not the right color for me," he said.

"You're not supposed to look good. Wrap this purple throw around you and hide your hands," Helen said. "You're my sickly auntie. We're checking into the Lauderdale Las Olas Hotel."

"But I have to go to work," Miguel Angel said.

"And I have to sneak you past the TV cameras. Move over into the passenger seat."

Helen drove Miguel Angel's Jeep to the hotel's check-in side. A valet rushed out to meet them.

"My aunt is recovering from surgery," Helen said. "She feels ill and needs a wheelchair. Do you have one?"

"We can get one," the valet said. He returned with a folding wheelchair and helped Miguel Angel into it. Helen carefully arranged the purple throw to cover the stylist's lap and hands and tipped the valet ten dollars.

"I'd like to leave my car here and get my aunt breakfast, then take her down Las Olas for some fresh air. We'll be back in a bit. Can we keep the chair for the day?"

"Certainly," the valet said. "There will be a thirty-dollar rental charge."

"Terrific," Helen said. She filled out the paperwork. Miguel Angel handed the valet forty dollars. The valet started to give him change, but Miguel Angel shook his head.

"Thank you, ma'am!" the valet said.

Helen wheeled the chair toward the hotel's front door. When she looked back, the valet had driven off with the Jeep. She pushed the chair two blocks up Las Olas. Their progress was slow and the chair felt like it was going to tip over.

"Can you go faster?" Miguel Angel said.

"I'm trying, but the pavement is uneven and you're heavier than you look."

"It's my arms and hands," he said. "They're all muscle."

"It's your Cuban sandwiches," Helen said. "Good thing you're a cross-dresser. It makes it easier to carry this off."

"I am not a cross-dresser!" Miguel Angel said, his voice fierce with anger. "That is someone who does not know who he is. I know who I am. I am gay. I am a hairdresser."

"I've known straight hairdressers," Helen said, "and please lower your voice."

"In Cuba, if you style hair, you must be gay," Miguel Angel hissed. "No real man plays with women's hair."

"That's stupid," Helen said, steering the chair toward the alley. "Miguel Angel, call Ana Luisa on your cell. Ask her to open the back door when we knock three times. Promise me you won't say a word while I get us through the press corps and inside."

Miguel Angel speed-dialed and delivered the message.

"Put your head down," Helen said. "I don't want anyone to get a good look at your face."

"Me, either," Miguel Angel said.

"Keep your hands under that throw," she said. "They look too strong to belong to a sick old woman."

Helen was rolling the chair around the news vans when the first reporter approached, a bleached blonde with dark roots. She could have used a consultation with Miguel Angel.

"Excuse me," the reporter asked. "Do you feel it's safe to come to this salon?"

"Miguel Angel has been doing my poor, sick aunt's hair for years," Helen said. "She's not feeling well. Please let me get her inside, out of this heat."

Miguel Angel hung his head like a wilting violet. The wave of reporters and videographers parted.

Helen wheeled the chair up to the back door, knocked three times, and Ana Luisa opened it. One more push over the threshold, and Miguel Angel was inside. Ana Luisa slammed and double-locked the door.

Miguel Angel stood up, pulled off the wig and shook out his own hair.

"How is it going?" Helen asked.

"Horrible," Ana Luisa said. "*Manhattan Fashionista* canceled their shoot, and so have three other New York magazines. The television bridal show canceled. LaDonna suddenly doesn't need Miguel Angel for her tour."

"That ingrate," Helen said. "After Miguel Angel saved her career."

"There's more," Ana Luisa said. "Three MTV dancers called to say they won't need their hair done after all. Valencia is sending her assistant to pick up her extensions. Someone else will put them on her."

Helen watched the color drain from Miguel Angel's face. He knew what this meant: slow death. The major magazines and celebrities that gave the big stylists their earning power were running away.

Miguel Angel's fame—and his fortune—would soon be gone. He would no longer be able to afford the pricey shop on Las Olas. The glittering Miguel Angel salon would slowly sink into the sleepy, low-paying life of a neighborhood beauty shop.

The dead King would drag him down into ruin.

Chapter 15

A re you sure you want to cancel?" Ana Luisa whispered into the salon phone. Her computer screen glowed in the darkened room.

She listened a moment, then said, "Yes, ma'am."

Ana Luisa clicked some keys and said, "I've canceled your appointment for tomorrow, but you may not be able to get another one at the last minute." She hung up and sighed.

Miguel Angel hovered nearby. "Who else canceled?" he asked.

"Kim Hammond."

"The supermodel who said she couldn't live without me? Now she cancels at the last minute?"

"She said she didn't need her hair fixed after all," Ana Luisa said.

"She has a South Beach photo shoot," Miguel Angel said. "I don't think so. Last week, I was a genius. Now I don't exist."

The lights were off in the front of the salon, and the shades were drawn. The phones hadn't stopped ringing. Helen, Miguel Angel, and Ana Luisa were huddled in the darkened store like burglars, hoping the reporters wouldn't notice them. Carlos hovered and looked worried.

"We're down to one celebrity for the week." Ana Luisa's voice was gloomy. Even her blond hair seemed to droop. "The good news is we're getting lots of appointments from people we don't know, so we're still booked. But they only want Miguel Angel, not Richard or Paolo. I think they're tourists."

"They're vultures," Miguel Angel said. "I am a scandal, and they want to see me."

"The first vulture arrives shortly," Ana Luisa said. "We'd better turn on the lights. Carlos, guard the front door. If any reporters want in, Miguel Angel is not here."

"How can I tell who they are?" Carlos asked.

"The real customers have confirmation numbers," Ana Luisa said. "If you have any doubts, I have the numbers here."

"But what about your hair?" Carlos asked. He'd been trying to talk Ana Luisa into dyeing her blond hair red. "You have beautiful skin. If Mother Nature knew what she was doing, you'd have been born with red hair."

"No," Ana Luisa said. "The last stylist cut my hair so badly it took a year to grow out."

"But he was fired. I am good," Carlos said.

"I know you are," Ana Luisa said. "But I want my children to recognize me when I go home. And they're blond like their mother. Besides, we're going to be too busy for you to fool around with my hair."

In the slow times, the salon staff styled one another's hair the way little girls played dolls. They cut long hair short, added extensions and

145

experimented with highlights. Some experiments were more successful than others. Stylists liked to run their fingers through other people's hair. They enjoyed the color, the texture, the feel.

"I've always loved hair," Miguel Angel told Helen. "Even as a little boy, I liked to play with hair. I styled my sister's hair."

"Lucky her," Helen said.

"Unlucky me. My father was furious. To have a gay Cuban son was a great shame. He did not want a hairdresser son. It was not a manly thing to do."

"I'm sorry," Helen said.

"Don't be. They like my gay money. But they keep trying to fix me up with nice Cuban girls."

"They don't get it, do they?" she said.

"No," Miguel Angel said. "I am not going to settle down, no matter how many novenas they say."

Helen laughed. "My family doesn't get me, either."

"Vulture alert," Ana Luisa said.

The new clients arrived in pairs, as if they were afraid to come alone to the salon. The first two were typical: women from Mississippi with short, curly blond hair and *honey-chile* accents. One was Luann. The other was Carrie. They were at least fifty, but dressed much younger.

"Everyone down here speaks Mexican," Luann said. "I thought this was America." Her pale blue shirt was a waterfall of ruffles. Her ring had a diamond the size of an ice cube.

"Where are you ladies from?" Helen asked.

"Olive Branch, Mississippi," Carrie said. Her purple muumuu was embroidered with bold yellow flowers. She had matching sunflower earrings.

"I'm not familiar with that town," Helen said.

"It's the ninth largest city in Mississippi," Luann said. Her dangly earrings danced and swayed.

"It's really a suburb of Memphis," Carrie said.

"Now, that city I've heard of," Helen said. "May I get you coffee or some water?"

"Is there an extra charge?" Luann said. "Because the boys—our husbands—said we could treat ourselves to an afternoon of beauty while they went deep-sea fishing, but these prices are scaring me."

"No charge," Helen said.

"Do you have sweet tea?" Luann asked.

"I have iced tea, but you'll have to add your own sugar," Helen said. "Are you here on vacation?"

"We leave tomorrow," Carrie said. "I thought if I went here, I'd have a story to tell the girls at bridge."

Vultures, Helen thought. Miguel had correctly identified these birds. She handed each one a hanger and directed the two women to the dressing rooms.

She'd just turned around when Carrie said, "Did he do it?"

"Do what?" Helen asked.

"Your boss. Did he kill that King guy?"

147

"Of course not," Helen said. "Do I look like I'd work for a murderer?"

"Oh no," Carrie said. "But that TV show—"

"Was wrong," Helen said, chopping off the discussion.

She wished the vultures would all flock back to Mississippi, Missouri or wherever they came from.

The next hour was slow torture. More vultures arrived. The only good thing, if you could call it that, was a five-car pileup on I-95. That accident sent the news vans heading for the highway. The press quit camping outside the salon. Helen dusted surfaces that didn't need dusting and swept an already clean floor. Again.

At twelve thirty, she slipped out to order her wedding cake. She noticed a plain white van in a no-parking zone across from the salon. It won't be there long, she decided. The ever-watchful parking patrol would have it moved. Helen walked to Kakes by Kitty, a tiny store no bigger than a phone booth. Cats abounded in the shop— stuffed toy cats, cat photos, stained-glass cats, everything but live cats. Kitty herself was a motherly woman with blue eyes and yellow hair who resembled a large tabby. Helen remembered her grandmother saying, "Never trust a skinny cook." By Grandma's standards, Kitty was trustworthy.

"A wedding cake reveals a lot about your relationship," Kitty said. "Do you want a traditional round cake, or something offbeat, like a hexagon or a square?"

"I'll stick with the round, tiered cake," Helen said. "I'd like a chocolate cake with white icing and sugar roses. I love sugar roses."

"And what about the cake topper? Do you want a bride and groom, a bell or a pair of doves?"

"How about more sugar roses?" Helen said. "Can we have one layer that's carrot cake?"

"We could do that," Kitty said. "We could also make a groom's cake. That's a Southern tradition that's being revived. A groom's cake can reflect your man's special interests—his favorite sport or hobby."

Does sex count as a sport? Helen wondered. Never mind. That wasn't something she could put on a wedding cake.

"Does he have an animal he likes?" Kitty asked.

"He likes my cat, but I don't think a cat wedding cake is manly," Helen said. "Wait, Phil loves Eric Clapton."

"We can do a Clapton carrot cake with a guitar."

"Perfect," Helen said.

Helen paid the deposit and gave Kitty the wedding information. She was back at the salon by one o'clock. Strange. That white van was still in the no-parking zone. The van should have been ticketed and towed hours ago. The tinted glass windows gave Helen the creeps. She'd read that kidnappers and killers liked anonymous vans.

More vultures arrived. Helen caught snippets of their conversations. "He's very handsome. . . ." "Do you think he's gay?" "Do you think he killed that man?"

The afternoon dragged on while Helen made a list of wedding to-dos, including inviting Peggy to be her bridesmaid. How could I have been so negligent? she wondered. Peggy will think she was an afterthought.

It wasn't true. Helen wanted to marry Phil, but she didn't have the obsessive interest in the perfect wedding. I did that last time, she thought. The perfect wedding didn't lead to the perfect marriage. Now I just want my friends to have a good time.

Mr. Carmichael, the only noncelebrity regular, arrived for his four o'clock appointment. He was at least ninety, and so thin he was almost transparent. His hair was even thinner. His pink scalp shone through the sparse, gray-white strands. His hair was long and frizzy from the humidity. Helen wasn't sure why he came to the salon at all, except that his wife, Adriana Carmichael, ordered him there.

Helen had never met the woman, but salon gossip said Adriana was nearly fifty years younger than her husband, and she'd married him for his money.

Mr. Carmichael clutched three glossy magazine pages in his blue-veined hands. "My wife wants you to fix my hair like the men in these pictures," he said, handing Miguel Angel the pages.

The stylist's eyebrows shot up almost to his hairline and stayed there. Helen had seen women bring in magazine photos with their favorite celebrity's style, but Mr. Carmichael was the first man who did this. She peeked over Miguel Angel's shoulder and saw photos of three hunks in their twenties. Mr. Carmichael was old enough to be their great-grandfather.

The young man in the top photo had a soft face and a long golden fringe over his right eye. "She wants the front of my hair like that," Mr. Carmichael said.

The second photo showed a Don Johnson look-alike in profile, complete with beard stubble, stern jaw and sunglasses. "She wants the sides like that," he said.

The third showed the thickly waved back of a man's head. "That's how the back of my hair is supposed to look," Mr. Carmichael said.

The poor man hadn't a clue that this mission was impossible. Most of his hair—and all of his youth—were gone.

"We'll try our best," Miguel Angel said solemnly.

"What can I get you?" Helen asked Mr. Carmichael.

"I'd like hot coffee, black," he said. "If that's not too much trouble."

"None at all," Helen said. "I'll put on a fresh pot."

She poured out the sludge in the pot, made a fresh one, and brought him a mug. Mr. Carmichael held it in his shaky hands.

It was nearly five o'clock when Miguel Angel finished clipping and snipping the old man's hair. Mr. Carmichael paid his bill without a murmur and tipped generously.

Helen thought his hair looked a bit thicker. Miguel Angel had treated it to bring out the silver, but the man looked stoop-shouldered and tired as he left the salon.

"What was his wife thinking?" Helen said. "Does she even see that man?"

"She sees a lot of men," Miguel Angel said. "In her dreams. I doubt if she looks at any part of Mr. Carmichael but his wallet."

Helen swept the gray hair from the floor, cleaned the coffeepot and washed the single cup. It was five p.m.

"Unless you need me, I'm leaving now," Ana Luisa announced.

"You can go," Miguel Angel said. "So can Carlos and Helen. I need to stay and work on some accounts."

Helen left for the Coronado, feeling low. That strange van was still sitting in the no-parking zone. Odd. A pizza delivery car pulled up behind it. The red-and-blue uniformed driver got out and carried a pizza box to the passenger-side window. A minute later, the pizza car drove away. The white van remained.

Something was wrong.

Helen started running. She arrived at the Coronado, sick from the heat. Phil looked impossibly cool stretched out, shirtless, on a chaise by the pool. He was reading a news magazine and drinking a Diet Coke. His skin was bronzed by the evening sun, and his thick silver hair shone.

"Are you okay?" he said. "You look pale."

"The heat got me," Helen said.

"Then sit in the shade and I'll get you some water."

Helen sat at an umbrella table. Phil came back with cold water and a ham sandwich on whole wheat. "I bet you forgot to eat, too," he said.

"I was ordering our wedding cake," she said. "I absorbed a lethal dose of calories looking at the sample photos." She bit into the sandwich. "Mm. Just the way I like it."

"Why were you running?" Phil asked.

"There's a strange van parked across from the salon," she said. "It's not a news van. It's in a no-parking zone. Someone delivered a pizza to the passenger side."

"Finish your sandwich," Phil said. "Then let's take a stroll on Las Olas. We could go to Kilwin's for a chocolate-covered strawberry, and I could check out that van."

Ten minutes later, they were back on Las Olas, threading their way through the slow-moving tourists, who called everything from a cat sculpture in a gallery to a display of men's underwear "cute."

Kilwin's had the intoxicating perfume of chocolate. Helen passed the tubs of ice cream and sherbet and the slabs of fudge. She felt virtuous choosing a fat strawberry dipped in dark chocolate. Phil bought a milk chocolate one. They strolled by the van, talking about their wedding plans and nibbling their treats.

"I got extra sugar roses for the wedding cake," Helen said. "It's chocolate with white icing."

"What about my carrot cake?" Phil asked.

"I wouldn't forget that," Helen said.

When they were in front of the van, he grabbed her and kissed her soundly, which gave him a good view of the vehicle over her shoulder. It gave whoever was inside a good view, too.

Phil guided Helen toward the alley behind Miguel Angel's shop. "Definitely a surveillance van," Phil said. He rang the back doorbell. Helen knocked three times, just in case Miguel Angel thought they were reporters. He answered the door, a cup of Cuban coffee in his hand. Phil and Helen mimed silence and slipped inside the salon.

"I think your shop is under surveillance by that white van across the street," Phil said. "It may be the police."

"Why? I didn't do anything," Miguel Angel said.

"I'm guessing the cops don't have enough to arrest you, but you're a person of interest in the King Oden murder," Phil said. "Until they arrest someone, be careful. And don't use your cell phone. They can track you with it."

Helen saw the folded wheelchair in the corner. "I have to deliver my sick old auntie to her Jeep," she said.

Miguel Angel slapped on the black, curly wig and a little makeup, then put on the dowdy blue blouse. Helen and Phil wheeled him through the alley to the hotel parking entrance. The valet brought the Jeep. Helen and Phil helped Miguel Angel inside. He tipped the valet and drove away.

"Good-bye, Aunt Angela," Helen called, waving at the Jeep.

She could swear her sweet old aunt flipped her the bird.

Chapter 16

"How did you know that was a police van parked across from the salon?" Helen asked Phil. They walked hand in hand through the warm June night. Helen wished they could keep walking forever.

"Because no vehicle could park that long on Las Olas without being towed," Phil said. "When we walked by—"

"We didn't exactly walk by," Helen said.

"When we were standing by the van," Phil said.

"And you were kissing me," Helen said.

"I saw shadows behind the tinted windows," Phil said. "Plus I saw the lighted dial of a cell phone. And someone inside was definitely smoking. I could see the glowing cigarette end."

"You noticed all that while you were overcome with passion?" Helen asked.

"An ordinary man wouldn't have," Phil said. "But I'm experienced at undercover work." He winked. Helen kissed him again. "Besides, you noticed that pizza delivery to the van. That was a major tip-off. Someone isn't taking this stakeout seriously."

"Is that good news?" Helen asked.

"No, Miguel Angel still needs to be careful."

"Why don't they arrest him?" Helen asked. "They caught him with a little heroin."

"Drug dealers are a dime a dozen," Phil said. "King's murder is high profile. I'm guessing his hair sample came back clean and they're buying the story that he was set up—for now."

"Thanks for helping him," Helen said.

"I like Miguel Angel," Phil said.

"He's doing my makeup and hair free as a wedding present," Helen said.

"That's nice. But what's in it for me?" Phil said.

"He can do your makeup, too," Helen said. "I wouldn't let him cut your hair, though. I like it the way it is." She gave his silver ponytail a playful yank.

"And I like you better without makeup," Phil said.

"Don't say anything to Miguel Angel. You'll hurt his feelings. What are we doing about dinner tonight?"

"How about Ferdos Grill? They have good kibbe. They're about the only place in town that still serves it."

Helen made a face. "I don't know how you can eat raw lamb. But their chicken kebabs are good."

"Cooked meat is so conventional," Phil said.

"Only circus geeks eat raw meat," Helen said.

"It's a little far to walk," Phil said. "Let's take my Jeep. I'll have to stop by my apartment for my car keys."

Margery Flax flagged them down from her front door. Their landlady looked like a giant eggplant in her dark purple dress. "Helen, your sister Kathy is on my phone," she said. A lit cigarette dangled from her lips.

"Cool shoes," Helen said. "Wish I could wear purple gladiator sandals."

"Nobody's stopping you," Margery said.

"I don't think they'd look good on me," Helen said.

"You've got great legs. You're too conventional," Margery said.

"Phil just told me that," she said.

"Well, listen to the man," Margery said.

"I am not eating raw lamb," Helen said. "He thinks I'm conventional because I don't like raw meat."

"Will you talk to your sister, please?" Margery said, handing her the phone. "She's waiting."

Kathy gave Helen a subdued hello.

"What's wrong?" Helen asked.

"Mom went ballistic, just like you predicted. She says you'll burn in hell."

"I probably will," Helen said. "But I won't be lonely. All my friends will be there."

"Helen, this isn't funny," Kathy said.

"Mom lives in another century, Kathy. I'm sorry you had to listen to her."

"You don't sound upset that she won't be at your wedding," Kathy said.

"I'm not," Helen said. "I'd be more upset if you disapproved—but I would have still ignored you. I asked Mom because I didn't want to perpetuate a grudge. I've done my duty, and so have you. Thank you."

"Mom isn't herself these days," Kathy said. "She's getting a little strange."

"Mom has always been strange," Helen said.

"No, I mean strange even for her," Kathy said. "She's so spooky religious, she's starting to worry me."

Helen could hear a child wailing in the background. "Is that my niece, Allison?" she asked.

"Yes. I'd better go," Kathy said.

"Thanks again," Helen said. "I can't wait to see you." Helen hung up the phone.

Margery stood with her arms crossed in front of her. "Let me guess. Your mother refused to come to your wedding."

"She said I was going to hell," Helen said. "Poor Kathy had to listen to the hellfire lecture."

"I don't understand people like your mother," Margery said.

"Neither do I," Helen said.

"Well, you tried. That's all I asked. I'll marry you and Phil."

"Okay," Helen said, "but you're sending me on the road to hell."

"I think you set yourself on that path without my help," Margery said.

Phil unfolded his long body from a kitchen chair. "We're going to dinner," he said. "Want to join us?"

"Thanks. You kids run along," Margery said. "I'll have a cold drink and sit outside. Call it my meditation session—or getting plastered."

"I meditate a lot," Phil said.

Ferdos, a quiet restaurant with white tablecloths, was a good place to talk. Helen had something important to discuss with Phil. She waited until they'd placed their orders. After their hummus and warm pita bread arrived, Helen said, "How can we help Miguel Angel? I know he didn't kill King."

"Any idea who did?" Phil said.

"It could have been King's bitter ex-wife. But his former business partner had a good reason to kill him. So did his stripper girlfriend and any woman he'd hit on, including the photographer's assistant. And let's not forget the celebrities whose careers he ruined with his gossip blog and TV show."

"What about the bride?" Phil said.

"Honey didn't kill him," Helen said. "She's too sweet."

"She's a gold digger," Phil said.

"If gold fell into her lap, she'd take it. But Honey's not violent."

"Oh, Helen," Phil said. "You barely know the woman."

"I've seen her at the salon," Helen said. "That tells me a lot. People pull tantrums there that would embarrass a two-year-old. Honey is not demanding. She has a fairly realistic view of herself—except she thinks she's old at thirty-eight."

"She was pregnant and desperate to marry. Two good motives," Phil said, using a hunk of pita to scoop up more hummus.

"But she was safely married to King—without a prenup. Why would she be desperate?"

"The prospect of having to live with King would make any woman desperate. How come I can't find pita bread this good at the supermarket?"

"Publix isn't known for its Middle Eastern cuisine," Helen said. "I understand what you're saying about Honey, but for a Miguel Angel client, she's fairly sane."

"You're talking about people who pay three hundred dollars for a haircut," Phil said.

"That includes a blow-out, too. Some of the salon customers expect miracles. They get furious because Miguel Angel can't make them look thirty years younger. You'll find more delusional people in that salon than in an insane asylum."

Phil mopped up the last of the hummus with the pita bread as their entrées arrived. Then he spread a chunk of white onion with raw chopped lamb. Helen averted her eyes from the bloody sight.

"I wonder why more restaurants don't serve this," Phil said.

"Because it's Florida and it's hot," Helen said. "In a less careful kitchen, people can get sick from raw meat. Salmonella is not the catch of the day."

"They don't know what they're missing," Phil said. "I meant to ask you something about King's wedding. There was a photographer, right?"

"A photographer with a very pretty assistant who took still photos and videos," Helen said.

"What about security cameras?" Phil said.

"I know there were security guards," Helen said. "I don't know about the cameras."

"What's the name of the security force?"

Helen gave him the name she'd seen on a lawn sign.

"Good. I know someone who works there. I

should be able to find out. I can check around for the autopsy report."

"Can you get one during an open investigation?" Helen asked.

"I have my ways," Phil said, and waggled his eyebrows.

"The only way to help Miguel Angel is to find the real killer," Helen said.

"Yep," Phil said. "If the pressure mounts, the police will quit ordering pizza and arrest Miguel Angel. The Hendin Island force is small and underfunded, and that could be the easy way out for them."

"We need to talk to some people who were at the wedding," Helen said.

"I'll talk to Tiffany," Phil said.

"King's stripper ex-girlfriend? You volunteered for that assignment in a hurry," Helen said. "I bet you'll interview her at her work, too."

"Do you want me to help or not? You know she's not going to talk to a woman."

"You're right," Helen said.

"I usually am," he said.

Helen resisted the urge to throw her plate at his head. "I'll visit the new widow's sister, Melody," she said. "I can leave after work."

"I'll drive you," Phil said.

"I'll take the bus," Helen said. "It's better if this is a girl talk. Two of us might make her feel like we're ganging up on her."

"Suit yourself." Phil finished the last of his kibbe.

It was nearly dark by the time they arrived back at the Coronado. The sky was a soft mauve with flamingo pink clouds. Margery was lounging by the pool, drinking a tall, cold screwdriver. A rumpled Peggy dragged herself up the walk. Her dramatic red hair was cut short for the summer. Peggy was pale, especially for a Floridian. Tonight, she looked tired, with drooping shoulders and dark circles under her eyes.

"Wait! Peggy! I need to ask you something," Helen said.

"I'll be back as soon as I check on Pete." Peggy unlocked her door and disappeared inside. She was out in five minutes, wearing a bright green shirt and shorts. Pete, her Quaker parrot, was perched on her shoulder like a feathered accessory.

"How are the wedding plans going?" Peggy asked.

"I've made a mistake," Helen said.

"Don't tell me the wedding is off," Peggy said.

"No, no, that's fine. But I want you to be my bridesmaid, and I forgot to ask you."

"Okay, I'm asked, and the answer is yes," Peggy said. "What should I wear?"

"Whatever you want," Helen said. "I'm not putting you in chiffon with dyed-to-match shoes. You can even wear Pete on your shoulder."

"Awk!" Pete said.

"Are you still seeing Daniel the lawyer?" Helen asked.

"We're going out tomorrow," Peggy said. "He's quite a change after the losers I've dated."

"If you want, he can be one of Phil's groomsmen," Helen said.

"Shouldn't that be Phil's decision?"

"Daniel will be fine," Phil said. "I may need a good lawyer someday."

They heard the back gate squeak, and a soft, fluttery voice said, "Yoo-hoo. Anyone home?"

Elsie, Margery's seventy-eight-year-old friend, was wearing her most startling outfit yet: a tight pink leather vest covered with grinning black skulls and a sheer pink chiffon skirt. Her wispy hair was dyed hot pink. The varicose veins on her legs made Elsie look like she was wearing purple stockings. Her arms were flabby toothpicks. Black biker boots completed the ensemble.

"What do you think?" Elsie asked, twirling around. "I wanted something summery."

"I've never seen summer leather before," Margery said.

"Helen invited me to be her bridesmaid," Peggy said.

"How wonderful," Elsie said. "I've always wanted to be a bridesmaid. I never had the opportunity. I married young, and I was pregnant with Milton when most of my girlfriends married. You couldn't have a pregnant bridesmaid in those days."

"You can be my bridesmaid," Helen said.

164

"What kind of dress do you want me to wear?"

"Anything you want," Helen said. "Pick your favorite style and color."

Margery choked on her drink.

"Would you like some white wine, Elsie?" Helen asked.

"No, no. I can't stay," Elsie said. "I stopped by to show you my new look. I can't wait to shop for my bridesmaid dress. Thanks for inviting me. It's never too late to have your dreams fulfilled."

Elsie clomped off in her biker boots.

Margery waited until Elsie left, then said, "I hope you know what you're doing. Elsie wears some weird getups."

"Have you looked at bridesmaids dresses?" Helen said. "They're weirder than anything Elsie dreams up. Let her have some fun."

"Okay," Margery said. "But I warned you."

Chapter 17

The white van was still in the no-parking zone across from the salon the next morning. Helen walked past it, studying the van's reflection in a shop window. She saw no shadowy movement, glowing cell phones, or red-eyed cigarettes through the darkened glass. How did Phil spot them? The man must have X-ray vision.

At least the press was not camped in front of the salon.

Miguel Angel's was open for business. The shades were up, the lights were on and Ana Luisa was at the reception desk.

"How is Miguel Angel?" Helen asked.

"He's not here yet," Ana Luisa said. "Good thing his first appointment isn't until ten."

"Is business any better?"

"More vultures," Ana Luisa said. "All tourists. When we're no longer a sensation, they won't come back here. We need celebrities to survive. A hint of stardust attracts the media and the big names who will pay the big prices. You know we don't get many walk-ins."

With that, the front door opened and a woman of size strutted into the salon. She had a generous bottom and gigantic breasts shoved into white spandex. Her red hair was piled into a towering beehive. Black fishnet stockings clung to her legs and her large feet were forced into red heels. Her false eyelashes fluttered like black butter-flies.

Helen was speechless. No one dressed like this had ever entered the ultrahip salon.

Ana Luisa was her usual cool self. "May I help you?" she asked, as if the woman was fresh from a Paris runway.

"I am Cachita," the woman announced dramatically. Her accent was as thick as Cuban coffee. "I want you to fix my hair for a party."

"Where is the party?" Ana Luisa said.

"I am the party," Cachita said, sticking out her massive chest. She ripped off her red wig and said, "Don't you recognize me?"

"Miguel Angel," Helen said, "where did you get that outfit?"

He was laughing so hard he nearly fell out of his spike heels. "I went as Cachita one Halloween," he said. "Even my own sister was fooled."

"I'm going to kill you," Ana Luisa said.

"How did you grow a double-wide rear end?" Helen asked.

"It's foam," he said, waggling the massive bottom. He pulled the fake pink-orange flesh out of the tight white miniskirt and pointed to its lumpy surface. "See, it even has cellulite. Just like the bosoms."

He yanked the enormous fake breasts out of the oversized halter top. Collapsed spandex pooled around his body.

"I have my regular clothes in here," he said, holding up a red purse the size of a suitcase. "I wanted to get past the police. They didn't recognize me."

"Just don't disguise yourself as a pizza," Helen said.

Miguel Angel looked puzzled.

"The cops had one delivered to the van yesterday while they were watching the salon," she said.

Miguel Angel stowed his disguise in the back room and washed off his bright makeup. He was combing his wig-flattened hair when Ana Luisa told him, "Suzi is here."

Suzi had squeezed herself into sky-high heels, tight jeans and a ruffled crop top as if she were sixteen instead of fifty-six. She was a regular with country-singer hair who resisted Miguel Angel's efforts to update her look. Her rumpled husband, Dave, dressed as if he'd robbed a Goodwill donation box. Helen guessed his age at seventy.

"Miguel Angel!" Suzi squealed and kissed him on the cheek. "I missed you, sweetie."

Helen saw Miguel freeze at the unwanted contact.

"May I bring you something to drink?" Helen asked her.

Suzi wanted a diet soda. Dave asked for black coffee. He gave Helen a sneaky pat on the rump when she passed him. She moved backward and stepped hard on Dave's sandaled foot, then gushed apologies.

"I'm so sorry," Helen said. "I didn't mean to be clumsy."

Miguel Angel caught her eye and winked. He must have seen Dave's sly pat-down.

Suzi bounced out two hours later, her hair artfully cut and curled. Dave paid the bill and left generous tips all around. Even Helen got a twenty for the coffee and the foot crush. Apparently, clumsiness paid.

After that, the day was a dreary repeat of yesterday. A society wedding canceled. So did another magazine photo shoot and a fashion show.

Even Honey, the woman who started their trouble, canceled her regular weekly appointment.

"She's devastated from planning the funeral," Ana Luisa told Miguel. "The doctor has ordered her to stay in bed."

"Poor thing," Miguel Angel said.

"Poor us," Ana Luisa said. "We're losing one major client after another. I hated to lose that fashion show."

"Why? Cookie is a nobody," Miguel Angel said. "He designs clothes for drag queens."

"I thought they were pretty," Ana Luisa said.

"Would you wear a swimsuit that had one arm?"

"Well, no."

"And what about those swimsuits where the models had scarves around their necks—long scarves, for winter. With summer swimsuits. They cover up drag queens' Adam's apples. No real woman would wear them."

"Well, I couldn't afford them, anyway," Ana Luisa said.

The flock of vultures gossiped. Helen could hear their sly, knifing whispers swirl through the salon:

"Do you think he killed King? He doesn't look like a killer."

"They never do."

"Is he . . . you know . . . gay?"

"Do you think he does drugs? They all do, don't

they? Drugs and little boys. I hear he goes to Jamaica. . . . Mitzi says it's probably sex tours of Thailand. She says they all do it."

Whenever Miguel turned off his dryer, the conversations stopped suddenly. There were loud silences while the women sipped their diet sodas.

At one thirty, Helen was relieved to escape. She virtually ran out the door, eager to order her wedding bouquets. She ran smack into Honey. The new widow waddled. Her ankles were puffy and her hair was straggly. She was carrying a garment bag from the ultrachic shop Las Olas Baby Mama. A small shopping bag bulging with pink lace hung from one arm.

"Honey? Is that you? I thought you were sick," Helen said.

Honey turned a blotchy red. "Oh. Yes. Right. I needed some fresh air. I had to pick up my black maternity suit for the funeral."

Helen could see the red SPECIAL ORDER tag. That black suit had been ordered three weeks before Honey's wedding.

"King wanted to take me to New York next week," Honey said. "For his show. I bought black because you have to wear that color in New York. It's a law or something. I'm lucky I can use it for the funeral."

"Lucky," Helen repeated. "At least you bought something cheerful for later. That's a pretty shade of pink."

"Clothes for my little girl," Honey said, holding up the shopping bag. "That silly tech read the ultrasound wrong. She called this morning. I'm having a girl. Isn't that wonderful? Poor King would have been so disappointed. He had his heart set on a boy. I don't care what I have, as long as the baby is healthy. But a little girl will be so much fun to dress. Well, I hate to keep you. Better run."

Honey moved fast for a pregnant woman.

Helen stood on the sidewalk, frozen with shock. The tech made a mistake? And Honey just found out, right after King's death? And she just happened to special-order a black suit that arrived in time for his funeral? Helen didn't think so. Honey was a nurse. Wouldn't she be able to read the ultrasound herself? Maybe she bribed the tech to give a false report, with the promise of big money later. When King was safely out of the way.

The cheery bells on the door of Orlando's Blooms jarred Helen out of her trance. The tiny shop was bursting with colorful flowers. Pink, white and red roses, stargazer lilies, and birds of paradise filled the flower coolers with a riot of color. A fiftyish woman with spiky blond hair stood behind the counter, snipping the stem on a pink rose. Her skin had been mummified by the Florida sun.

"I'd like to order flowers for my wedding," Helen said.

"Lovely," the woman said. "My name is Patrice. When is the happy event?"

"A week from Saturday," Helen said.

"Then we'd better hurry, hadn't we? What is the color theme for your wedding?"

"I don't have one. The bridesmaids are wearing whatever color they choose."

"Oh." Patrice clearly didn't approve of bridal anarchy.

"We're getting married in a friend's backyard," Helen said

"An outdoor wedding can be fresh and informal. How many bridesmaids?"

"Three," Helen said.

Patrice pulled out a sample book with photos of bouquets. "We have a gorgeous bridesmaid bouquet with white orchids," she said. "It's only three hundred dollars."

Helen gulped. "Uh, that's a little out of my price range."

"How about pretty pink gerbera daisies, dark blue irises and yellow freesias for one hundred fifty?"

There went a big bite of the reception food budget. "Uh, no," Helen said.

"Still too high?" Patrice said. "Maybe blue irises and lavender roses for thirty-five?"

Helen quickly estimated how much she had in the emergency fund she hid in the belly of her teddy bear, Chocolate Truffle. Maybe she should buy a couple of supermarket bouquets and tie ribbons on them. "I might be able to afford that."

Patrice must have heard the doubt in Helen's voice. "May I suggest our budget bridesmaid bouquet?" Her nostrils flared at the word *budget,* as if the bouquet smelled bad. "It's petite, pretty and only sweet sixteen dollars."

She pointed to another page. *Petite* wasn't the word for this bouquet. *Pathetic* was more like it. The sad flowers seemed like wadded Kleenex. The bouquet looked cheap.

Well, this is a cheap wedding, Helen thought. She'd had high-priced bouquets when she'd married her first husband, and they hadn't helped. The flowers were dead and so was her marriage.

"That looks lovely." Helen forced herself to smile at the budget bouquet.

"Good," Patrice said. "For the bride, may I suggest a single rose? Very inexpensive." Again, the nostril flare. Patrice couldn't keep her contempt hidden.

"I'd prefer a small bouquet," Helen said. "Something in the forty- to fifty-dollar range."

"We can do some nice carnations with a stargazer lily," Patrice said.

"I'd like that," Helen said. She signed the papers and left a cash deposit.

Helen hurried back to the salon, feeling bluer than the delphiniums. Should she have spent more on her flowers? Would it make any difference?

The salon was no place for someone in low spirits. Helen listened to the squawks of the vultures and the odd silences whenever Miguel Angel passed them. Paolo was amusing himself by giving Carlos' dark hair yellow highlights. Helen didn't like them, but she kept her mouth shut. She'd been called too conventional twice yesterday—once by a seventy-six-year-old woman.

At five o'clock, Helen caught a bus to Melody's home in Pompano Beach, north of Fort Lauderdale. The bride's sister lived in a pink stucco duplex three blocks from the ocean. Melody answered the door and looked blankly at Helen.

"Hi, I was with Miguel Angel the day of your sister's wedding," Helen said.

"Ah," Melody said. "I remember now. That hairdresser guy."

"The police keep asking me questions about what happened that day," Helen said. "I was working most of the time. I thought you might be able to help."

"Come in," Melody said.

Helen was amazed by how much puffy, pale furniture was stuffed into the tiny living room. Nearly every surface was covered with clothes, magazines, soda cans and dirty plates. Floor-to-ceiling mirrors reflected the chaos.

Melody picked a pile of dirty clothes off a chair and dropped them on the floor. "Excuse the mess.

I've been helping my sister and haven't been home much. You're lucky you caught me here."

"How is Honey doing?" Helen asked.

"Well, she's upset, as you can imagine. And the baby is making her uncomfortable. She's big as a house. But Honey will land on her feet. She always does. My sister got all the breaks—looks, money and men. Her baby turned out to be the girl she really wanted. Now her husband up and dies and leaves her rich. I never had her advantages."

Helen tried to hide her shock. Did Melody just say that a dead husband was an advantage?

"Do the police really think Honey killed her husband?" she asked.

"Well, the wife is always the first suspect, as they say on the TV shows," Melody said. "But I don't believe it. Honey had a soft heart. That's why she became a nurse."

Helen had known nurses with hearts as tough as combat boots, but she kept silent. Melody was anxious to talk. "I remember when our cat Smokey was sick. Honey took it to the vet. Smokey was eighteen years old, and it was time for that cat to die. But Honey spent two hundred dollars to have it treated. Cat lasted another four months. She could have spent the money on something better than a mangy old cat. I could have used a new dress."

Helen felt chilled as Melody talked, and it wasn't the air-conditioning. This woman was cold.

Melody's blond hair was a little brassier than her sister's. Her skin was limned by the sun. She looked tough and a little mean.

"But really," Melody said. "I don't know how I can help you. I didn't see anything at the wedding. I told the police that. I was at the head table when Honey asked me to look for King. I figured he'd went into the bathroom for a quick snort—"

"You knew he did drugs?" Helen said.

"He did drugs, strippers and for all I know, French poodles. My sister saw what she wanted, and she wanted his baby and his bank account."

"Oh," Helen said.

"I don't mean to run her down, but Honey was practical. She cleaned up vomit and hauled bedpans. She could put up with King for several million bucks."

"Right," Helen said. Was she comparing her brother-in-law to vomit?

"But Honey didn't kill him. She told me his health was bad and she doubted he'd live long. You can stand anything—or anyone—for a while."

Chapter 18

Helen was stunned by the way Melody had talked about her sister. On the bus back to the Coronado, she brooded over the conversation.

Was Melody honest—or jealous? She practically said that Honey wanted to get rid of King. His

176

murder was convenient: The couple was legally married. The bride didn't sign a prenup. The groom died before he knew his treasured son was really a daughter. And the ultrasound tech made a mistake—or did she make a mistake? Did clever Honey trick King into marriage?

Helen wanted to run this conversation by her landlady. Margery was a shrewd judge of people. When Helen arrived at the Coronado, Margery was even more anxious to talk to her.

"You've got a letter," her landlady said.

"I do?" Helen asked. "I never get anything but junk mail."

"No, this one is personally addressed to you."

Helen looked at the ordinary white envelope. Her name and address were in printed in blue ink. There was no return address.

Helen opened the envelope. On a plain sheet of white typing paper, in black letters cut from newspapers and magazines, was this message: *STOP OR YOU WILL BE PUNISHED.*

"What's wrong?" Margery asked. "You look sick. You're as pale as milk."

"I am sick," Helen said. "Look at this anonymous letter. It says I will be punished."

"For what?" Margery said.

"I don't know. The letter is only six words. It tells me to stop."

"Sensible advice," Margery said. "Which means you won't take it. What is the postmark?"

"Ocean City, Maryland."

"Do you know anyone there?"

"No," Helen said. "But this letter is creepy. The words are cut from newspapers and magazines like some weird ransom note."

"You've been messing around in a murder again, haven't you?" Margery handed Helen the letter.

Helen picked it up between two fingers, as if it were a scorpion. "A little. I was trying to help Miguel Angel."

"He can help himself. He shouldn't have run from the police after that gossip guy died."

"Miguel Angel got scared," Helen said. "He's not from this country."

"So what? Most of South Florida wasn't born here. More than half of Miami doesn't speak English. Does that mean everyone should run?"

"No," Helen said. "But I can see why Miguel was worried. He's a gay Cuban."

"Former Cuban," Margery said. "He's a U.S. citizen now. As for gays, Fort Lauderdale may have more gays than San Francisco. They're hardly an oppressed minority in this city. Helen, why don't you leave this puzzle to the professionals? You've been conducting your own amateur investigation, haven't you?"

"I asked a few questions," Helen said. "That's all."

"And you went alone, without Phil?"

"I can take care of myself," Helen said.

"King Oden was big and strong and a lot more powerful than you," Margery said. "Now he's dead."

"He was easy to kill. King was using drugs and alcohol," Helen said. "And he was sick."

"Everyone is easy to kill, if the killer is motivated," Margery said. "You can be pushed under a bus, or hit on the head and dropped in the ocean, or rolled in a rug and taken to the Everglades. No one will ever find your body."

"Thank you for those lovely thoughts," Helen said. "But I doubt that a pregnant woman could drag my body to the Everglades."

"You think the widow did it?" Margery asked.

"I ran into Honey today. She was hugely pregnant. And her little boy suddenly morphed into the girl she's always wanted. A very convenient sex change, now that Daddy is dead—and before he found out his marriage was a mistake."

"Honey won't have to haul your body around. If King is really worth ninety million, she can afford to hire a killer," Margery said. "And you're walking around unguarded. Where's Phil?"

"I think he's interviewing someone right now."

"For work?" Margery demanded.

"For me," Helen said.

"Terrific," Margery said. "Do you two want a double funeral? I can perform that service, too."

"No, I just want King's murder solved, so I can have a normal life."

"You'll never have a normal life," Margery said. "But now we're back to the question I wanted to ask: What are you wearing for your wedding?"

"I have a nice off-white suit I've only worn once," Helen said.

"I love the symbolism," Margery said. "Slightly used—just like the bride. What is the matter with you?"

"I've been broke for so long, I got out of the habit of shopping."

"If you don't have the money, I'll buy you a wedding dress," Margery said. "Is Phil wearing a tux?"

"He's renting one. But I can't see myself in a long white gown with a veil," Helen said. "Been there, done that, tried to forget it."

"So you picked a bad husband the first time around," Margery said. "Big deal. You think you're the only woman who ever got divorced? Rob is gone, and you're marrying a good man. Not many women get a decent second chance. Celebrate your fresh start. Even tough guys are romantics at heart."

Margery pointed a bloodred nail at Helen's chest. Her cigarette's angry glow matched her eyes. The landlady looked like an ancient goddess demanding a sacrifice. Helen knew there was no escape.

"Okay," Helen said. "I'll look for another dress. But I'll only buy one if I like it."

"We're going to three places. You'll find something, or get married in the nude," Margery said.
"Go change, and feed your cat, while I ask Peggy
to come with us. Maybe she'll talk some sense into
you."

Helen did as she was told. She was greeted by a
howling Thumbs. She fed her big-pawed cat, then
opened the old Samsonite suitcase she kept in her
bedroom closet and took out her emergency cash.
A root canal had pared it down to $750. She found
another hundred bucks in her teddy bear. The bear
stash would cover the flowers.

She changed into fresh clothes and put on her
best heeled sandals. Margery was pacing the sidewalk in front of Helen's apartment, Peggy walking
alongside her. The three women piled into
Margery's roomy white Lincoln Town Car.

"Where are you registered for your wedding?"
Peggy said.

"Tiffany and Williams-Sonoma," Margery said,
her voice dripping sarcasm.

"Really? That's nice," Peggy said.

"It's also not true," Helen said. "Phil and I don't
need another toaster or more china. We'd rather
you donated money to our favorite charities."

"That's what the movie stars do," Peggy said.
"It's a nice trend for adult weddings."

"I like Kiva," Helen said. "Phil would like
money donated to Habitat for Humanity."

"Is Kiva the organization where you give small

loans to people in developing countries to help their businesses?"

"That's it. And Habitat for Humanity builds houses for people."

"Very uplifting," Margery said. "But we're at our first stop, Britt's Bridal Boutique."

A sign in the window screamed FREE TIARA!

"A tiara—just what I need for a backyard wedding," Helen grumbled.

They were met by a bubbly brown-haired saleswoman. "I'm Stacey," she said. "Who's the lucky bride?"

"I am," Helen said.

"Oooh. A mature bride," Stacey cooed.

"She's not young, but I wouldn't call her mature," Margery said.

"What style of dress are you looking for?" Stacey asked, bravely attempting her job.

"Ask her," Helen said, pointing to Margery.

Stacey looked confused. "I thought you were getting married," she said to Helen.

"I am," Helen said. "But she's directing the dress search."

"Are you the mother of the bride?" Stacey asked.

"I've made a lot of mistakes in my life, but she's not one of them," Margery said.

Stacey's smile dimmed. She looked like a hurt puppy. Peggy took pity on her. "My friend Helen has a bad case of bridal nerves. She'd like something for an outdoor wedding."

Helen told Stacey her dress size, and the three women crowded into the shop's largest dressing room. It had a triple mirror and a small dais for the bride-to-be. The carpet was littered with straight pins, tags and white threads. Margery sat in the only chair. Peggy propped herself against the wall.

"I hate looking at myself in dressing room mirrors," Peggy said. "I look all saggy and horrible."

"At least you get to keep your clothes on," Helen said. "If I could dress in the dark, I would."

"Quit whining," Margery said. "When you're as old as I am, you'll both wish you looked as good as you do today."

Stacey thrust a white dress into the room. "Try this mermaid gown," she said, and ran as if she were pursued by an ax murderer.

Helen climbed into the stiff white satin gown. The strapless dress fit tight at the bust, waist and hips, and then fanned out like a mermaid's tail below the knees.

"I look like a forties torch singer," Helen said. "Unless you're holding the marriage in a cocktail lounge, this dress is out."

"It's a little formal," Peggy said.

Stacey knocked timidly on the dressing room door. "Well, what do you think?"

"Pretty, but not for me," Helen said. "Satin is too warm for an outdoor wedding."

Stacey was back with a simple white dress. "Here's a nice, cool linen."

Helen tried it on. Margery zipped up the back while Helen buttoned the cuffs. Stacey waited for the verdict.

"Too wrinkled," Peggy said.

"She's talking about the dress, not the bride," Margery said.

"Wrinkles are the hallmark of natural fabrics," Stacey said. "First Lady Nancy Reagan had wrinkles painted into the suit she wore in one portrait."

"I'd better try something unnatural," Helen said. "I'll look rumpled halfway through the ceremony."

"How about this lovely cotton dress?" Stacey said. "It will look fresh. It has sheer sleeves and an empire waist."

Helen tried on the dress and looked at herself in the mirror. "The sixties live," she said.

"Looks like a nightgown," Margery said.

After four more dresses, they waved good-bye to Britt's.

Margery and Peggy dragged Helen through the discount Bridal Barn. They made snarky remarks while Helen struggled in and out of wedding dresses.

A long dress with masses of white lace ruffles "makes you look like a country singer," Margery said.

"I don't want to remind Phil of Kendra, his ex-wife," Helen said.

"I like the trumpet sleeves on that one," Peggy said.

"Too bad you have to wear the dress that goes with them," Margery said.

A high-necked dress was "too matronly." A plunging neckline was "too slutty." A princess style was "too young." A dress with creamy layers of satin looked like "melting ice cream."

The rude comments didn't upset Helen. She needed to be distracted from memories of her disastrous first marriage. Her mother had lectured her on purity and faithfulness while they shopped for dresses. Too bad Mom didn't lecture Rob, Helen thought, as she adjusted a halter-top gown.

"That halter is a seventies throwback," Peggy said.

"More like a seventies throw-up," Margery said. She and Peggy both nixed a simple white cocktail suit that Helen liked. "Makes you look like an accountant," Margery said.

"I am an accountant," Helen said. "At least, I used to be."

"It usually doesn't show," Margery said. "Are you getting married or going for an audit?"

"It's easier to find the right man than the right outfit." Helen was starting to despair. Peggy kept collapsing into fits of giggles.

"Okay, ladies, we're getting silly," Margery said. "Let's go to Nordstrom. That department store has good clothes."

Three dresses later, Peggy zipped Helen into a short cream dress with a scoop neck.

"Perfect!" Peggy said.

"Shows lots of leg," Margery said. "Phil will like that."

"I like it, too, if that counts for anything," Helen said.

"Well, praise the Lord," Margery said. "Those sandals you have on will work, unless you want to buy new ones."

"I wore new shoes at my first wedding," Helen said. "My feet were blistered the next day. These are comfortable. If they look good, I'll keep them."

"What are you going to wear on your head?" Margery asked.

"Flowers are nice," Peggy said.

"How about a short veil?" Helen said.

They quickly approved a small, sheer veil. The ordeal was over.

"You have the perfect dress and the perfect man," Peggy said. "The weather is supposed to be good. What more could a bride want?"

"I'd like the wedding day to go without a hitch," Helen said.

"Won't happen," Margery said. "You can count on that."

Chapter 19

Thunka. Thunka. Thunka.

The music was loud, fast and hard, like bedsprings rocking. Am I thinking about bedsprings because I'm getting married, Helen wondered, or because I'm at a strip joint?

King's Sexxx was as sleazy as its name. The shabby pink stucco building was striped with rust stains. It squatted in a black, nearly empty parking lot, broiling in the late-afternoon sun like a crab cake on a griddle. The club was nearly empty at five o'clock. Helen was glad. She didn't want anyone to see her in King's old strip bar.

Helen opened the door and blinked at the smoky darkness. She was hit by waves of pounding music. The bouncer looks like he should be wearing a prison jumpsuit, she thought. "You here for the audition?" he asked.

What audition? Helen wondered. But she had to see King's old partner, Wyllis Drifford.

"Yes." Her voice sounded small and shaky.

Helen followed the stoop-shouldered bouncer down a dark hall. The walls were painted dark brown, unless that was mold. The bouncer knocked on an office door and said, " 'Nother one, boss. Should I send her in?"

The bouncer interpreted the answering grunt as a yes. He opened the door to a room with plywood paneling and a ratty green sofa. A greasy-looking guy with zits like measles sat behind a cheap desk, smoking an even cheaper, smelly cigar.

"Are you Wyllis Drifford?" Helen asked.

"Speak up," he said. "I can't hear you. You auditioning? Take off your blouse so I can see your tits."

"What?" Helen said.

"Look, sweet cheeks, this is a strip joint, not a tea shop. You gonna show me your tits?"

"Can't you say hello like any other man?" Helen asked.

"Not when I'm hiring dancers."

"I'm not a dancer," Helen said.

"You're too old for the job, anyway."

Helen longed to break his jaw. Instead, she said, "Then why did you want me to take off my blouse?"

"Wouldn't hurt to look," he said.

"I don't want your disgusting job," Helen said.

"Hey, don't get so high and mighty. You came to me. I'm not in your office. My girls make three thousand a week in tips. I'll bet that's more than you make."

"I bet their mothers are real proud," Helen said.

Drifford crushed out his cigar on the yellow tile floor—adding another layer of grime—and said, "Why are you taking up my time?"

Here goes nothing, Helen thought. All he can do

is throw me out. "Why did you sue your old partner?" she asked.

Drifford stood up. "He was a crook. Good-bye." He shoved Helen out into the hall and slammed the office door. "Don't come back."

Helen nearly fell into the tattooed arms of the bouncer. "Where's your car, lady?"

"I came by bus," Helen said.

The bouncer smirked, as if he thought that was funny, and said, "Bus stop is over there."

Helen was relieved when the bus finally rumbled up. All the way home, her cheeks burned in anger and embarrassment. Phil had never looked so good. He met her at the Coronado gate and greeted Helen like a fifties sitcom wife. "Hi, honey. How was your day?"

"Lousy," Helen said.

He gave her a beer-flavored kiss and said, "Tell me all about it."

Phil led her to an umbrella table by the Coronado pool and handed her a cold glass of white wine. On the table was a roast chicken, a salad and warm rolls. The table was set with blue plates, silverware and yellow paper napkins. A branch of purple bougainvillea was stuck in a beer bottle for a centerpiece.

Helen kissed him back. "This could make up for it. You've fixed dinner. That's so sweet."

"Well, I bought the chicken at Publix. I didn't cook anything," Phil said.

"And neither will I," Helen said. "I'm so lucky to have you." She kissed him again.

"Sit down and eat, before the chicken gets cold and the salad gets warm," Phil said. "How many days till the wedding?"

"You know perfectly well it's next Saturday," Helen said between kisses. "At seven o'clock. Eight days from right now, unless I decide to take the job."

"Miguel Angel offered you a different job?"

"No, I had a chance to audition at King's Sexxx."

"You what?" Phil said, nearly spitting out his beer. "You auditioned at King's old strip club?"

"Well, not exactly. I thought I'd better check with my future husband in case he had any objections to my new career as a stripper."

"Please tell me that's a joke," Phil said.

"Sorta. Let's eat. Then we'll talk." Helen clinked her wineglass against Phil's beer bottle, then cut herself a generous portion of chicken breast. Phil only liked the dark meat—a sure sign to Helen that they were compatible.

"You're going to make me wait until after dinner?" Phil asked.

"Anticipation adds spice," Helen said.

When the chicken was reduced to a bony carcass and the salad bowl was empty, Helen lined up her knife and fork on her plate and said, "Now we can talk."

"You go first," Phil said. He was still gnawing a chicken leg.

190

"Things are not going well at the salon," Helen said. "The police van is still camped out across the street and none of the big names are booking appointments. We're overrun with nosy tourists, and most of them don't tip. They'll be gone once Miguel Angel is no longer in the news. Unless his name is cleared, I may not have a job when we return from the Keys."

"Guess we'll have to live on love," Phil said.

"Or find out who killed King." Helen gave him a chicken-flavored kiss.

"You've delayed long enough," Phil said. "What did you learn when you talked to King's old business partner?"

Helen told him about her botched "audition."

"He said that to you?" Phil asked. "Where's his office, so I can put out that cigar in his eye?"

"Oh, calm down," Helen said. "I handled the jerk. I didn't learn a darn thing, except that King's ex-partner is a pig."

Helen helped Phil carry the dinner dishes into his apartment. "Let me get dessert," he said, producing a plate with one perfect chocolate cupcake.

"Aren't you going to have one?" she asked.

"I have a beer to finish," he said.

Helen ate the cupcake while sitting on his couch. They went back outside by the pool and watched the sun set. They sat in chaise longues side by side, holding hands.

"I didn't do much better questioning Tiffany,

191

King's stripper ex-girlfriend," Phil said, and took another sip of beer. "I tracked her down at Desiree's Porthole."

"Subtle name," Helen said. "Where is this place?"

"It's a dive near the airport. The Porthole is on a canal, which is the excuse for the nautical name."

"Nice view?"

"If you like concrete-block buildings and pot-holed asphalt. The canal banks are covered with rusty boats and beer cans."

"I hope it was nicer inside," Helen said.

"The interior stunk like cigarettes and Pine-Sol. The strippers were old, bored and tired."

"I thought you went there yesterday."

"I did. The bouncer told me Tiffany wouldn't be onstage until Friday afternoon, so I bought the booze for the wedding instead. Today I went back to see Tiffany. She appeared on stage as Monique, with a French maid outfit and a feather duster."

"She never struck me as the domestic type," Helen said.

"She isn't. She quickly stripped down to a black thong," Phil said.

"Black, hmm? She must be in mourning for King," Helen said.

"She was a sad excuse for an exotic dancer, that's for sure. A few old coots pushed dollar bills into her G-string, and she patted their bald heads with the feather duster."

"They must have loved that," Helen said.

"Not if they saw where she put that feather duster during her act," Phil said.

"Gross," Helen said. "Did she pat you?"

"No, I tipped her a twenty, and she promised me a private session in the Velvet Room in the back."

"Is the Velvet Room really velvet?" Helen asked.

"It had some kind of dark, plush fabric on the walls, the ceiling and the couch," Phil said. "I didn't want to look too closely. Tiffany charged me a hundred bucks for the private session, even though I told her I didn't want sex. She said talking was more work."

"Did you learn anything useful for your money?" Helen asked.

"Tiffany hated King. She said, 'I stayed in shape, I got new tits and Botox, and he still married that bitch, Honey.'

"She said King used drugs. He didn't sell them, but he knew people who did, which makes sense if he was a user. I asked if Honey had killed King. Tiffany said, 'Hell, yes. Can I prove it? No, but I'd like to.'

"Then I asked, 'Did you kill him?'

"Tiffany said, 'If I'd killed him, it would have been a lot more painful.'"

"She's not bitter," Helen said.

"Don't interrupt," Phil said. "I'm getting to the good part." He finished his beer, deliberately making Helen wait. "I said, 'You don't like men, do you, Tiffany?'

" 'If you worked here, you wouldn't like men, either,' she said.

"I wasn't going to let her get by with that. 'I mean, you prefer sex with women. That's why King dumped you, isn't it?' "

"Wow, what happened next?" Helen asked.

"She let out a screech like a parrot, and two bouncers came roaring through the door. They were the size of refrigerators, and just as dumb. I rolled behind the black couch and crawled out the side door. It was so dark in there, they couldn't see me."

"So you got away without getting hurt?"

"Well, I've been washing my hands all afternoon. God knows what diseases I picked up on that floor."

Helen quickly dropped his hand.

"Hey, you're getting me for better or worse, including the cooties."

Helen laughed, then said, "How did you know that Tiffany was gay?"

"Men like to believe strippers are dancing for them. But most of those women are really dancing for the money. She would have married King for the money, too."

"That was a shrewd guess," Helen said.

"Well, I also saw a short, gray-haired woman drop Tiffany off at work this afternoon, and the way those two kissed good-bye was not sisterly. Tiffany is on that stage for the money, not the men."

"What's the difference between Honey and Tiffany?" Helen asked.

"Honey wears more clothes," Phil said. "Also, I don't think she can twirl tassels."

"Do you think Tiffany killed King?"

"She's mad enough to kill. But I don't know if she did."

"Then neither one of us got much today," Helen said.

"Well, I saw the autopsy report," Phil said. "After reading it, I know why Miguel Angel didn't want to listen to the TV news. King was murdered, like the news said. The report said there was chlorine water in his lungs, so he was alive when he hit the pool. There was bruising that might indicate a fight. His right hand was stomped with a heel from a dress shoe. That left an impression, like a spike in the back of his hand. There was also a slight abrasion on the palm of the same hand, where King was hanging on to the pool coping."

Helen shivered. "King tried to crawl out of the pool and the killer stomped his hand. That was nasty."

"So was the groom, from what I could tell."

"Was the killer's shoe a skinny heel, or a fat one?" Helen asked.

"Skinny. Probably a spike heel or high-heeled sandal."

"That's what the bride wore, too," Helen said. "Maybe Honey did kill him."

"But we don't have any proof," Phil said. "Just a lot of motives. We need to look at the women in the blue dresses and check their shoes."

"At least that information leaves out Miguel Angel as the murderer," Helen said.

"Unless he'd already changed into the bride's blue dress and high heels," Phil said. "Didn't he disappear before the groom died?"

"Yes. But Miguel Angel disguised himself as a woman so he could escape the police after King's body was found."

"That's what he told you," Phil said. "Honey told King she was having a baby boy. She lied about that. Maybe Miguel Angel was lying, too."

"No, Miguel Angel wouldn't kill anyone," Helen said.

"Helen, you don't really know these people," Phil said. "You work with Miguel Angel, but you don't know him personally. He's worked a lot of weddings. He knew this was being photographed. There were cameras everywhere. If he killed King, he'd be identified unless he disguised himself as a woman."

"Too bad he chose a blue dress when half the women there wore the same color," Helen said.

"Maybe," Phil said, "it was the best way to hide."

Chapter 20

"M iguel Angel, would you put on my veil, please?" Honey asked.

She had said those same words one week ago, but then the veil was white.

Today, the bride wore black. Her severe maternity suit looked like dark armor, and she needed it. Her late husband's gossip rivals had branded Honey a murdering gold digger. They gleefully revealed that the bride was a "person of interest" in King's murder investigation.

HONEY'S IN A STICKY MESS gloated one blogger. Another gossip site showed a video of the dazed bride leaving the emergency room on her fatal wedding day, escorted by her lawyer. She was still wearing her bridal gown, but it no longer resembled the magnificent *Sex and the City* dress. Honey's wedding dress was torn and wrinkled, and her expensively coiffed hair straggled down her shoulders. Her pregnancy was obvious in the drenched dress, and one gossip columnist gleefully asked, "Is that a King-sized baby bump?"

The new widow looked even more pregnant today. Despite her bulk, she seemed fragile in her dark mourning suit. Her face was pale and lined, and shiny patches of concealer showed where she'd tried to cover the dark circles under her eyes. Honey's beauty and confidence were gone. She moved and spoke with such slowness Helen wondered if the bride was on heavy tranquilizers. She couldn't be, could she? Not with the baby?

Was King's death really only a week ago? Helen couldn't tell if Honey was suffering from the dreadful publicity or if she'd really loved her husband of one hour.

"I'm so glad you came to the house," Honey said, her voice dying to a whisper. "I wouldn't blame you if you didn't want to see me anymore."

Honey had called the salon and begged Miguel Angel to style her hair for King's memorial service. Miguel Angel had refused, and Honey doubled his fee.

Helen talked Miguel Angel into it. "I'll go as your assistant," she said. "How else can we get into that house? Maybe we can find something that will clear your name. Besides, you don't have any important appointments today."

"Or next week. Or the week after that, thanks to her," Ana Luisa said. "It's all vultures. Miguel Angel, you can't afford to say no. Honey is rich and famous. She tips. Go."

Miguel Angel went. Helen rode with him in his rattling Jeep. He dodged the news vans parked along the narrow street and pulled into the semicircular driveway.

King's mansion still showed the chaos of his death. The burned tent and overturned tables were gone, but Helen saw the glitter of crushed crystal stars in the pink pavers. The flower beds were trampled and the shrubbery broken.

The lawn had been resodded to cover the tire marks gouged into it from the emergency vehicles. One side of the house was streaked with black smoke and some windows were boarded, but the repairs had started. Helen heard the pounding of hammers and the screech of a power saw. Yellow CAUTION tape blocked the entrance to the back-yard.

The front door had a black wreath. Its dark ribbon fluttered in the heavy, damp breeze. A maid in a white uniform answered the doorbell and ushered Helen and Miguel Angel upstairs to the master bedroom, where Honey now slept alone in the huge round bed. There was no sign of Honey's wedding finery. What had the bride done with her bedraggled twenty-thousand-dollar dress? Packed it away? Given it to charity? Thrown it out?

Probably not that last choice. King's competitors would stoop to searching his garbage in the name of news. The fatal dress would be quite a find.

Honey was seated at the vanity. She rose when they entered the room, and Miguel Angel took her hand. "How are you doing?" he asked.

"As well as can be expected," she said.

"Sit. Let me fix your makeup," he said.

"I plan to hide my face under a veil," she said. "It will give me some privacy."

"You can do that, but let me fix you up a bit."
Miguel Angel wiped away her amateur makeup
job and began repainting her face. Honey let him
work without saying a word. For the next half
hour, there were only his soft commands—"Look
up. Up," "Don't blink," "Hold still"—while he
used pencils, brushes and sponges to hide the rav-
ages.

When Miguel finished Honey's makeup, he said,
"There. That's better. Now you look dignified."

Miguel Angel styled Honey's hair in a severe
updo, while Helen handed him pins, brushes and
hair spray from his salon case. The police still had
the black traveling case he'd brought here for the
wedding.

Then he pinned on the black mourning veil, as
she requested.

Honey stood up and twirled around, in a parody
of last week's performance. "What do you think of
my suit?" she asked. "Jessica Alba wore one just
like it."

"Very attractive," Helen said.

"The veil is a copy of the one First Lady Jackie
Kennedy wore to John F. Kennedy's funeral,"
Honey said.

"Oh," Helen said. It was all she could manage.

Helen had seen the funeral photos of the wid-
owed first lady holding the hands of her two
orphaned children. On Jacqueline Kennedy, the
black veil seemed dignified and touching. On

Honey, it was overdone and tasteless. She was the widow of a gossip columnist, not a world leader.

"The veil is classy," Honey said. "King always liked class."

Miguel busied himself packing away his brushes, possibly to avoid talking.

"I'm having King cremated today," Honey said. "I don't think he'd like being buried."

"Who does?" Helen asked.

Miguel Angel glared at her. Honey didn't seem to hear Helen's remark. Instead, she babbled about the funeral plans. "King's memorial service is at the crematorium chapel at three this afternoon. I didn't want to have a wake with his body on display. That would attract the most awful people, and security would be impossible. I've only invited his close friends to the service. I hope you don't mind that you weren't on the list, Miguel Angel."

"We weren't friends," he said. "Everyone knew that. It would be improper for me to attend."

"That's what I thought," Honey said.

Helen was relieved that Miguel Angel wouldn't be at the memorial service. Phil had told her that the police frequently videoed murder victims' funerals, looking for persons of interest. It would be better if Miguel Angel—and Helen, for that matter—were absent.

"I didn't want his body on display," Honey said. "I think that's a horrible custom. Instead, we'll have my favorite photos of King. That way, people can remember King the way they saw him in life."

How was that? Helen wondered. As a crude drunk? A cokehead? A philanderer? A vicious gossip who destroyed careers? Perhaps King's daughter would mourn him sincerely. Cassie was too young to know what her father was really like. But Helen doubted there would be many tears shed for the dead King. Even Honey's eyes were tearless. Did murderers cry for their victims?

"It's a sad business," Helen said, which was as close to the truth as she wanted to get.

"Cremation is so much nicer and cleaner," Honey said. "It's better than having him rotting in the ground."

"King should definitely burn," Helen said, then stopped. Miguel Angel's glare could have stripped the skin off her face. "It's how many cultures give final tributes to their kings and warriors. What are you going to do with his ashes?"

"King loved the ocean. That's his boat docked behind the house. I've hired a charter captain to take us out at sunset and scatter his ashes at sea."

Helen heard the screech of a power saw and jumped. "Sorry," she said. "I thought it was one of the peacocks."

"They're gone," Honey said. Helen thought the widow might be smiling under the heavy veil.

"Gone where?" Helen said.

"I got rid of them. I couldn't stand the noise. It reminded me of King."

Who thought the noisy birds sounded like money, if Helen remembered right. Maybe Honey preferred quiet money.

"I know King's death is hard for you, but it's also caused problems for Miguel Angel," Helen said. "The video of their disagreement just before the wedding was on television."

"I know. I'm sorry," Honey said. "I didn't give that terrible video to the TV station. I don't know how they got it. My lawyer is looking into the situation. I just want this horrible mess to go away."

"So do we," Helen said. "But all that's going away right now are Miguel Angel's celebrities. They're canceling bookings right and left."

"What can I do to help?" Honey said. "May I write you a check to cover the salon's losses?" She pulled a checkbook out of the vanity drawer.

"Yes!" Helen said.

"No!" Miguel Angel said. "There were no losses. We had many appointments."

"All tourists," Helen said. "The big names are gone."

"Do you want me to make some calls?" Honey asked.

"I won't beg people to come to my salon," Miguel Angel said. "If they don't want my services, they can go to hell."

Helen could see Miguel Angel was angry with

203

her for telling Honey about his troubles. He was a proud man.

"You can help Miguel Angel by letting us examine the wedding photos and videos," Helen said. "Maybe we can find something that will give us a clue to the killer."

"I don't see how you can, since the police already took copies. But you might as well have them," Honey said. "I can't bear to look at those pictures and videos. I've paid the photographer for his work, but Marco Antonio still has the originals. Take them if you want."

"Where's his studio?" Helen asked.

Honey gave Helen the address.

"Will you give us written permission?" Helen asked.

"I'll write something now," Honey said.

Miguel Angel ducked outside on the balcony for a cigarette while Honey typed a permission letter on a computer in King's home office.

She's being very cooperative, Helen thought. Was Honey innocent of murder? Or did she already know there was nothing useful in those photos? Helen couldn't read the woman.

She slipped into the bride's dressing room. It was the size of Helen's Coronado apartment, and organized like a fine library. Flat mahogany drawers held scarves, sweaters, socks and lingerie. Sweaters were arranged in clear drawers by color. Dresses hung on a revolving carousel. They were a rainbow of color: red, yellow, green, black, turquoise, pink and coral.

So why did Miguel Angel choose the peacock blue dress that nearly everyone else had?

Chapter 21

I never gave that wedding video to Channel Fifteen," Marco Antonio said. "I swear it on my mother's grave."

The photographer's smooth, dark hair stuck up like a field of weeds, probably because he kept running his fingers through it. His pleated guayabera shirt had a mustard smear on the front and sweat circles under the arms. He looked old and tired.

Helen couldn't believe this was the same photographer who'd been so cool and controlled throughout the chaos of Honey's wedding. Now Marco Antonio seemed sick with worry.

She and Phil were crowded into his tiny office in the back of his photography shop. The air conditioner clanked and rattled and poured out air barely cooler than the June heat.

Marco Antonio talked fast, even for a Cuban. "I will be ruined. I am sorry that Mr. Oden died. Very sorry. But I signed legal papers that I would not release any pictures or videos to the media. King insisted on that in the contract. He didn't want his competitors scooping him on his own wedding.

Now his widow has turned her lawyer loose on me. She says she'll sue and take everything I have."

He threw out his arms to embrace his dusty office and desk piled with greasy takeout bags. "Everything" was not much, even if he included the gold-and-white couch and framed bridal portraits in the lobby.

Helen felt a stab of pity for Marco Antonio. Phil pressed him for more information. "You gave the police the original video the day of the murder, didn't you?" he asked.

"No! I pretended to, but I only gave them a copy. That video on the TV news has ruined my business. Four brides canceled and I had to return their deposits. Now I can't afford to fix the air-conditioning—and it's June. This is supposed to be my busy season."

Helen handed the photographer Honey's permission letter. "We may be able to help you," she said. "I talked with Honey this morning. We need the Oden wedding photos and videos. Phil, my fiancé, is a private detective. We can't make promises, but if Honey has some answers to King's murder, she might leave you alone."

She certainly can't sue you if she winds up in jail, Helen thought.

Marco Antonio patted his damp forehead with a white handkerchief. "Thank you," he said. "I'll get them now."

"A copy will do," Phil said. "But I also want the

video and photos your assistant shot. Did the police get those?"

"No," Marco Antonio said. "They never mentioned Mireya, and I didn't tell them about her. Who needs more complications? I think it was Mireya who sold the video to the television station. She is greedy."

"When does she come into work?" Phil asked.

"She quit."

"What's she doing now?" Phil asked.

"I don't know and I don't care," Marco Antonio said. "Mireya had a chance to be a good photographer and she threw it away." He sat on the edge of his desk and started an avalanche of fast food bags.

Phil caught them. "Where does she live?"

"Three blocks north behind the Publix shopping center. It's a bright blue two-bedroom house with white awnings. You can take the alley that runs alongside this building to get there."

Helen felt like she'd spent all day in a Jeep. First, Miguel Angel had driven her to Honey's and back to the Coronado. Then she and Phil had rushed off to see the photographer. Now she was bouncing up the rutted alley to Mireya's block. Phil turned onto the street and pulled up to a house the color of a blueberry snow cone.

"Mireya!" Phil pounded on the front door and called her name. No answer. Finally, a tiny older woman with impossibly black hair peered out of the house next door. Her hair was piled in an elaborate style Marie Antoinette would envy. The woman wore a flowered housecoat and gold slippers.

"She's not here," the woman said. "I am her neighbor, Gracie." Helen was fascinated by her thick eyeliner and false lashes. Gracie moved toward them in a cloud of sweet perfume.

"Do you know when she'll return?" Phil asked.

"She won't," Gracie said, batting her false lashes at Phil. She pulled her housedress closer to her body, so it showed her buxom figure. "Mireya is too good to live in our neighborhood now. It has too many Cubans, she says. What does she think she is? She's moved to Palm Beach County."

"Do you have her address?" Helen asked.

"Yes. She expects me to forward her packages."

"We can take her some things, if you want," Helen said.

"Let her pick them up herself," Gracie said. "Do you know what she gave me for a good-bye present? Some dusty old silk flowers and a half-empty jar of mayonnaise. I threw them out. You can have her address. Tell her I said the neighborhood is better without her."

"Do you know where she works now?" Helen asked.

"Mireya says she doesn't have to work anymore. She has an annuity from a rich auntie. Rich auntie, my eye. Her family are no-goods. They're all on welfare."

Helen and Phil thanked Gracie. On the drive back to the Coronado, Helen said, "Mireya must have gotten a lot of money for that video if she's living in Palm Beach County."

"Not necessarily," Phil said. "Not everyone in Palm Beach County is rich."

"True," Helen said. "I've seen some *Cops* shows set in Palm Beach County. The police were chasing drug dealers out of trailer parks. I bet those episodes made the society types wince."

"The county has a ragged side the socialites would rather forget," Phil said. "Do you want to go to Mireya's house now?"

"Let's go back home and check out the wedding pictures she shot first," Helen said, "in case we see something important. I can't believe we'll be on our honeymoon in the Keys next week. I'm really looking forward to that."

"Me, too," Phil said, and kissed her.

"I hope King's murder will be solved by then. How did your interview with King's ex-wife go?"

"I haven't seen Posie yet," Phil said. "Her condo is on the way home. Want to go with me?"

"Sure," Helen said.

An elderly guard waved their Jeep into Posie's development without checking. The condos were stacks of storage boxes with screened-in porches built around an artificial lake.

Helen thought the palm trees and greenery made a pleasant setting. But Posie, banished from King's palace with her daughter, probably saw the condo as a comedown. She was home, and looked younger in jeans and a T-shirt. Posie ignored Helen and flirted outrageously with Phil as she led them to a wicker couch on the porch. She fluffed her hair and tucked in her shirt to show her bust and narrow waist.

"You weren't at the wedding Saturday," she said to Phil. "I would have noticed."

"He was helping get ready for our wedding," Helen said, then wished she hadn't. She sounded defensive.

"We wanted to ask you about King's wedding," Phil said. "You're an important witness."

"I'm so important the police hardly bothered talking to me," Posie said. "Honey wanted everything perfect, but it was a massive screwup." Her hard eyes were lit with malice.

"I wasn't surprised by the fire. King had already let that woman set fire to his money. He watched every nickel when we were married."

"Do you think Honey killed King?" Phil asked.

Posie didn't blink at his blunt question. "All I know is this: If King had stayed married to me, he'd still be alive."

"Then why did you leave him?" Phil asked.

"I didn't. He dumped me. King said Honey was younger and classier—and she was giving him a boy. I ruined my health trying to give him a son. I had four miscarriages. Then I gave him a beautiful daughter, but Cassie wasn't good enough. It had to be a boy—a prince for King.

"Honey knows how to suck up to the old broads at those society parties King liked," Posie said. "He'd kiss their asses, and he wanted me to do the same. But I had too much pride. I gave one old bag a little fashion advice and she got insulted. I was only telling the truth: A face-lift would have made a big difference. She said she preferred to look natural. There's nothing natural about wrinkles, and I told her so.

"King dropped me because of that. He said it wasn't classy. He was obsessed with class because he didn't have any himself. Classy, my ass. How classy is it to marry a man for his money? What does she have that I don't?"

Fewer face-lifts, Helen thought. Softer manners. Bitterness and hate were etched in Posie's tightly stretched skin. Her collagen-filled lips looked ready to pop, like angry balloons.

"So, yeah, sweet little Honey killed him. That gold digger was after his money, and she got it. If Honey had signed a prenup, King would be safe. But he was thinking with his little head."

"How come no one saw Honey kill her husband?" Phil asked.

"They did," Posie said, "They're just not coming forward. Sorry, I have to throw you out. I have to pick up Cassie at soccer practice."

When they were in the parking lot, Helen said,

"Wow, three rooms aren't big enough to hold all her hate. I was glad to get away from her."

"I bet King was, too," Phil said. His Jeep rumbled back to life. Phil made a right turn and almost wiped out a bicyclist who blithely cut in front of him.

"Did you see that?" Phil said. "I nearly hit that guy."

"Do you think that's true?" Helen asked.

"What? That Honey killed King? I don't know," Phil said. "We don't have any proof, just lots of motives. Did someone see the murder? We may find that out when we look at those wedding videos."

"My place or yours?" Helen asked.

"I have the better system," Phil said.

Half an hour later, Helen and Phil were stretched out on his black leather sofa, watching Mireya's wedding video and eating spicy Thai noodles. Helen kept track of the blue dresses. She saw at least five on the video: the bride's sister, Melody. The groom's ex-wife, Posie. King's daughter, Cassie. King's former lover, Tiffany. Miguel Angel's assistant, Phoebe.

Miguel Angel made six. All wore spike heels.

Helen and Phil looked through the wedding photos until Helen had trouble telling everyone apart. One photo nagged at Helen: It showed a blonde in a blue dress arguing with King. They were standing by the pool.

"Can you turn up the sound?" Helen asked.

"There isn't any sound with this video," Phil said. "I don't know if it's defective or Mireya didn't record it."

"Look at this," Helen said. She pointed to something at the edge of the photo. "That looks like a white tablecloth. Why would a tablecloth be on the ground by the pool?"

She stared at the white shape until something clicked in her mind. "Wait!" she said. "That's not a tablecloth. Look at how it's draped. That's the poufy part of Honey's wedding dress. See the satiny fabric? And she wore spike heels. She could have killed him."

"Let me check the notes," Phil said. "That picture was made off a shot in the second video." Phil raced through the video until it came to the section where the photo came from. First they saw a blonde in a blue dress arguing with King. Then the camera jumped to Barry, the embarrassing best man, announcing the toast that wouldn't stop.

"Back up there. Does it look to you like several frames are missing?" Phil asked.

"Yes," Helen said. "But I can't tell if the deletion is deliberate or if the camera was trained on something else, like Barry's toast. You should have heard him. There's a memory the bride won't want to keep."

The camera swung back to the groom again. He

was arguing with the blonde. "Is that still the same blonde in the blue dress?" Phil asked.

"I can't tell," Helen said. "They all look alike. What's that on the woman's back, near the shoulder blade?"

"It's a blue smudge," Phil said. "Maybe it's a flaw in the photo."

The hair was the same color as Miguel Angel's wig, and the blonde's large feet were crammed into too-small sandals. Sandals with very high heels.

"Is that Miguel Angel in that dress?" Phil asked.

"I don't know," Helen said. "I can't tell."

"Why is Phoebe wearing a blue dress? How could she afford it? It looks expensive," Phil said.

"Good questions," Helen said. "Maybe we need to know more about little Phoebe."

There was a knock on the door. "It's me, Margery," their landlady said. "Are you two decent?"

"At what?" Phil asked, as he opened the door.

Margery was wearing a purple caftan trimmed in silver. Phil whistled. "I like the outfit."

"Thanks," Margery said, waving away his compliment and her cigarette smoke. "I wanted to remind your future wife that her bachelorette party is tomorrow. Helen, you need to be outside at ten thirty in the morning."

"Who's invited?" Helen asked.

"Your minister and your bridesmaids," Margery said. "That's Peggy, Elsie and me. Your sister is welcome, but she won't be in town until next Friday and you don't want a party the night before your wedding."

"I don't want to get married with a hangover," Helen said. "You never told me where we're going. What should I wear?"

"What you have on now is fine. Don't dress up. It's Florida. Oh, one more thing. You got another letter." Margery handed it to Helen and left.

Helen opened it and choked.

"What's wrong?" Phil asked.

"It's another one of those creepy anonymous letters. This one says, *DEATH IS THE ONLY SOLUTION.*"

"What's that mean?" Phil said.

Helen shrugged.

Phil got out his fingerprint kit and checked the letter for prints. "Only a few useless smudges on the envelope," he said. "Besides, we don't have any suspects to compare them to."

"I must be getting somewhere with this investigation," Helen said. "I'm getting death threats."

Chapter 22

"More champagne?" Sister Mary Rebecca asked.

"Sure," Helen said. She'd never had anyone in a nun's habit pour champagne. But then, Helen had never been waited on by a nun in drag.

Margery had one hell of a surprise for Helen's bachelorette party. She took the women to the drag queen gospel brunch at Lips in suburban Fort Lauderdale. Lips was a nightclub that offered "the ultimate in drag dining." The decor was high-camp glitter—cheesy gold statues guarding the stage, oodles of pink and purple, mirrors and sequins.

A gospel singer in a gold choir robe and enough makeup to stock a Revlon counter was belting out a song.

"These gospel singers are divine," Elsie said, and raised her glass of champagne and orange juice. She'd convinced herself that mimosas were a healthy way to get vitamin C.

Helen thought Elsie was too buzzed to know she was punning.

Sister Mary Rebecca poured Helen more champagne and topped off Elsie's mimosa. Elsie looked right at home among the sequins and shimmering beads. The drag queens—the Sisters of Sequins—made her feel welcome.

"Heavenly dress, sweetie," Sister Mary Rebecca said, nodding at Elsie's blue sequin, strapless tube topped with a ruffled cobalt chiffon coat. The tube bulged like a water balloon. Elsie's short, spiky hair was dyed lime green. It looked startlingly good with the blue.

"Oh, do you like it?" Elsie blushed like a young girl. "I got the outfit for ten dollars at a resale shop.

It's so important to recycle. That's what my grand-daughter says."

"Go green," Sister said, and flitted to the next table. Elsie patted her lime hair, slightly missing the point.

The gospel show was fast, funny and lip-synched. Helen thought most of the tunes weren't traditional gospel, but she and her friends hadn't been in a church for so long, they wouldn't know gospel music if it walloped them in the key of G.

Sister Mary Rebecca put down her champagne bottle and ran onstage for an energetic version of "This Little Light of Mine."

"She has a nice voice," Elsie said.

"Just like Milli Vanilli," Margery said.

Elsie looked puzzled.

"She's lip-synching," Peggy explained. "Sister is singing along with a recording. Milli Vanilli got in trouble for doing that."

"Amazing," Elsie said. "I'd never guess that wasn't Sister's voice."

Sister went back to serving champagne, and Nicollette, the glitzy emcee, was back on stage. Nicollette strayed often from the path of good manners and good taste. She told one young blond female, "You've got more roots than Alex Haley."

She called another woman with short hair and a baseball cap "my little dyke tyke" and asked, "Would you change my oil?"

Helen prayed the emcee would ignore her, and

she did. Instead, Nicollette turned her attention to a visitor from England. "Don't they have enough queens there?" she asked.

The audience sang along: "If you're gay and you know it, clap your hands. If you're gay and you know it, then your fashion sense will show it."

The straight version was: "If you're straight and you know it, then your Kmart clothes will show it."

There was a lot of hand clapping for all the songs, and each table got tambourines. Elsie never let go of hers. Her arms shook like Jell-O in an earthquake when she clapped along to the music. Her chins wobbled in time.

The Sisters of Sequins escorted a muscular man onstage to a chair covered with crystals and sparkles. He was blond and pouty. The drag queens serenaded him with "There She Is, Miss America."

"Are you single?" Nicollette asked.

"Yes," he said in a hesitant voice.

Nicollette plopped herself in the lad's lap and said, "Then you want me. Because when I take off this drag, I'm a man, and that will make you happy. But I look like a woman, which will make Mommy and Daddy happy."

"I wonder if Milton would enjoy this," Elsie said as she finished her fourth mimosa. "The food is really quite nice and the music is lovely. The sisters are very kind."

Margery put her hand over Elsie's glass when a

sequined server came by with another pitcher of mimosas. "That's enough alcohol for you," Margery said. "Your son is so straight, he wore cuff links on his onesies. Take him to this place, and I'll be visiting you at the assisted living facility before Nicollette can whip off her wig."

"Milton's not like that," Elsie said, but she quickly shut up. She loved her conservative son, but the massively uptight Milton was too clenched to tolerate Lips.

"Those drag queens are beautiful," Peggy said, in a frantic effort to change the subject. "I feel sort of scraggly compared to them, and I've got the factory-installed equipment."

In the glittering light, Peggy was an exotic creature with her shock of red hair and elegant nose.

"They are beautiful," Helen said, "if you like the way women looked fifty years ago. Drag queens go for the heavy glamour that we women liberated ourselves from long ago—except on special occasions."

"But looking at them, I'm getting lonesome for sparkly dresses, chandelier earrings and evening gowns cut down to there," Peggy said.

"Most of these men have a pretty good 'there,'" Helen said. "I know those are probably implants, but the guys walk and talk like real women. I suspect some have had their Adam's apples altered— I didn't see much evidence of that telltale giveaway."

"The only figure fault I can see is that some of

the drag queens are a tad chunky around the waist," Peggy said. "But then, so are many of the genuine women in the audience."

"That's why I'm glad the kitchen ran out of Hollandaise sauce for my eggs Benedict," Helen said. "I have to fit into my wedding dress on Saturday."

A drag queen flounced past them in a fabulous bias-cut sequin gown. "How would I look in bias-cut fringe?" Helen asked.

"Excuse me," Margery said, grinning wickedly over the top of her champagne glass. "Is that Miss I Think I'll Wear My Old White Suit for My Wedding? He's a man, sweetie. You'd look terrific in that sequin outfit. You could wear it lounging around the pool or feeding the cat."

"Look at that!" Elsie said. "How did that per-former step off that stage wearing four-inch heels? She—"

"He," Margery interrupted.

"She or he negotiated a drop of nearly three feet in those high shoes. Even when I was young, I'd cripple myself trying that."

The Sisters of Sequins passed long-handled col-lection plates while the emcee reminded the audi-ence to tip the performers. "It takes a lot of money to look this cheap," she said.

Helen pulled out a ten-dollar bill. Margery coun-tered with a twenty. "This is my party," she said, shoving Helen's money aside.

"And I live on tips," Helen said, dropping the ten in the plate on top of Margery's money. "Easy come, easy go."

The brunch was over by three o'clock. Helen and her friends staggered out into the merciless Florida sunlight. Helen was pleasantly dizzy from the champagne. The four waited under a canopy emblazoned with enormous red lips while the valet fetched Margery's car. Helen's landlady lit a cigarette with an addict's trembling fingers and inhaled deeply.

The hunky valet drove up in Margery's white Lincoln Town Car and opened the doors.

"This car is becoming a white elephant in more ways than one," Margery said, buckling up.

"It's so nice to sit in a big, comfortable auto," Peggy said, as she climbed into the backseat.

Helen tried to steer Elsie to the front passenger side, but she said, "No, dear, you're the guest of honor, and you have long legs. You sit in front. There's plenty of room for me in the backseat."

Elsie staggered slightly as she slid into the car. "This party was lovely, Margery," she said, as she settled herself. "So unique. Helen, dear, what would you like for your wedding? Do you need a nice toaster oven? I sometimes find that young couples who've been living on their own neglect the basics for housekeeping."

"Thanks, but we already have one," Helen said. "Phil and I are asking guests to donate to our favorite charities."

"That's very generous," Elsie said, her words slightly slurred.

"We really don't have room for any more stuff," Helen said. "I'll get you the information for the charities when we're back at the Coronado."

"Thank you, dear. Not many people turn down gifts, no matter how many things they have. I'll be happy to make a donation in your honor."

Elsie pulled a colorful brochure out of her purse and perused the Lips schedule. "I'd like to come back for the drag karaoke. I've always wanted to sing onstage. The brochure says, 'Remember . . . frozen cosmos alleviate stage fright!' That's so true."

Margery nearly swallowed her cigarette in surprise.

"I was brought up Catholic," Helen said. "I'm tempted by the Bitchy Bingo with Misty Eyez on Wednesday nights."

"I'm going for Dinner with the Divas," Peggy said. "I can 'dress to impress' and dine with drag versions of Cher, Madonna, Diana Ross, Tina Turner and Bette Midler."

"If you want to dress up, you should go for the Glitz and Glamour Las Vegas Style on Friday and Saturday," Margery said.

"Those are my date nights," Peggy said. "I don't think Daniel would enjoy it."

"But they'd like him," Margery said. "Daniel is cute."

"I can't wait to meet your new gentleman," Elsie said. "Helen, thank you so much for letting me be in your wedding. You've made me very happy. I've had such fun choosing my bridesmaid dress."

"What color is it?" Helen asked.

"Pink," Elsie said. "But the rest is a surprise."

"Whatever you wear is always a surprise," Margery said.

Helen glared at her landlady. She didn't want anything to interfere with Elsie's fun.

"My granddaughter went with me and helped me pick out the outfit," Elsie said. "I hope you'll like it."

"I'm sure I will," Helen said. The bachelorette party had been hilarious, but something about it bothered her. There was something important Helen had to remember. Something she had to tell Phil.

"Now, you must tell us how the wedding plans are going," Elsie said, interrupting her thoughts. For the rest of the trip home, Helen talked about ordering the flowers, the food, the cake and all the other wedding trivia. She was bored by it, but they seemed interested.

They reached the Coronado at the peak of the afternoon heat. The old apartment complex had a sunburned look. Josh and Jason, the renters in 2C, were sunning themselves by the pool. Both had bottles of beer and matching sneers.

Margery introduced them to Elsie. "So pleased to

meet you," Elsie said in her fluttery voice. "You look familiar. What do you do?"

Josh and Jason pointedly ignored Elsie.

"They're in construction," Margery said.

"I have that charity information in my apartment," Helen said, hurrying Elsie away from the rude boys. She didn't want that gentle soul to get her feelings hurt.

"I know I've seen them before," Elsie said. "I think those are the young men working on my neighbor's house."

"You're drunk," Margery said. "Guys that age all look alike."

"I am drunk," Elsie said. "But I know what I saw. Those boys are repairing my neighbor's roof. They said they had a special discount for people over sixty-five. I'm thinking of asking them to look at my roof, too."

Helen had a sick feeling that the curse of 2C had struck again.

Chapter 23

Miguel Angel came into the salon Monday morning, drenched from a tropical downpour. He was so angry, the water seemed to rise off him in a cloud of steam. He tracked damp footprints across the salon floor. Helen wiped them up with a mop.

"I can't believe this," he said. "Mrs. Morton

wanted me at her house at eight o'clock this morning—all the way up in Palm Beach. I drove there in my Jeep, which has a leak in the driver's window. I got there at eight, and her maid says she is asleep. Asleep! I am wet and she is asleep. The maid won't wake her. I got up at six thirty to be at her house on time. That's it! She is off my list. I will never go there again. Never. I have her credit card, and I will charge her for a missed appointment. She deserves it."

Miguel Angel grew angrier as he talked, and his Cuban accent thickened. But Miguel didn't yell when he was angry. The madder he got, the more he lowered his voice. His furious whispers carried over the other salon noise.

Blow-dryers roared. Clouds of hair spray hovered in the salon air. Helen, like an acolyte, bore glasses of water trimmed with lemon slices and artfully folded in napkins to two clients wrapped in salon robes. They were regulars from before King's murder. Helen could hear them gossiping about a television reporter.

"Lydia is divorcing her husband," said a skeletal brunette in her sixties with unnaturally tight facial skin. "She caught him in bed with a blonde."

"How boring," a buxom redhead said. "Can't he think of an original sin?"

"The blonde was a man," the skeleton said.

"Well, Lydia is built like a boy," the redhead said.

They giggled maliciously.

Other women lounged in the salon chairs, talking on their cell phones and reading glossy magazines. Their handbags and shoes were branded with logos. They were so rich they didn't care if the pouring rain ruined their six-hundred-dollar shoes.

"You have just enough time to dry your hair before your ten o'clock appointment," Ana Luisa said. The receptionist was not afraid to interrupt Miguel Angel's tirade.

That ominous white police van was still watching the salon, but some longtime customers were back, and tipping generously, for the first time since that dreadful video. There were still no celebrities. When it came to major names, the appointment book was empty as the Gobi desert.

But Helen saw the returning regulars as a hopeful sign. The celebrities would be next, wouldn't they? Maybe Miguel Angel's salon would be saved if she and Phil could find King's killer.

"Who is my appointment?" Miguel asked.

"Mrs. Rodriguez wants her roots done and her hair blown out."

Miguel Angel made a face, but didn't protest. He was in no position to object to anyone. But Helen didn't like the woman.

Mrs. Rodriguez wore gold bracelets that jangled and clothes that clung to her gym-toned body.

Salon gossip said her husband was unfaithful. Mrs. Rodriguez behaved as if she were a queen and spent like an empress. Her only talent was shopping, but she condescended to Miguel Angel as if he were a peasant.

Mrs. Rodriguez was robed and waiting in the chair when Miguel returned. He'd changed into a fresh black shirt, and his dark hair was dried and styled.

"How do you want your hair?" he said.

"Not short," she said, tossing her dark curls. "And not frizzy, either."

Mrs. Rodriguez would strut naked down Las Olas before she would admit she was in the throes of menopause, but she'd reached the age when her hair had lost its glossy, youthful thickness. Miguel Angel could give her young hair, for a price.

As he worked, she chattered about the things she'd bought. "I got my son an Alexander McQueen tie with little skulls to wear with his tux for the school dance."

Helen tried to hide her surprise. Mrs. Rodriguez had bought a teenage boy a designer tie that cost more than two hundred dollars—and the kid would wear it maybe once.

"You must have the coolest kids in school," Miguel Angel said.

"I want them to have everything I didn't," she said. "My family ruled Cuba for centuries before we came here in 1960."

Helen was beginning to understand this was the Cuban version of "my family came over on the Mayflower"—a way of bragging. Mrs. Rodriguez was letting them know she was part of the Latino elite.

"You wouldn't understand, since you came here so much later, Miguel Angel," she said. "It was 1980, wasn't it?"

A double slap, for those in the know. That was the year of the Mariel Boatlift, when more than 120,000 Cubans came to South Florida from the port of Mariel. Many of the older, often conservative immigrants looked down on the Mariel refugees, considering them criminals and homosexuals. Many right-wing Cubans did not tolerate gays.

Miguel Angel said nothing at the implied insult, but he held the blow-dryer a fraction closer to her head.

Mrs. Rodriguez yelped. "Ouch! Be careful, you fool! You burned me."

"Oh, I'm so sorry. So very sorry," Miguel Angel said. His voice was a soft, insincere coo.

Helen suspected Miguel Angel had burned the woman's scalp on purpose. Helen didn't know when the stylist came to the United States, and she'd be fired if she told Mrs. Rodriguez what she really thought: If Fulgencio Batista and his cronies did such a terrific job running Cuba, Castro would have never taken over the island.

Many Batista supporters left the island when Castro came into power in 1959. They took their ill-gotten gains in suitcases—if they hadn't already stashed fortunes in foreign banks. They had a rich cushion when they landed in the United States, but they weren't above playing the "poor immigrant" routine when it served their purpose.

After Mrs. Rodriguez hobbled out on her Jimmy Choos, Miguel Angel spent ten minutes mumbling to himself in the prep room. Then he fixed a Cuban coffee with enough caffeine to power IBM headquarters and went back to work.

Miguel Angel spent the afternoon spinning hair like straw into sensuous gold.

Connie, his two o'clock customer, confided that her husband was having an affair with his office assistant. George had just told her he wanted a divorce, and Connie ran to her hairstylist for comfort and a makeover.

She looked like a portrait on a candy box. Her hair was curly blond and her makeup was perfect. She moved in a welter of ruffles, ribbons and lace, and wore a big-brimmed white hat to shade her delicate complexion. Connie reached into her little pink purse and pulled out the only lace handkerchief Helen had ever seen used by a woman under thirty.

"He took me by surprise," Connie said. "Until George told me our marriage was over, I thought we were happy. I feel like such a fool." She twisted the handkerchief, then blotted her wide blue eyes. Helen didn't see any tears.

"Then you deserve some fun," Miguel Angel said. "I will give you a new hairstyle so that he will regret wanting another woman. Has he cut off your credit cards?"

"Not yet," she said.

"Then I advise you to buy some new clothes as soon as you leave, before it's too late. Zola Keller on Las Olas has a fabulous sale. I will call Zola and tell her to take good care of you."

A conversation between a woman and her stylist was as intimate as talking to a confessor, Helen decided. Except hairdressers passed judgment on your style, not your sins.

Connie clip-clopped out of the shop in her pink high heels on her way to a new husband-funded wardrobe. After she left, Helen said, "Did you know George was cheating on her?"

"Everyone did, except Connie. She will find another man soon. He'll be just as bad as this one, but she will believe she is happy—for a while."

At four o'clock, the shop was quiet. The roaring blow-dryers and hissing cans of hair spray were silent. "You might as well go home," Miguel Angel told Helen. "If you sweep the floor one more time, I will go crazy."

Helen left. She arrived at the Coronado slightly sick from the walk in the heat. She saw Josh and

Jason tanning themselves by the pool and went over to say hello. "I hear you have a special discount for older people," Helen said.

"Yep," Josh said. Jason took a big gulp of beer.

"And you want to help my friend Elsie," she said.

Jason belched loudly. "Gotta go," Josh said. "Later." The sullen pair left their beer bottles by the pool. Helen thought they were slippery, and it had nothing to do with their Coppertone. How could Margery like them?

Helen unlocked her door, fed Thumbs and gave him an ear scratch. Then she changed out of her work clothes into shorts, fixed herself a cold drink and knocked on Phil's door. He met her, carrying a cup of coffee. Once again, Helen was struck by her lover's cool good looks. She kissed him and said, "Mm. You're wearing my favorite blue shirt. How many days before you're mine?"

"If you're counting today, four and a half," he said. "I've spent the day working for you. First, I checked out your latest anonymous letter and found nothing useful—no fingerprints. The letters were cut from a newspaper, but I don't know which one, and stuck on with ordinary Elmer's Glue. The letter was postmarked Dover, Delaware."

"I don't know anyone in Delaware," Helen said. "The other one was from someplace in Maryland."

"I did find out a little information on your excoworker, Phoebe. She was a runaway who had connections with the sex industry before she went to beauty school and hired on with Miguel Angel."

"What kind of connections?" Helen asked.

"Looks like a little prostitution, some drugs, maybe some porn or nude modeling."

"Where did she run away from?" Helen asked.

"Granite City, Illinois," Phil said. "I've never heard of it. Is it a mining town?"

"No, Granite City was named for kitchenware," Helen said. "Graniteware is enameled metal that looked like granite, like those old turkey-roasting pans."

"My mom had one," Phil said.

"Everyone's mom did," Helen said. "Granite City is right across the Mississippi River from my hometown, St. Louis. It has steel mills, and parts of town can look pretty depressing. Granite City has some beautiful old homes, but many people still think it's a good place to be from. When I was in high school, there was a T-shirt that said, MY GIRLFRIEND WANTED ME TO KISS HER SOME PLACE DIRTY, SO I TOOK HER TO GRANITE CITY."

"Bet the city loved that," Phil said.

"Phoebe sounds like a dead end," Helen said. "Maybe we should investigate the groom. How did King Oden get in the strip club business? Where did he get the money?"

"I'll check that out, but you realize I may have to

look at a lot of women in skimpy outfits?" Phil asked.

"You can make the sacrifice for me," Helen said, and kissed him again.

Chapter 24

Helen sat straight up amid the sex-tossed sheets in Phil's bedroom. "It's not Miguel Angel," she said. "He didn't kill King."

"Huh? What?" Phil had his head buried in a pillow and his long legs tangled in the covers.

They'd fallen asleep in each other's arms about midnight. Helen had sighed contentedly, and the cares of the day slid away. So did her worries about her upcoming marriage. She began to think about the drag queen brunch. She'd seen something. Something important. Something she had to . . .

Helen didn't know when she'd drifted off to sleep, but she was wide-awake now, her heart pounding in the dark room.

"Sorry, I didn't mean to startle you," Helen said. "I just realized Miguel Angel didn't kill King."

Phil sounded groggy and slightly confused. "You've always said Miguel Angel is innocent. What time is it?" He rolled over and turned on his bedside light.

Helen blinked at the sudden brightness, then squinted at the bedside clock. "Three twelve," she said.

"In the morning?"

"I think so, since there's no daylight coming through the blinds," Helen said. "I can prove Miguel Angel is innocent. He doesn't have a waist."

"I still don't get it," Phil asked. "So what if he doesn't have a waist? He's a guy."

"Exactly. Let me show you." Helen climbed out of bed, put on Phil's blue shirt and ran to the living room, where the fatal wedding videos and photos were piled on the coffee table. She rooted through the photos until she found the picture of the blonde arguing with King. This photo had made her boss a "person of interest" to the police.

"Look at that picture," Helen said. "That's a woman."

"I could figure that out," Phil said. "Even at three in the morning."

"What I mean is the person has a very feminine shape," Helen said. "A narrow waist, rounded rear end, and a firm, high bust."

"Gee, if I say that, I get in trouble for being a pig," Phil said. "But I still don't see why that's a big clue."

"The waist is the key. Remember my bachelorette party at the drag queen brunch at Lips? The drag queens were beautiful, but they didn't have waists like real women. Miguel Angel did a good job in a hurry with his hair and makeup when he ran from Honey's wedding. He could pass as a female if you didn't look too close. But I had a chance to study him on the ride back to the Coronado. His bust was obviously padded. The dress he wore was too tight around the middle because Miguel Angel doesn't have a woman's figure."

"I can't believe we're having this conversation at three in the morning," Phil said. "How does that prove he's innocent?" He rubbed his eyes like a sleepy little boy.

Helen kissed him. "You are so darn cute," she said.

"True," Phil said, "but please explain why you woke me up."

"All the police have to do is make Miguel Angel wear Honey's blue dress."

"Where are they going to get it?" Phil asked.

"They pulled it out of the Dumpster behind the salon, remember? Once Miguel puts that dress on, the cops will see he's not the blonde in the photo."

"Okay, that makes sense," Phil said. "But we still have to find King's killer."

"And soon, before Miguel Angel is arrested," Helen said. "The police seem to be permanently parked outside the salon. I have tomorrow—I guess that's today—off work. We need to move quickly before Miguel Angel loses his salon."

"I promise I'll spend the whole day digging around in King's past," Phil said.

He was pacing the living room when he stopped

in front of his locked front door. "What's this?" Phil picked up a white legal-sized envelope.

Helen saw the block lettering and suddenly felt sick. "Looks like another anonymous letter," she said. "There's a sticky note on the envelope."

"The sticky note is from Margery," he said. "Do you mind if I open the letter?"

"Go ahead," Helen said.

Phil carefully prized open the envelope along the flap with a letter opener, then used a tissue to pull out a sheet of white paper with letters cut from a newspaper.

"What's it say?" Helen asked. She didn't want to know.

Phil showed her the letter. This one said, *YOU WILL BURN IN HELL.*

Helen wasn't even sure she believed in hell, but these notes were frightening.

"It's postmarked Rehoboth Beach, Delaware," he said.

"Another place I've never heard of," Helen said.

"Lot of mob connections in Delaware," Phil said.

"Lot of mobsters here in Florida, too," Helen said.

"Let me spend some time studying this letter." Phil went to his desk in the living room and booted up his computer, then made a pot of coffee and poured himself a cup. "Want some?" he asked.

"I need to get some sleep," Helen said, and went

back to bed. She awoke again at six in the morning. Phil was still working at his computer.

"Find anything?" she asked.

"Same old story on the anonymous letter," he said. "No fingerprints, plain typing paper and not a clue as to who sent it."

"Somebody hates me," Helen said.

"That's what worries me," Phil said. "Why don't you stay with me until the wedding?"

"It's not proper," Helen said.

"And what we did last night was?"

"No, but it's also bad luck to stay with the groom right before the wedding," Helen said.

"Says who?" Phil said.

"All the bridal guides. Honey and King lived together, and now he's dead."

"I'm sure that's what killed him," Phil said.

"Maybe it did," Helen said.

"Maybe she did," Phil said. "I'd feel better if you were someplace safe."

"What if I move in with Margery until Saturday? Kathy, Tom and their kids will be staying at my place on Friday. I need to get it ready for them."

"What about Thumbs?" Phil asked. "Margery hates cats."

"He can stay with you," Helen said. "He likes you better, anyway."

"Thanks a lot," Phil said.

"It's a great compliment," Helen said. "Thumbs doesn't fall for just any man. Is it really six in the morning? I'd better go feed him. What time do you want to leave?"

"About eleven," Phil said. "Sex-industry workers are not early risers."

"Are we going to King's Sexxx?" she asked.

"No, the current owner knows you and he's met me. We're going to the area near the bus station."

"Why?" Helen asked.

"Because the runaways hang out there. That's where King and his friends find fresh meat."

Helen kissed Phil good-bye and made the three-step trek to her door. A tail-lashing Thumbs met her, loudly demanding fresh water, more food and a clean litter box.

"Oh, hush," Helen said. "I have enough to do without waiting on a cat."

Thumbs slammed his nearly empty water bowl with his giant six-toed paw.

"That's enough, Mr. Nasty," Helen said. "If you want to eat, you behave yourself."

Thumbs stared at her with resentful yellow-green eyes. Helen did her feline chores, then started cleaning her apartment. The dust flew, the vacuum roared and Thumbs crawled under the bed to get away from the cat-killing Hoover.

While she worked, Helen brooded on who would send her threatening letters. Was it Honey? Phoebe? Did they have connections in Maryland and Delaware? Were they connected with the mob? King used to be a partner in a strip club, and some of those clubs were supposed to be mob owned.

The tiny apartment was sparkling when Helen heard Margery's door slam at ten thirty. Her landlady was padding out to the poolside umbrella table with a cup of coffee and a cigarette.

Helen changed into a fresh white blouse and jeans, then poured herself a cup of coffee and went out to talk to Margery. Her landlady looked tired this morning. Her brown face was like wrinkled chiffon. Helen was alarmed to see Margery huddled in her purple robe instead of dressed in some wild outfit.

"Are you feeling okay?" Helen asked.

"As good as I'm going to feel at seventy-six," Margery said. "I saw you got another anonymous letter yesterday." She took a long drag on her cigarette.

"This one says I'll burn in hell," Helen said.

"Probably." Margery looked demonic in the cloud of cigarette smoke. "But that's beside the point. Who is sending you threatening letters?"

"I don't know. Phil is worried. He wants me to stay with him before the wedding. I'd rather not. I'm wondering if I could sleep on your foldout couch."

"Nobody can sleep on that couch," Margery said. "It's stuffed with antlers and anvils. I bought it that way on purpose. One night on that couch and even the cheapest houseguest heads for the Days Inn.

However, I do have a guest room, and it's yours for a few nights. May I ask why you won't move in with Phil?"

"Call me old-fashioned, but I don't want to live with him before the wedding," Helen said.

"I don't think you're old-fashioned. I think you're nuts. That man is a hunk. Take your minister's advice and move in with him immediately."

"I'll take your guest bed instead," Helen said. She put down her coffee cup. "I hate to drink and run, but I need to meet Phil. We're looking for King's killer."

"Please don't get yourself into something dangerous," Margery said. "I want to marry you, not bury you."

"Do we get a group rate if we're both dead?"

Margery threw her cigarette butt at Helen.

Chapter 25

The girl's eyes were lined in black, like an Egyptian princess in a tomb painting. Her face was sprinkled with zits, badly hidden under thick makeup. Her pink-and-black hair fell to her shoulders.

Helen and Phil were parked in his Jeep on a sun-baked street at the edge of downtown Lauderdale. The Egyptian princess noted the Jeep and the two passengers, and moved on to a hunchbacked red SUV going way below the posted speed limit. She cocked her hip to show off her black leather teddy, leather shorts that bared half her cheeks, and high-heeled boots that rose to her knobby knees.

"Those boots look hot," Helen said.

"That's the idea," Phil said. "The young woman is selling herself."

"She's not old enough to be a woman," Helen said. "She can't be more than fifteen."

"She's probably younger than that," Phil said.

"By hot, I meant the boots look uncomfortable, not sexy," Helen said. "What kind of sleaze likes sex with children?"

"That one," Phil said, pointing to the red SUV.

Helen studied the driver. He had a face like a slab of beef. His shoulders had gone to flab, and his arms were thick and hairy. The man was bald, fat and frowning. The Egyptian princess opened the passenger door to his misshapen SUV, smiled coyly, and slid inside.

"Can't you stop them?" Helen said.

"I'm not a vice cop," Phil said. "Even if we save her, what about her friends?"

He pointed at a Tila Tequila wannabe in a teeny skirt, fishnet stockings and green platform heels, smoking a cigarette. Beside her, a short blonde with braids, Daisy Duke cutoffs and a shirt tied under her big breasts chewed gum and talked on a cell phone. A third woman in a plaid school jumper and white blouse stared at Phil's Jeep and licked her shimmering pink lips.

"I'd guess the schoolgirl is probably the oldest," Phil said.

These weren't the tanned-and-toned hookers of the movies. Tila had a wide bottom, Daisy Duke had a doughy midsection and the schoolgirl was heroin-thin. Helen wondered if that hint of sickness was part of their attraction.

The SUV driver roared off with the Egyptian princess. "That fat old guy should be ashamed," Helen said, nodding at the departing SUV.

"He should be, but he's not," Phil said. "This is runaway central. The pervs know where to find what they want. The bus station is only blocks away, so there's always a new supply of girls."

Phil drove past a boarded-up funeral home with a FOR SALE sign. "Must be a good neighborhood if the funeral home is out of business," Helen said.

"It's a bad neighborhood," Phil said. "People get shot, mugged and killed here. I wouldn't walk down these streets after dark. That funeral home used to be family owned. It was bought out by a big chain."

"I thought there were runaway shelters around here," Helen said.

"There are," Phil said. "Those juvie hookers may have stayed at a shelter when they first hit town. But some runaways don't like the shelter's rules. The good ones insist on no drugs, no smoking and no booze. The kids have to go to school, do their homework, go to counseling sessions, avoid gang clothes and weapons. They're kicked out if they don't abide by the rules. That's one shelter there."

He pointed to a windowless stucco building, white as a bleached skull and surrounded by a spiked iron fence.

"Not very friendly-looking," Helen said.

"It's not supposed to look friendly," he said. "It's a refuge for kids in trouble. The shelters hope the runaways will get off the bus and head there for help. Some will make a decent life for themselves. Others can't follow the rules and land back on the streets. Around here, there are too many ways to make easy money. They can sell themselves, like those girls." He nodded toward the salacious schoolgirl and the teeny-skirted Tila.

"Do you think Phoebe went to a shelter?" Helen asked.

"Maybe. There's no way I can find out," Phil said. "Most shelters aren't police- or PI-friendly. They refuse to say if someone is staying there. I tracked a guy wanted for murder to one shelter. He was nineteen—a year over the cutoff age to stay there. I saw him go inside, but the shelter refused to admit he was there. I couldn't get in. But I can go to the places that attract runaways."

He drove past an adult bookstore and turned down a potholed alley. Behind the bookstore was a big parking lot and a boxlike photo studio painted dusty red. AWESOME ART PHOTO MODELS! PASSPORT AND PORTFOLIO PICTURES! a faded sign proclaimed. A yellowing notice in the window said, NUDE MODEL WANTED. NO EXPERIENCE NECESSARY. ASK FOR AL.

"Runaways can get quick cash posing for so-called art photos," Phil said, as he pulled into the parking lot.

"That looks like my next job." Helen opened the Jeep's door.

"What are you doing?" Phil said.

"Al will talk to me before he says anything to you." Helen hopped out and slammed the door. "Wait here and don't fuss, or the wedding's off."

"Helen, come back!" Phil said.

He's not bossing me around, Helen thought, as she opened the photo studio door—then wished she hadn't. The man behind the cluttered desk smoked a cigar that smelled like a trash fire. His thin, pockmarked face seemed to disappear into a nest of red wrinkles above his dingy shirt collar.

"Are you Al?" she said.

Helen guessed the pus-green walls had been painted about the last time Al took a shower. The room stank of cigars and sweat.

"That's me," Al said. He tilted his head, and his neck wrinkles moved like an accordion. "What can I do you for?" He grinned as if that was a clever line. Al smiled like a hungry reptile. If Phil hadn't been outside in the Jeep, Helen would have run.

"Uh, I'd like some portfolio pictures," Helen said.

"Nudes." Al grinned that snaky smile.

"Node. I mean, no. I'm an actress."

"You're all actresses, baby. Some of you perform standing up, some on your knees and some on your back."

"I do summer stock," Helen said. She cursed the quaver in her voice. "I want to see samples of your work."

"Riiiiight," Al said, as if he didn't believe her. "Book is right there. Knock yourself out."

Helen cleared a pile of girlie magazines off a scummy leatherette couch and sat down gingerly.

The pages in the sample book were stuck together. Helen peeled apart the plastic sleeves and saw the photos of barely dressed young women. Some pouted, some sucked their fingers, and one licked a phallic-looking lollipop. They had names like Kimberlee, Kaylee, and Kellee. They promised to be "open-minded, wild and playful."

A series of ads for what looked like escort services and strip joints—except they were called "gentlemen's clubs"—followed the photos. Helen almost dropped the book when she saw a nearly nude Phoebe winking at her. That had to be a mistake. She studied the photo. It was definitely Phoebe with long brown hair, winking over one bare shoulder.

The ad headline said, FOLLOW MY STAR TO KING'S SEXXX. Helen could see a blue star on Phoebe's right shoulder. Phoebe was photographed

245

from the back, wearing only high heels and a thong no thicker than dental floss.

"Find something you like?" Al took another puff on his smelly cigar. The neck wrinkles contracted.

"How much for this photo?" Helen asked.

"Let's see—lighting, makeup and studio rental, plus prints—that would run you a thousand dollars. But we could work out a better price if you were nice."

"I don't want you to take my photo," Helen said. "I want to buy this photo."

"You a muff diver?" Al asked.

"I beg your pardon," Helen said, and stood up.

"Hey, don't get huffy on me. If you want the photo for your personal entertainment, it's fifty bucks. I have to make a copy."

"Twenty," Helen said. "I don't want a copy. I want this ad right here."

"Twenty-five," Al countered.

"Sold." Helen found twenty-five dollars in her purse, threw it on Al's desk and pulled the ad out of the plastic sleeve.

"Listen, lady, I don't judge anybody, but if you ever need a real man—"

Helen was out the door before Al could finish. She jumped into the Jeep and said, "Let's leave, quick."

"Are you okay?" Phil asked, as he threw the Jeep in reverse.

"At least I can't die of disgust," Helen said. "I've

found something you have to see. Do you want to wait till we get home, or stop somewhere?"

"Let's get lunch," Phil said. His dented Jeep rocketed down the alley. He made a dizzying series of turns and they were back on Federal Highway, where Helen felt safer. Phil drove into the tunnel just past Broward Boulevard, then turned in to a restaurant called Dogma.

"What's this?" Helen asked.

"Possibly the best hot dog stand in South Florida. I thought we could talk here."

Dogma was devoted to hot dogs, from the plain classic to the Sedona, embellished with spicy salsa, grilled bacon, sliced avocado, sour cream and tomatoes. Most of the dogs were less than five dollars.

"What about the Athens?" Phil said. "That's a hot dog with cucumbers, olives and feta cheese."

"I'm not up for cucumbers and hot dogs," Helen said.

"Maybe a nice, healthy salad?"

"If I want healthy, I'll go to Whole Foods," Helen said. "Today, I'm going to the dogs. Let's mainline nitrates and nitrites. I want the Pitchfork with barbecue sauce, cheese, grilled bacon and grilled onions."

"I'll take the classic with raw onions and mus-tard—and a beer," Phil said.

The hot dogs were deliciously messy. Helen wolfed hers down in four bites.

"Do you want another?" Phil asked.

"Not if I'm posing nude for Al," Helen said.

"Please tell me you're joking," Phil said.

"I am. Let me show you what I found." She handed Phil a wad of paper napkins and said, "I don't want any grease on this ad. I just paid twenty-five bucks for it."

"You bought an ad from a free newspaper?" Phil said.

"I'm pretty sure it's not on the stands anymore," Helen said. "Look at the winking girl. That's a younger Phoebe."

"I thought she was blond," Phil said.

"She is now, but I've seen her roots. Phoebe is really a brunette."

"A very young brunette," Phil said. "She was born in 1992."

"That makes her seventeen now," Helen said. "How old was she when she worked at King's strip club?"

"This ad is two years old," he said, looking at the date at the top of the page. "So she would have been about fifteen."

"King would still be responsible for having an underage minor working at his club, right?" Helen said.

"I think so," Phil said. "He might beat the underage rap in court, but it would ruin his entry into Lauderdale society. Someone who exploited young girls wouldn't be invited to the A-list parties. Those old dowagers would bar the door when he showed up, no matter how fat his charity checks were."

Helen looked at Phoebe's nipped-in waist and large breasts—and her enormous feet in those high heels—and felt like someone had stuck a stiletto in her brain. "She's the blonde who fought with King right before he died. That was her in the blue dress. We've got to see Mireya, the photographer's assistant. She's in danger."

"I've missed something here," Phil said. "We were talking about Phoebe."

"Phoebe's the killer," Helen said. "Mireya photographed her pushing the groom into the pool and stomping on his hand."

"Why didn't Mireya go to the police?"

"She let King die so she could blackmail Phoebe," Helen said. "Why else would Mireya give up a good job in this market? What's she going to live on now? Phoebe is out of work and can't pay her. If Mireya has been pushing Phoebe for more money, she's in danger."

"You've just set an Olympic record for jumping to conclusions," Phil said.

"No!" Helen said. "I'm serious. We have to warn her. I have Mireya's new address from her neighbor. We have to drive there."

"Now?" Phil said.

"It's only two o'clock, and I don't have her phone number."

"How do you know the bride didn't kill King? That was Honey's white wedding gown in a corner of the photo."

"The bride didn't try to frame Miguel Angel for the murder," Helen said.

"That makes no sense."

"Humor me," Helen said.

Chapter 26

M ireya!" Helen called. "Are you home?"
She knocked loudly on the town house's red-painted door and rang the bell.

No sound of footsteps. No flick of the mini blinds. Helen wondered if Mireya could hear her over "Stairway to Heaven" blasting from the place next door.

Mireya had moved into a narrow pinkish-beige town house at a development called Three Palms. The entrance was flanked by three royal palm trees, trunks straight as concrete columns. One was alive and lush with greenery. Two were topless trunks, their fronds probably blown away in a hurricane.

"They ought to change the name," Helen said.

"They could buy two new palm trees," Phil said, "but it looks like they're cutting corners."

0% DOWN! FIRST MONTH FREE! U CAN'T LOSE! screamed a banner strung between two of the dead trees.

"Yep, Palm Beach County is really exclusive," Helen shouted over the neighbor's blaring music.

Mireya's front yard was the size of a bath mat and landscaped with brown pebbles. Her front steps were cracked. A pot of pink impatiens was dying in the searing sun. The crowded parking lot's flower beds were filled with beer cans and sun-blasted boulders.

Three Palms was near the railroad tracks and the Dixie Highway—not a prestigious location. But Mireya could say she lived in Palm Beach County.

Helen rang the doorbell. Phil beat on the door and kept one eye on his Jeep, parked illegally by the Dumpster.

Small, dented cars were crammed into every spot in the parking lot. Stenciled on the white concrete barriers were the town house numbers. A black Neon with a broken trunk was in spot 117 in front of Mireya's town house.

"She has to be here," Helen said. "That's her car."

"Maybe," Phil said. "But these people don't seem to respect parking rules." Vehicles were parked haphazardly in the fire zone.

The lot's exit was partially blocked by a yellow pickup stuffed with a mattress, a table, and a fat plaid couch.

"I'm guessing these are investment properties," Phil said. "The owners buy them cheap, then rent to anyone who scrapes together enough money to cover the loan payments. The average renter is mid-to-late twenties with an entry-level job. Four to six people are packed into two bedrooms. There's no homeowners' association to complain about the noise, the renters or the parking violations."

Helen pounded on the door again and rang the bell. No answer. Phil joined her. "Mireya!" they screamed. "Are you there?"

Silence. At least from inside Mireya's town house. Next door, the music was cranked another notch to rap-concert level.

"Now what?" Helen said.

"It's only three o'clock," Phil said. "Maybe she's at work."

"Her neighbor said she doesn't need a job anymore," Helen said. "Mireya struck it rich."

"The blinds are shut on the front windows," Phil said. He pulled out a pocket handkerchief and tried the front door. "Locked. Let's go around to the back. Maybe we can see inside."

"What if the neighbors call the cops?" Helen asked.

"At this place? I could kick in the door and carry out everything she owns, and nobody would notice."

"Hey, assholes! Watch it!"

Helen and Phil turned and saw a big-bellied guy yelling at three sweating men hauling a huge television. Big Belly's face was stroke red. "You drop that flat-screen TV, and I'll kill you," he screeched.

"How do we know those guys carrying out that monster TV aren't stealing it?" Phil asked.

Helen nodded at an upstairs window two doors down. A ruffled curtain fluttered slightly. "How do we know whoever is watching behind that curtain isn't writing down their license plate number—or our description?"

"We don't," Phil said. "But if you're worried, I've got just the thing." He ran back to the Jeep, reached inside and pulled out a clipboard with a yellow legal pad.

"This looks official," he said. "I can say I'm a city inspector. Nobody ever challenges that excuse."

"I smell smoke," Helen said.

Phil sniffed the air. "Barbecue," he said. "Probably ribs. Let's go."

Helen started tiptoeing toward the sidewalk that led around the back.

"Helen!" Phil whispered. "Don't walk like that. You look like a housebreaker. Act like you live here."

He walked boldly around the privacy fence, armed only with his confidence and his clipboard. Helen followed. The air was thick with chlorine and coconut oil as they passed the pool. Helen peered through the fence slats. Bikinied bodies were roasting on chaise longues, iPods plugged into their ears. The sun worshipers looked like greased corpses.

A chunky man used a long-handled barbecue fork to poke at a rack of ribs on a grill. He splashed beer on the ribs, then chugged the rest and tossed the bottle on the ground. Phil waved and smiled. The rib poker waved back.

"See? That's how you do it," Phil said. "People move in and out of this place every week. He has no idea if we live here or not."

"You're good at this," Helen said. "That makes me nervous."

"I have to be," Phil said. "It's my job."

Mireya had a small concrete slab behind her town house. More plants roasted in the sun, along with plastic patio furniture. "No curtains on the sliding glass doors," Helen said, as she stepped around a chair.

"Sliding glass doors on the ground floor. The burglar's friend." Phil used his handkerchief to tug on the door handle. It slid open. "Careful," he said. "Try not to touch anything."

"Mireya!" he called once more, but there was no sound. The walls seemed to throb with the neighbor's music.

"Brrr. It's cold in here," Helen said, when she stepped inside. Her heart was pounding. She was now officially guilty of trespassing. "Mireya keeps the air conditioner high. Was this place ransacked, or is she just moving in?"

"Hard to tell," Phil said. "It's a mess."

The living room was a maze of upended cardboard boxes. Towels, clothes and kitchenware spilled out of them. A fat brown recliner lay on its side next to a smashed end table.

"I don't like this," Helen said.

"The kitchen was definitely ransacked," Phil said.

Broken cups and glassware were thrown on the beige kitchen tile. Sugar and flour were dumped on the floor, and cooking oil poured over the white mounds. The refrigerator door hung open, and an overturned milk jug dripped on the floor. The stink of spoiled milk was overpowering.

Phil used the handkerchief to flip on the kitchen light. A fat roach scuttled away.

"Ohmigod, is that blood dripping off the counter?" Helen said, her voice shaky.

Phil stuck his finger in the red goo, tasted it, and said, "Ketchup. Brooks, I think."

"How do you know?" Helen asked.

He pointed to an overturned Brooks ketchup bottle in the corner. Phil wiped away the spot of ketchup he'd touched with a dishtowel on the counter. "Don't go in any farther. We'll leave footprints in this mess."

"I hope Mireya wasn't hurt," Helen said.

"Maybe she spent the night with friends, and someone broke in," Phil said, but Helen could tell he didn't believe that. "Let's check the rooms upstairs."

They sprinted up a short flight of steps to a bathroom. Phil turned on the bathroom light with his handkerchief.

Helen screamed. "That's blood in the sink," she said. "Real blood. That's not ketchup."

Red-black lines had dripped and dried on the blue sink. A bloody towel had been dropped on the toilet lid. A large red shoe print was stamped in the pale throw rug. There were more blood spots on the tile.

"Looks like someone tried to wash up," Phil said. "Don't come in."

Helen backed away from the bathroom door, hoping she wouldn't throw up. "Hurry, Phil. We have to get out of here. Something is wrong."

"One more room to check, after I look behind that shower curtain." He used the handkerchief to pick up a long-handled bath brush and moved the blue plastic curtain. "Tub is clean," he said.

Helen sighed with relief and ran to the bedroom. The curtains were drawn and the room was dark. Helen nearly flipped on the light when Phil called, "Stop!"

He turned on the light with his handkerchief. A king-sized brass bed with a flowered spread and a maroon pillowcase took up nearly the whole room. Mountains of clothes, costume jewelry and under-wear were tossed on it. A teddy bear wearing a Marlins cap topped the pile. The only other furni-ture was a bedside table and a mirrored dresser. All the drawers were open and their contents were dumped on the floor.

"Somebody has already searched this room," Phil said.

"Papers are scattered on the dresser top," Helen said. "That's a check register."

Phil used the handkerchief and a pen from his pocket to open the check register and flip through the recent pages. "Mireya deposits $623.43 every two weeks, like clockwork," Phil said. "There are small withdrawals for checks to Publix, the utilities, Marshalls. Then the deposits stop and whoa—what's this? A deposit for twenty thousand dollars."

"That's major money for a young woman making minimum wage," Helen said. "When was the money deposited?"

"Last Monday. The day before that video ran on Channel Fifteen."

"It smells funny in here," Helen said. "Smells like—"

She saw Phil's jaw go rigid and his mouth tighten into a thin line.

"Does Mireya have a poodle?" Helen asked. She was talking too fast, trying to stave off the inevitable awful discovery. "I see curly dark hair on the pillow." She edged closer to the bed and realized the spread wasn't covered with flowers. Blood, bone and brain matter were spattered on the powder blue spread. The pillowcase wasn't maroon. That was blood.

"No," she said. "No, no, no!"

She started to pull back the spread when Phil grabbed her arms. "Helen," he said. "That poor woman is dead."

"Was she shot?"

"She was beaten with a baseball bat. It's beside the bed. You can't help Mireya. We need to leave."

"But what about the police?" Helen asked.

"You've already been interviewed in connection with one murder. If you're involved in two, they'll lock you up—and I'll lose my PI license."

"But you've used your handkerchief on all the light switches and doors," Helen said.

"I've still tampered with a crime scene. I've left hairs, fibers and probably shoe prints all over this place."

"Shouldn't we search for the wedding video?" Helen asked.

"It's either at the TV station or the killer has it," Phil said. "Let's go."

"How long has Mireya been dead?"

"The air-conditioning was turned down to sixty, but the body is pretty bloated. My guess is she's been dead about a week."

"We can't just leave her here," Helen said.

"We won't." Phil steered Helen toward the hallway. "We'll make an anonymous call to the police from a big shopping mall north of here."

"If you get the Jeep," Helen said, "I'll search her car trunk."

"You don't have a key," Phil said.

"The trunk is broken and held shut with a bungee cord," Helen said.

"Someone will see you," Phil said.

"They may see a person, but they won't see me," Helen said. "Give me your shirt."

"My shirt? Why?"

"I need a man's shirt." She picked an oversized T-shirt off the pile of clothes on the bed and said, "Put this on."

"It's pink," Phil said.

"Good. You didn't come in wearing a pink shirt."

Phil unbuttoned his blue shirt, and Helen put it on over her white blouse. She looked heavier wearing two shirts. For once, she was glad she looked fatter. She pulled her long brown hair into a knot on top her head, plucked the Marlins cap off the bear and put it on. Then Helen reached into her purse and pulled out a dark brown eyeliner pencil.

"We don't have time for you to put on makeup," Phil said.

"This isn't makeup. It's a mustache." Helen drew a heavy, dark handlebar mustache on her face.

"It looks fake," Phil said.

"No one's going to get close to see," Helen said. "I'm tall enough to pass as a man, and I'm wearing jeans and running shoes."

"Not many men carry purses, even in Florida," Phil said.

"Good point," Helen said. She shoved her purse

down her blouse. "That should hide my chest. Now I have a manly beer gut. I'll carry your clipboard. Phil, you get the Jeep. Park it outside the town house complex. I'll join you as soon as I can. Let me borrow your handkerchief to close the sliding door."

Phil left the town house first by the back door. Helen counted to thirty and followed, pulling the door shut with her hand wrapped in the handkerchief. She tried to walk macho. Helen was relieved that the chunky guy was no longer torturing ribs on the grill. The pool was deserted, except for a single, sleeping sunbather.

Helen marched briskly to parking spot 117. Phil's Jeep was gone from the illegal spot by the Dumpster.

She saw the curtain flutter in the town house two doors down. With her hand wrapped in the white handkerchief like a bandage, she unhooked the bungee cord. The trunk sprang open with a haunted house creak.

Inside was a rusty beach chair and an empty canvas tote, but no tape, CD, or MiniDV. Helen quickly ran her hand around inside the trunk and came up with stray hairs, threads and bits of rust.

She heard a car honking on the other side of the complex fence and suspected it was Phil, growing impatient. One more quick swipe around the trunk, and she saw the spare tire. She ran her hand inside the wheel well. The MiniDV was taped to the tire, out of sight. Helen pried it loose and stashed it in her purse, hoping Phil didn't see it.

She was securing the trunk's bungee cord when Phil roared into the parking lot.

Chapter 27

"You look funny with that hand-painted mustache," Phil said to Helen. He'd broken every speed limit to get back on I-95. Now his battered old Jeep was creeping in rush-hour traffic. Helen sucked in smog and wished for air-conditioning, or even fresh, hot June air.

She scrubbed at her self-inflicted mustache with a tissue and checked the rearview mirror. The dark eyeliner wasn't coming off. It seemed embedded in her skin, a dark brown, greasy splotch.

"Can we get off the highway and stop at a drugstore?" Helen said.

"Are you sick?" Phil said.

"I feel all right. But unless you want me wearing a mustache for our wedding, I'd better remove this fast. I used waterproof eyeliner. I need some cold cream."

"Do drugstores carry cream?" Phil said. "I could get you half-and-half at the supermarket."

"Not that kind of cream," Helen said. "Face cream, like Pond's. For removing makeup. It comes in a jar."

Phil had many fine qualities, but the man was shopping impaired. Still, he edged into the slow lane and turned off the interstate toward US-1, prepared to brave the stores.

"There's a Walgreens," Helen said.

"I can go in and ask for cold cream," Phil said. "But aren't they going to look at me funny?"

"It's Florida," Helen said. "Nothing is weird here. Say you're buying it for your mother. Or you're an actor."

"Well, okay," Phil said. "But won't you come in with me?"

"We're supposed to be traveling under the radar," Helen said. "We drove all the way north to the Wellington Green mall to use a pay phone to report Mireya's murder. The cops should be at Three Palms by now. If they've interviewed the neighbors, the curtain twitcher could mention that the person searching Mireya's car trunk had a mustache. If I walk into this store with a smeared painted-on mustache, someone will notice. I'll be on the store's video."

"Okay," Phil said. But he still sounded reluctant. He squared his shoulders and marched into the drugstore like a gunslinger facing a bar packed with surly bikers. He ran back out ten minutes later with a bag. "Is this right?"

Helen took out the jar of Pond's cream. "Perfect," she said.

"You don't know what it was like in there," he

said. "They didn't just have Pond's cold cream. They had a nourishing moisturizer pack, some towelettes coated with the stuff and an antiwrinkle cream I didn't get because you don't have wrinkles."

Helen interrupted him with a quick kiss. "Thank you," she said.

"I finally settled on Pond's Classic. I figured that was like Coke Classic. I couldn't go wrong with the original. Did I do right?"

"You did right," Helen said. "I didn't realize I was putting you through that."

"You women have no idea what men go through in stores," Phil said. "You think it's simple to run in and pick up something. But whenever I go, the store is out of the item you want, or they don't carry that brand but they carry something similar or—"

"It's over," Helen said. "You survived the ordeal." She began smearing the fake mustache with globs of cream, then rubbing it with another tissue. "It's coming off. Do I have a big red mark on my upper lip?"

"Of course not," Phil said.

"I'm worried about Elsie," Helen said.

"Margery's older friend?" Phil asked.

"Yeah, the cute one. She's my bridesmaid. She recognized those two sneery creeps in apartment 2C—Josh and Jason. She says they're working on her neighbor's roof and she's thinking of hiring them to do hers. Elsie can be a little ditzy some-times, but she's good with faces. And I don't trust those guys."

"Why? Because everyone else in apartment 2C has been a crook?"

"Yes, and Josh and Jason don't look like con-struction workers," Helen said.

"And how does a construction worker look?" Phil said. "Should they wear hard hats?"

"They don't have the right kind of muscles," Helen said. "We had a lot of construction workers staying at Sybil's Full Moon hotel when I cleaned rooms there. Even the skinny ones had serious muscles—their arms were like braided ropes. Josh and Jason look like they've never lifted anything heavier than a beer bottle. Also, the construction workers' necks and arms were burned deep red. The 2C guys have pool tans. Their skin color is too even and pale for outdoor workers. Look at their hands. They aren't calloused. Josh and Jason aren't roofers."

"So you want me to check them out?"

"Please," Helen said. "Elsie's a sweet lady and an easy target. I don't want her or her friends hurt."

"Okay, I'll go tomorrow," Phil said. "As a present for you."

It was six thirty when Phil drove into the Coronado parking lot. Helen was relieved to see Margery decked out in a cool, pale lavender caftan and purple kitten-heeled sandals, looking like her old self. She had a screwdriver in one hand and a cigarette in the other.

"Why do you have that red mark on your face?" Margery asked.

"I'll explain later," Helen said.

"And since when did you become a Marlins fan?" Margery asked.

"Oh, the hat? I found it."

"I'll see you tomorrow," Phil said, and kissed her.

"Oh no," Margery said. "You're not getting away. I need to talk to you two about the wedding. Have a seat by the pool."

"Can I go get a beer?" Phil asked.

"Of course," Margery said.

"Helen, do you want anything?" Phil asked.

"White wine."

Helen and Margery sat down at the umbrella table. "Good evening," Helen said to Josh and Jason. They grunted, got up and went inside, leaving their beer bottles by their chaise longues again.

"Hey," Margery called after them. "I said no glass by the pool."

"Whatever," Josh said. Unless it was Jason. Their door slammed and the beer bottles stayed on the concrete pool deck.

"I'm raising their rent," Margery said. "They're renting on a month-to-month basis. That's the easiest way to get those slugs out of here. They've snubbed my guests and broken my rules."

"But Phil drinks beer out by the pool all the time."

"That's different," Margery said. "Phil picks up after himself. He doesn't leave bottles lying around. I want these two gone."

"You used to think they were cute," Helen said.

"You talking about me?" Phil was balancing a beer bottle, a white wine, a roll of paper towels and a bowl of fresh popcorn.

Margery rescued the bowl of hot, buttery popcorn and took a handful. "This is the real thing. It's not microwaved. You make terrific popcorn. I like that in a man."

"Great little cook," Helen said. "Think I'll keep him."

"You wanted to see us?" Phil asked.

Between popcorn crunches, Margery said, "Who is going to be your best man?"

"I was thinking of asking Cal the Canadian," Phil said, reaching for a handful of popcorn.

"Are you sure he's back in Lauderdale? I haven't seen him," Helen said.

"He's here," Margery said. "He's spent his time in Canada and is now eligible for his government health insurance. He came in the other night. Phil, is he the best you can do for a best man?"

"Helen vetoed the vice cop."

"I did not," Helen said. "I just wasn't enthusiastic about having a vice cop in my wedding."

"Why? You're all wearing clothes, aren't you?"

Margery asked. "Who are you getting for Peggy's escort?"

"Her boyfriend—Daniel the lawyer—said he'd escort her," Helen said.

"Good," Margery said. "He probably has his own tux. I didn't know Phil knew the man."

"I don't, except to say hello," Phil said. "But guys don't get all sentimental about who's in their wedding. He's not in vice, is he?"

"Depends," Margery said. "He is a lawyer. Who should we get to escort Elsie?"

"She's a bridesmaid, too?" Phil said.

"I told you that," Helen said, then wondered if she had.

"Uh." Phil didn't know what to say.

"Never mind, I'll find someone," Margery said. "Helen, your sister Kathy is going to be your maid of honor, right?"

"Yes. Unless Phil has any objections, Cal can be her escort. I don't want to put poor Tom in a monkey suit."

"And your niece is a junior bridesmaid?"

"Allison is only three," Helen said. "She's too young. We could make her brother the ring bearer, but Tommy Junior is a little old for that honor."

"Make him the cat wrangler," Margery said. "I gather that fur ball of yours is invited to the wedding."

"I thought we'd lock Thumbs away for the ceremony," Helen said.

"He'll howl through the whole service," Margery said. "I can hear him yowling at mealtime, even with my door shut. Tommy can watch him and make sure the cat doesn't go over the fence."

"I'll get Thumbs some shrimp for the wedding feast," Phil said. "We don't need a ring bearer. Cal can hold the wedding ring."

"What about your mother, Helen?"

"She can get her own shrimp," Helen said, helping herself to more popcorn.

"Will you please talk sense," Margery said, and puffed out an angry cloud of cigarette smoke.

"Mother is not coming to our wedding," Helen said in clipped tones. "We've already discussed this. She won't change her mind. She's going to stay home and disapprove."

"Well, at least you made the gesture," Margery said.

"And she made a gesture right back," Helen said. "Mom is not the forgiving type."

"What about your family, Phil?"

"Don't have one," he said. "I'm an orphan, and my ex, Kendra, is not invited."

"Any children?" Margery asked.

"Not that I know of."

They chomped popcorn and discussed plans for the food, chairs, flowers and tiki torches for the seven o'clock ceremony. "I've checked the long-range weather forecast," Margery said. "Saturday is supposed to be hot and sunny."

The wedding cake was being delivered to the Coronado. Phil promised to pick up the food and ice.

"What time do you want me to help set things up for the wedding?" Helen said.

"You are not doing anything the day of your wedding," Margery said. "You are the bride. And don't tell me you're going to work at Miguel Angel's salon."

"I have Saturday off," Helen said. "Though I do go in for a few hours tomorrow."

"Is Miguel Angel coming here to do your hair and makeup?"

"No, I'm going to the shop."

"Then you'd better take my car," Margery said. "You'll look a mess if you try to walk home or ride in Phil's un-air-conditioned Jeep."

"I'm going with Cal tomorrow to get our tuxes fitted," Phil said. "I'll take him out for a beer tonight."

"Bring your wallet," Margery said. "If you take Cal, you'll pay for the pleasure of his company."

Margery turned to Helen. "What are you doing tonight?"

"Moving in with you," she said.

Chapter 28

A twenty-three-year-old woman was found beaten to death in her town house at the Three Palms complex in Palm Beach County," the television announcer said.

Flashing emergency lights and solemn law enforcement officials filled the screen, followed by the inevitable black body bag being wheeled to an ambulance. Clumps of neighbors stood at the edge of the parking lot.

Helen shivered and felt sad. She remembered Mireya's dark hair and enthusiasm for her job. She was so young. Such a cruel death.

"The victim's name is being withheld pending notification of relatives," the announcer said. "The police are looking for a man wanted in connection with the killing. Witnesses say a white male in his late thirties was seen leaving the victim's home by the back door. The man is described as about six feet tall and two hundred pounds. Here is a composite drawing."

A beady-eyed man with a Marlins cap and a Snidely Whiplash mustache flashed on the screen.

"If you see this person, do not try to apprehend him," the announcer said. "Call the police immediately. He is believed to be dangerous."

Helen choked on her white wine.

"What's got into you?" Margery asked.

"Nothing. I'm tired. It's after ten. I hauled my clothes over here and cleaned my apartment for Kathy and her family."

The shock of finding Mireya's body was also taking its toll, but Helen didn't mention that. Her brain felt stuffed with sawdust. Little bits seemed to ooze out her ears. Her eyelids were heavy.

"You're lying," Margery said.

"I'm exhausted," Helen said. "I'd like to take a shower, then go to sleep."

"Suit yourself," Margery said. "But I will find out what's going on."

"I told Phil about your renters in 2C. I think they're crooks."

"Don't change the subject on me, Helen Hawthorne," Margery said.

"I wanted to give you a heads-up, that's all," Helen said.

"Normally, I don't appreciate you two butting into my business. You are both prejudiced against any renter in 2C. But if you can find a way to get rid of those buzzards, I'll be happy. I don't want them in my apartment."

"I don't want them at our wedding," Helen said.

"So don't invite them."

"They'll show up, anyway, drink our beer and sneer at our guests," Helen said. "I hated how they treated Elsie. If we throw them out at the wedding, it will cause a scene."

271

"Why do you and Phil think those guys are crooks instead of plain rude?" Margery asked.

"Elsie says she knows them," Helen said. "She says Josh and Jason are working on her neighbor's roof, and the neighbor gave them money. She's thinking of hiring them, too. Phil is going to check them out tomorrow, after he orders the tuxes."

"That's all you're going on?" Margery said. "You're relying on Elsie?"

"Yes. Elsie dithers a little, but she's not stupid."

"She is pretty gullible," Margery said.

"She's too nice, if that's a fault," Helen said. "I'd feel safer if Phil checked out Jason and Josh. Do you have Elsie's address?"

"I'll look it up now," Margery said.

Helen tossed the Marlins cap in the trash while her landlady looked through her address book.

Margery handed her an address written on a piece of paper. She spotted the cap in the wastebasket. "I'm glad you're throwing that out. It doesn't suit you."

"That's what I thought," Helen said.

"Maybe your nephew would like it," Margery said.

"He's a St. Louis Cardinals fan," Helen said. "Besides, I found this cap. I have no idea who wore it before me. What if it was a kid with head lice?"

"Would you mind washing your hair before you

use my pillow?" Margery asked. "What time do you go into work tomorrow?"

"I don't have to be at the salon until ten o'clock. I'm exhausted. I'd like to turn in. Thanks again for putting me up."

"No problem," Margery said. "I just want to see you two safely married."

"Me, too," Helen said.

Helen showered and washed her hair, then tossed and turned for the next three hours. A slide show from Mireya's town house of horrors played in her head. Helen saw the ransacked kitchen. The bloody sink. The beaten body in the brass bed. Again and again, Helen saw herself sneaking out of the town house in her painted mustache. She imagined herself being arrested by the police, with the bright lights of the interrogation room. The lights seared her eyes and the police wouldn't turn them off.

Then Helen realized that wasn't a bright light. It was summer sunshine. She glanced at the bedside clock: 8:02.

Helen got up, washed, and dressed in her work clothes. She followed the fragrant smell of hot coffee to the kitchen. Her landlady handed her a steaming mug.

"Phil's out by the pool," Margery said. "I assume you'll want to talk to him. Would you like eggs and toast for breakfast?"

"No food, thanks," Helen said. "I'm not a breakfast eater. I'll just pour myself some coffee."

Helen kissed Phil good morning and said, "I hope Saturday is this nice for our wedding."

"The weather is supposed to be clear," Phil said, "but it may be hotter."

"How was your drink with Cal?"

"Fine," Phil said. "He's an entertaining guy. He's going with me at eleven this morning. Peggy says her boyfriend has his own tux, and he'll be happy to escort her."

"Good," Helen said. "Some dates panic at the thought of going to a wedding. They're afraid it may be catching. Margery gave me Elsie's address." She handed the paper to Phil.

"It's only a few blocks away. I'll go there now," Phil said. "The guys' truck is gone, so I assume Josh and Jason are working now."

"I'll finish my coffee and stare at the pool until I go to the salon," Helen said.

Phil was back by nine o'clock, roaring mad. "Those two creeps are ripping off widows."

"What? Did you see them?"

"No," Phil said, pacing up and down the pool deck. "They weren't around. I want to beat the little bastards to a pulp."

"Easy," Helen said. "I don't want you in jail on our wedding day. Sit down and tell me what happened."

Phil sat, but he could barely contain his fury. "Elsie has a neighbor who lives alone. Mrs. Berger is eighty-two years old. Her husband has been dead for a decade, and they have no children. Her roof was leaking and the water had ruined her bedroom ceiling. Josh and Jason said they'd fix the roof for two thousand cash, which was a lot less than any other estimate she got. They called it a special senior discount. They got the job done quickly, according to Mrs. Berger. She gave them the money. Then we had that downpour Monday morning and her roof still leaked. I climbed up there—"

"You actually got up on the roof?" Helen said.

"Of course. How else could I see what they did? Josh and Jason hadn't fixed a thing. Mrs. Berger's house has one of those white tile roofs you see here in Florida. All they did was paint over the leak and take the poor lady's money."

"So they got two thousand cash for pouring a little paint on a roof?" Helen said.

"That's it," Phil said. "They hung out on the roof for a couple of hours, spread the white paint around and collected their money. Nice, huh? I went looking for the creeps, but they weren't in the area."

"But we know where to find them, don't we?" Helen said.

"Do you have to be at work right now?" Phil asked.

"I've got a little time. It's only nine ten. Let's go see Margery."

Their landlady was outraged. She took her key, marched upstairs to apartment 2C, and threw open the door.

"Look at this place," Margery said. "It's a train wreck."

"Stinks like a locker room," Phil said.

Dirty T-shirts, paint-stained cutoffs and moldy towels littered the floor. Grease-stained pizza boxes were stacked three deep on the couch. The TV clicker sat on a slice of pepperoni pizza.

"Look at my lampshade!" Margery said.

Thick white socks were drying on the shade.

"An old bachelor trick. Saves spending money on a clothes dryer," Phil said. The laughter died in his throat when Margery and Helen glared at him.

"They're out of here today," Margery said. She dragged two suitcases and a gym bag out of the hall closet.

Phil and Helen threw Josh and Jason's belongings into the bags. Helen delighted in wrapping their toothbrushes in a pair of dirty socks.

Margery searched the apartment. "Aha!" she shouted in triumph. "I found cash in the freezer." She pulled out a plastic bag and started counting the money. "Five thousand dollars." Margery helped herself to all but a hundred dollars. "That should get them back to Maryland," she said.

When the three bags were packed and set by the door, Helen said, "What do we do now?"

"You go to work," Margery said. "Phil, you and Cal have to order your tuxes. I'm going to wait here until those two birds come home. I expect I'll see them between three and four o'clock. That's when they turn up at my pool, sunning themselves like the snakes they are."

"I should be back by then," Helen said.

"Me, too," Phil said. "Helen, you want Cal and me to get blue polyester tuxes with butterfly bow ties, right?"

"It will shave years off you," Helen said. "You'll look just like my junior prom date."

She kissed Phil and was out the door. This morning, the salon was infested with vultures who gossiped just as much as the regulars. Two women from Moberly, Missouri, were typical.

"Do you think anyone back home will recognize me with my new hairdo, Sally?" She patted her chic blond style.

"You may need a new wardrobe to go with it, Darleen," her friend said.

"I think I do. But I'll buy carefully," Darleen said. "Did you see that outfit Betty wore to church last Sunday? It was too short, too tight—"

"And way too young," Sally finished. "She's stew meat who thinks she's prime rib."

"That lady is way past her prime," Darleen said. "Nobody has seen Betty's ribs in ages. You're too tasteful to dress like a two-dollar whore."

Sally lowered her voice. "Do we have to tip the

girl who brought us that water? We're never coming back here."

"We should at least get a glass of water for what they charge," Darleen said. "I'm not made of money."

Neither am I, Helen thought, and wished she'd dumped the ice water in their laps. Darleen gave her a measly dollar when she and Sally left on their shopping expedition.

"Tomorrow will be better," Ana Luisa said to Helen. They watched the women leave without regret. But more vultures flocked to the salon.

Helen was relieved to be home by three thirty. She knocked on the door to 2C and found Phil and Margery sitting on the couch.

"You two look grim," Helen said.

"Not as grim as that shower stall," Margery said. "It's black with mold. They've turned this place into a toxic waste dump."

"I'll help you clean it up," Helen said.

"No, you won't," Margery said. "I'm hiring someone. I may have to call in the EPA."

They heard a key rattling in the lock. Phil went to the door, crossed his arms and straightened his shoulders, which made him look even taller. Margery and Helen stood behind him.

"Hey, dude, what are you doing in our place?" Josh asked.

"It's my place," Margery said, fury flashing in her eyes. "I didn't realize I was renting to a pair of swindlers. Ripping off an old woman. Shame on you. How could you cheat poor Mrs. Berger?"

"Hey, we didn't rip her off. We fixed her roof."

"You painted it with cheap latex," Phil said. "I climbed up there and checked."

"You're out of here," Margery said. "Pick up your luggage and leave."

"Hey, you can't do that," Josh said.

"Yes, I can," Margery said. "You don't have a lease. But if you'd rather, I can call the police. They'd love to discuss your special senior discount. You'll get free room and board, too."

Jason ran straight to the fridge and opened the freezer. He pulled out the deflated bag of cold cash. "Hey, where's the rest of our money? You ripped us off."

"Now you know what it feels like," Margery said. "I took two thousand to return to Mrs. Berger. The rest is a cleaning fee. I'm cleaning you out to teach you a lesson. Unless you'd rather talk to the police."

"Come along, dudes," Phil said.

He grabbed Jason and Josh by their shirt collars and shoved them out the door. Helen and Margery followed with their bags.

Chapter 29

"Y ou're the killer the cops are looking for, aren't you?" Margery asked.

Helen screamed at the sight of her landlady in the morning light. Margery was sitting at the kitchen table, wearing the Marlins cap Helen had swiped from Mireya's bedroom. Margery had a crazed grin. The air around her glittered with anger. Cigarette smoke surrounded her like fire from an ancient sacrifice.

"I thought I'd rescue this from the trash, in case the police need it for evidence," Margery said. "Those aren't strawberry jelly spots on that cap, are they? Those are blood flecks from that poor little photographer."

Helen felt dizzy, and grabbed the edge of the table. She'd crawled out of Margery's guest bed feeling like she'd been slammed in the head with a shovel. Funny, she didn't remember drinking that much wine last night. The three of them—Phil, Helen and Margery— had celebrated the departure of the crooked 2C renters. Helen had been happy when she'd fallen into Margery's guestroom bed at two in the morning. She didn't care that she'd missed supper.

This morning, she craved coffee.

"Don't stare like a halfwit," Margery said. "Answer me. Where did you get this hat? Is it off the dead girl?"

"No," Helen said. "Her head was—"

"Her head was a bloody mess because she'd been beaten to death," Margery said. "You were there, weren't you?"

"How did you—?"

"How did I figure it out? I saw this morning's *Sun-Sentinel.*"

Margery slapped the paper down on the table. Helen jumped.

"The police composite drawing of the 'person of interest' is on the front page," her landlady said. "The witnesses got the height right, but the rest wrong. You don't weigh two hundred pounds, and you're not a man. But you did come home wearing a baseball cap for the first time in your adult life, and you sure as hell are no Marlins fan. That red mark on your upper lip was where you had the mustache, isn't it? You think it's funny to screw around with a crime scene?"

"No," Helen said in a small voice. Her head was ringing from Margery's lecture. She desperately needed coffee. She reached for the pot, but Margery stepped between Helen and the kitchen counter.

"No coffee until I get a straight answer. What were you doing yesterday?"

"I tried to save Mireya, but I was too late," Helen said. "Phil and I drove to her town house. She was already dead when we got there, and her place was ransacked. There were neighbors all over the com-

281

plex. We had to get out of there, so I disguised myself."

"Did you find anything?" Margery asked.

"I don't know. Maybe. I found the wedding tape. I think Mireya was blackmailing the killer and that's why she was murdered."

"Has Phil seen it?" Margery asked.

"He was getting the Jeep while I found the tape. I slipped it into my purse."

"You didn't tell him?"

"We were too busy running for the highway. Then I forgot."

"Oh, you forgot, did you?" Margery's voice dripped sarcasm. "What a surprise that Phil doesn't know about that tape. He'd go straight to the police and probably lose his license. We can at least save him from himself. I've got a VCR right here. Let's take a look at that tape."

"It won't work in a regular player. It's a MiniDV tape," Helen said. "Do you have a camcorder that takes one?"

"No, but I think Peggy does."

"She's not home," Helen said.

"Then we'll go to her apartment and borrow it."

"You just can't walk into her place—"

"I can," Margery said. "I have a key, remember? But I won't. I'll call her at work and ask first—not that breaking and entering would bother you. But Peggy has this wonderful invention called a cell phone."

Margery punched a speed-dial number on her phone. "Peggy, is that you? Do you have a camcorder that takes MiniDV tapes? Can I use it? No, no, I don't want to video anything. I want to look at a tape. The camcorder has a display screen, right? Good. I'll look for it in the hall closet. Thanks."

Margery hung up her phone. "Now you can have that coffee while I get the camcorder."

Helen's hands were shaking so badly, she poured herself a cup over the sink. The coffee had cooled by the time Margery returned, but her landlady was still boiling mad. Helen kept staring at the teal Marlins cap.

"What are you staring at?" Margery said.

"I've never seen you in any color but purple," Helen said.

"I am wearing purple shorts," Margery said. "But these teal caps are classics. They go for twenty-five bucks on Amazon and eBay. Too bad this one was ruined by blood. Now, get that tape."

Helen fished it out of her purse. She was relieved when her landlady removed the ball cap and tossed it into the trash for the second time.

"Let's make sure I don't record over this." Margery popped the tape in the camera and opened a three-inch display screen on the camcorder. A shot of Honey with her sister, Melody, fussing over the bride's veil appeared.

"I think that was some of the first video Mireya took," Helen said. "That's in Honey's bedroom."

"Now, about when did the murder happen?" Margery asked.

"The last time anyone saw King alive was just before the toast by the best man. That would be almost an hour later."

Margery fast-forwarded through endless views of the bride, the ceremony, and the receiving line. Finally, the camera was on a man holding a glass of champagne.

"Is that him?" Margery asked.

"Yes," Helen said.

The camera swung toward the head table. Honey was smiling at her wedding party. The groom's seat was empty, but Honey didn't look worried.

Then the camera tilted. The next part was an out-of-focus jumble, before the camera settled on a blonde in a blue dress. She was arguing with King. They stood by the edge of the pool. Helen could see a close-up of a blue star on her back. King's hair was plastered to his forehead, and he swayed as he talked. His back was to the pool. His face was red and sweating. The blonde gestured angrily and waved her arms. King laughed. It sounded harsh, even with the tinny camcorder speakers.

The blonde pushed him, and King toppled into the pool with a tremendous splash. He thrashed in the water, clearly panicked. The blonde backed away to keep from getting wet. King managed to grab the pool edge with one hand. The blonde stomped on his hand.

King screamed and fell back into the water. The blonde watched him struggle. Blood trailed in the water from his damaged hand. The blonde turned her back on King and walked away. Helen could see her clearly. That was Phoebe.

The camera stayed trained on the man's struggles, until King went quiet and floated facedown. Water ballooned out the jacket of his ugly tux, and he slowly sank to the bottom.

"He's dead. Phoebe killed him," Helen said. "But Mireya is guilty, too. She watched him die when she could have saved him. No wonder she didn't go to the police. This video is proof Miguel Angel is not guilty. I could enjoy my wedding a lot more if I knew he was in the clear."

"And how are you going to do that?" Margery said.

"I'm going to talk with Phoebe."

"Alone! Are you nuts?" Margery said.

"Nope, I'm not going alone. You're driving me. You don't have to come in. You can wait in the car."

"Like hell I will," Margery said. "Who do you think you are, the Lone Ranger? Even he had Tonto."

"Okay, *Kemo Sabe*, will you drive me to Phoebe's condo?"

"Where does she live?"

"Near Commercial and Bayview in north Lauderdale," Helen said.

"Ritzy neighborhood for an assistant hairdresser," Margery said. "How does she afford it?"

"I don't think it's from salon tips," Helen said.

"Do you have that Hendin Island homicide detective's card?" Margery asked.

Helen found it in the bottom of her purse. "He's in the Crimes Against Persons Unit and his name is Richard McNally."

"Good. If anything goes wrong, I'll call him on my cell phone."

It was a tense half-hour ride to Phoebe's condo. Helen was glad Margery drove a big car. She hugged the door, but there still wasn't room for the two of them and Margery's anger.

Phoebe lived in a ten-story pink condo on the Intracoastal Waterway, with an ocean view from the upper floors. The view from the street was not as picturesque. The lawn and circular drive were piled with wood and rusting metal. The fountain and flowers were hidden by a noisy generator and a Dumpster overflowing with construction material. One-third of the building had a skeleton of scaffolding. Metal stages, like those used by window washers, hung at the seventh and third floors. Brown-skinned men with jackhammers tore at the concrete balconies and shouted at one another in Spanish.

"Are they building this place or tearing it down?" Helen asked.

"I'm guessing they're replacing the rebar," Margery said. "That's the ridged steel bars used in reinforced concrete. This salty ocean air destroys them. When the rebar goes bad, it has to be removed, then replaced and new concrete poured over it. These condo owners are looking at monster assessments. Do you know what unit she lives in?"

"Seven-seventeen," Helen said.

"How are you going to get up there? Most condo elevators require special keys. I see a security guard."

"He's reading a magazine," Helen said. "If this condo has a big assessment, buyers are going to be hard to find, right? What if I say I'm getting married and I'm looking at a condo for sale."

"Finally, you have a smart idea." Margery parked the Lincoln in a guest spot and waved at the guard, who stayed engrossed in his magazine. "There are always places for sale in these big buildings. Let's look around the grounds first."

They followed a path to the fenced pool, which jutted out over the Intracoastal. A crooked palm tree cast a grudging circle of shade on the concrete deck. Only one woman was out by the pool. She'd dragged her towel-draped chaise longue into the shade circle. The blonde, wearing a red bikini, was lying on her belly. Her bra clasp was undone to avoid a tan line on her back. The star tattoo was visible. A plastic water bottle the size of an oxygen tank sweated next to the chaise, along with a pair of black heels. Were those the same shoes that killed King's last hope of rescue?

"I think that's Phoebe by the pool," Helen whispered. "I'm going to talk to her."

"Don't let her back you into that pool," Margery said. "She's dangerous. Take a weapon."

"Like what?" Helen said. She could hardly hear Margery over the stutter of the jackhammers.

"That purse you have looks pretty hefty. Hit her with that. And carry this." She handed Helen a two-foot section of rusty rebar.

Helen slid the rebar into her purse so only a small piece stuck out, then strolled toward the pool gate. The jackhammers suddenly went silent as Helen opened the gate. She stood over Phoebe's chaise. The sun-roasted killer seemed to be asleep.

"Phoebe!" Helen said in the deafening silence.

Phoebe sat straight up and grabbed her bra to cover her bare breasts.

"Nice to see you again," Helen said, sitting in a deck chair next to her. "Florida unemployment must pay well if you can afford this luxurious condo. Did King buy this, or have you found someone else to blackmail?"

"I don't know what you mean," Phoebe said. Her voice was cold enough to chill the pool.

"Of course you do," Helen said. "You pushed King into his own pool, then stomped his hand when he tried to crawl out. You watched him drown."

"I don't know what you're talking about," she said.

"Sure you do."

"Prove it." Phoebe was a study in sunburned defiance.

"I have the wedding video," Helen said. "You have a star part in King's life and death."

"You never did make sense," Phoebe said.

"I mean the star tattoo on your back. It was in the newspaper ads when you danced at King's strip club."

Phoebe turned her back and said, "There's no tattoo there."

"Sure there is. It's on your—"

Phoebe grabbed a high heel, swung around abruptly and aimed for Helen's eye. The bikini top fell on the pool deck. Helen ducked and caught the blow on her head. Something warm dripped down her forehead, but Helen was too furious to notice. She swung her leather purse and knocked Phoebe flat onto the chaise. Phoebe took a second swing at Helen, using the hefty water bottle as a bat. Helen dodged it and nearly fell into the pool. She carefully backed away, anxious to avoid the water.

Helen reached for the rebar in her purse and swung the rusty metal at Phoebe's smooth, tanned legs. She connected, leaving a long, nasty scrape. Phoebe screamed, but no one heard her over the pounding jackhammers. She picked up the chaise and threw it at Helen. Helen easily sidestepped it. Waving the rebar like a sword, Helen aimed for Phoebe's ankles, trying to drive her away from the pool.

Phoebe leaped up on an umbrella table. The table tipped under her weight. Phoebe hung by the umbrella pole, six feet over the brown, polluted Intracoastal.

Helen whapped Phoebe's fingers with the rebar. The bare-breasted killer screamed and dropped straight into the dirty water. Phoebe splashed around, then swam to the condo's concrete seawall and tried to climb out. Margery was there with a tire iron.

"Put one finger on that concrete before the cops get here and I'll smash it to pieces," Margery said.

Helen heard the wail of sirens and felt dizzy with relief. She put her hand to her forehead. It was red with blood. Black spots formed at the edge of her vision, and she swayed in the heat.

"Don't you dare faint, Helen Hawthorne," Margery yelled. "Are you a woman or a wuss?"

Chapter 30

Helen managed not to faint like an overgrown Victorian maiden. She clung to the pool fence until the paramedics took her to the emergency room. She was grateful to lie on the gurney.

"Head wounds bleed freely," Margery told her, as the paramedics loaded her into the ambulance. Helen didn't find that reassuring.

Margery was allowed to see Helen in the ER two hours later. "The doctor says the X-ray of your head revealed nothing," she said. "I could have told her that."

"I think she meant I don't have a concussion," Helen said. "The doc put butterfly bandages over the wound. Those will look lovely with my wedding dress."

"Don't worry," Margery said. "The veil will cover them."

"But what about my hair?" Helen said. "She shaved off a patch."

"Your boy-wonder stylist can hide that by parting your hair on the left," Margery said. "I'll pick up the emergency room bill. I should just adopt you and put you on my insurance."

"You'd make a better mother than the one I have," Helen said.

"I'm hoping to marry you off and get you out of my hair," Margery said.

A gray-haired man wheeled a cart into their cubicle. "Juice?" he asked. "Crackers?"

Helen took a carton of juice and a pack of graham crackers, but her hands were so shaky Margery had to open them for her.

"I think this is dinner," Helen said, and sat up too fast. The little room shifted and the privacy curtain danced. "Ohmigod. Kathy and Tom are due in Friday and I wanted to get some food for them this afternoon."

"I've already thought of that," Margery said. "I sent Phil to the supermarket with a list of things they'll probably need. I got a call from your sister. They're making good time. They may get here a day early, on Thursday, depending on the traffic."

"Good. Did the cops arrest Phoebe?" Helen asked.

"You bet they did," Margery said. "I had them contact that Hendin Island detective, Richard McNally. He came rushing over to Phoebe's condo. I gave him the wedding video. Took a while to calm him down. He's not happy about you stumbling around in a murder scene. You're darn lucky he's pretending to believe my story that you found that video on the sidewalk outside Mireya's town house. I didn't mention Phil. He needs to stay clear of this."

There was a knock on the cubicle door. Helen said, "It's probably the hospital after more of my blood. All they've done is stick me with needles."

"Maybe they can give you a shot of common sense," Margery said.

Helen was surprised to see Richard McNally in the doorway. The white-haired detective was taller than she remembered. She hadn't forgotten those steel blue eyes. Now they were lit with an angry fire.

"May I have a minute with Miss Hawthorne?" he asked.

"You can have her as long as you want," Margery said. "I need a cigarette."

"Are you after my blood, too?" Helen asked McNally.

The lanky detective leaned against the wall and crossed his arms. "No, but I should be," he said. "What were you thinking, going after that young woman alone?"

"I had Margery with me," Helen said.

"An old woman. She can really protect you against a seventeen-year-old killer."

"Did Phoebe confess?" Helen asked.

"Oh yes. Once she knew we had the video, she decided to talk. She didn't want a lawyer. She believes she'll get away with murder because she was underage and sexually assaulted by the victim."

"It's going to be hard to figure out who the victim is here, isn't it?" Helen said.

"Mireya was definitely a victim," McNally said. "But I don't think there will be much sympathy for King Oden."

"Was Phoebe blackmailing him?"

"For more than a year. She got close to half a million dollars out of him. When King got engaged, he quit giving her money. She threatened to tell his blog competitors, and he laughed at her. She made one last attempt to convince him at his wedding. He said he'd married a woman with class and nobody would believe a hooker with a tramp stamp."

"I thought tramp stamps were lower-back tattoos," Helen said.

"I don't think he was in any position to argue. He was trying to get out of the pool. He had one hand on the pool edge when she slammed him with her spiked heel and said, 'I'll show you a tramp stamp.'"

"And he fell back into the pool and drowned," Helen said.

"While she turned her back on him. That's a cold woman, Miss Hawthorne. A jury might have let her get away with killing him if she hadn't beaten that little photographer. The only thing Mireya was guilty of was greed."

"Her death was sad," Helen said. "And useless."

"Don't think for one second I believe you found that wedding video on the sidewalk," he said. "I ought to throw you in jail, but I hear you're getting married on Saturday. I'll give you a wedding present: I'm not going to press charges."

"Thank you," Helen said.

"You get one pass from me, and one only," he said. "If I find out you've 'accidentally stumbled' onto any more murders, you'll be a guest of the Broward County correctional facility. Got that?"

"Yes," Helen said.

"Good. Keep your nose out of police business. And heaven help your husband."

McNally walked out. The room felt suddenly emptier. Helen was freezing in the cold cubicle. She crept to a cart in the hall piled with hospital blankets and helped herself to three. She was shivering under the thin blankets when she heard a man shouting above the chaos of the emergency room.

"And I say she's my fiancée and I can, too, see her." That was Phil.

"Sir, if you'll calm down," a nurse said in a professionally soothing voice. "I don't want to call security."

Helen sat up, grabbed the edge of the gurney to keep from falling, and stuck her head out of the cubicle. "Phil!" she cried.

"Do you know this man?" the nurse asked her.

"It's okay," Helen said. "We're getting married. He'll be paying the hospital bills after Saturday."

Phil loped over to Helen's cubicle, his tanned face several shades paler with anger. "What did you do to yourself?" he asked between gritted teeth.

"I had a little accident with a high heel," Helen said.

"Bull! You went off alone to catch a killer."

"I wasn't alone. I had Margery with me," Helen said.

"A seventy-six-year-old bodyguard. Then I had no reason to worry."

"Hey! She's tough," Helen said.

"You're damn right I'm tough." Margery materialized in the crowded cubicle, trailing the scent of cigarette smoke. "I can take care of myself—and your wife-to-be."

"I'm sorry, Margery," Phil said. "It's not your fault. This is between Helen and me. I thought we were in this together, Helen. Instead, you went running off to meet a killer without telling me. I found out what happened when I saw a breaking news story on television. I was putting the groceries away in your apartment and nearly dropped the eggs."

"The story is on TV?" Helen said. "Already?"

"Somebody at the condo called Channel Seven. Phoebe was nearly naked, and that didn't hurt. The station ran a shot of the cops helping the topless murderer out of the water. They called her the Bikini Killer. I saw you at the edge of the shot, holding on to the pool fence. You had blood running down your face."

"You could tell it was me?" Helen said.

"I could, because I'm the man who's going to marry you. I doubt if anyone else will recognize you. I drove to the condo, and the guard said you'd been taken to the hospital. I was afraid you were badly hurt."

Phil's blue eyes showed white all around, like a frightened horse's. Helen took his hand and kissed it. "Phil, I'm sorry if I upset you. I promise I will never, ever, chase a murderer without you."

"You better promise," Phil said. "Margery, you're my witness."

"I can't believe the Bikini Killer story has made the news already," Helen said.

"Made it? It's the lead local story on three stations," Phil said. "Only one channel had the arrest on tape, but the other stations rushed over to King's Sexxx and interviewed all the strippers who claim they knew Phoebe. There were so many half-naked women, I'm surprised Phoebe ever had room to dance on the stage."

"Then the word is out. Miguel Angel is safe," Helen said.

A nurse in hospital scrubs entered the room with a pile of papers. "I have your instructions and release," she said, "plus a prescription for pain medication. If you have a severe headache or vomiting, come back to the emergency room."

Helen signed the papers.

"I'll take her to the pharmacy for the painkillers," Margery said.

"Skip the pharmacy," Helen said. "I want to go home." She scrubbed at the dried blood on her face with a hospital washcloth. "Maybe I should put on some makeup."

"You'll look better if you don't try to cover up the damage," Margery said. "My car has air-conditioning. I'll drive her home, Phil."

"I'll pick up something for dinner," Phil said. "Mexican food okay for both of you?"

"Chicken burrito for me," Helen said.

"I want a side of guacamole," Margery said. "The nice thing about wearing a minister's robe is I don't have to watch my figure."

Helen was silent on the ride home. Her head throbbed. When they got to the Coronado, she was glad that Peggy and Cal weren't home. She didn't feel like talking to anyone.

Helen saw a blank envelope taped to Phil's door. Inside was a bill for $110 for the rental of a tux, cummerbund, shirt and shoes. A note from Cal said, "Thought you'd want to pay this, since it's your wedding."

"Of all the—" Helen said.

"What's wrong?" Margery said. Helen handed her the bill.

"Don't that beat all?" Margery said. "He wants Phil to pay for his tux. I think I'll raise his rent a hundred and ten dollars. That guy is too cheap to live."

"Don't bother," Helen said. "He is cheap, but he pays his rent on time and he's quiet."

Phil came up the walkway, carrying a fat takeout bag. Helen was hungrier than she thought. She finished the last crumb of food, then yawned.

"I've had a long day," Helen said. "I need some sleep."

Phil walked her to Margery's doorstep. Helen kissed him. "This time Saturday, we'll be married," she said dreamily.

"Can't wait," Phil said, kissing her again.

"One last kiss," Helen said, "then I go inside."

"Oh, wait," Phil said, "I forgot this letter. It was in the mailbox for you."

Helen opened it and grabbed on to the doorknob for support.

"What's wrong?" Phil asked. "You're the color of putty."

"It's another threatening letter. This one says, *YOU HAVE BROKEN YOUR PROMISE AND WILL DIE.* It's postmarked Berlin, Maryland. Where's that?"

"That's another town near the Eastern Shore," Phil said. "All the other letters are from the same area. I googled them."

"Aren't Josh and Jason, the ousted renters, from around there?" Helen asked.

"Close," Margery said. "Jason said he lived in Ocean Pines, Maryland."

"Maybe they've been sending those letters," Helen said.

"I doubt if they're smart enough," Margery said.

"Who cares? They're gone," Phil said. "Quit worrying. We're getting married Saturday. Nothing can stop us now."

Chapter 31

That bruise is a beaut this morning," Margery said. "Nice shade of purple. My favorite color."

Helen had to fight to keep from telling her hostess to shut up. "I'd better see Phil," she said. "He wants to talk about the wedding music." When she first saw the purple-red knob on her forehead, she'd wanted to cry. Helen downed two aspirin and carried her coffee outside to the umbrella table.

"Head still hurt?" Phil asked as he kissed her gently on the cheek.

"A little," Helen said.

"That means 'a lot.' I'm learning to speak wife. I've picked out the music, if you're ready."

Helen nodded and thought her head would roll off her shoulders.

"We can start with a classic, 'Wonderful Tonight.' Clapton wrote it for his future wife, Pattie. Then there's 'Promises.' And 'Layla.' All Clapton, all night."

"Okay," Helen said.

"What's wrong? You don't sound enthusiastic."

"Nothing's wrong," Helen said.

"That means something's wrong," Phil said.

"If something was wrong, I'd say so," Helen said.

"No, you wouldn't."

"I wish Clapton hadn't left his wife Pattie for another woman. Their marriage failed. That song is bad luck."

"Says who?" Phil said.

"You told me to speak, and now you don't want me to talk."

"Helen, you know I love Clapton—and you, too, of course. But you're being unreasonable."

"I am not!" Helen said.

Margery stormed out of her kitchen into the yard. "What's going on? I could hear you two arguing."

"Helen's having a case of bridal nerves," Phil said.

"That's not true. I don't think a song Eric Clapton wrote for a woman he dumped later is the right music for our wedding."

"Good musicians have messy lives," Phil said.

"What's the song?" Margery asked.

"'Wonderful Tonight,'" Phil said. "Clapton wrote it for Pattie Harrison."

"Who was married to George and hit on by Mick Jagger," Helen added.

"Nice bit of rock-and-roll history there, Helen," Margery said. "But that was the sixties, and from what anyone can remember through the drug haze, they were all in bed together. Ozzie and Harriet didn't write many songs. Phil, why don't you feed the cat while I talk to Bridezilla?"

Margery waited until Phil was inside. Then she

lit a cigarette and turned on Helen. "What's wrong with you? You're quibbling about songs because of the sex lives of the musicians? Are you insane?"

"I'm worried," Helen said. "I'm afraid something will go wrong with this wedding. The last one I went to, the groom was murdered."

"Too bad the groom was a freaking pervert," Margery said, "but that had nothing to do with his murder. I'm sure he drowned because they played Handel's *Water Music*. I'm worried, too. I'm afraid Phil is going to walk out when you start this crazy talk. Then I'll be stuck with you till death do us part. That will be soon, because I'm ready to strangle you. What music did you have at your first wedding?"

"The usual," Helen said. "Wagner's bridal chorus from *Lohengrin*—'Here Comes the Bride'—and Mendelssohn's 'Wedding March' after the ceremony."

"No wonder your marriage failed," Margery said. "Wagner had three wives. Mendelssohn died of multiple strokes at age thirty-eight. Talk about unlucky. That music doomed your marriage before you even left the church."

"You're being ridiculous," Helen said.

"I am, but you're not?" Margery's hair was wreathed in blue smoke. She was so angry, Helen couldn't tell if the smoke was coming from the burning cigarette or the irate landlady.

"You've had plenty of time to go over the playlist," Margery said. "But you let Phil pick out the songs, then second-guessed him and threw a hissy fit. Phil may excuse your behavior as bridal nerves. I think you're a jerk. You go apologize, then agree on some songs, or I'll provide my own music. I'll sing, 'Here comes the bride, short, fat and wide' when you march down my aisle. And don't think I won't."

Margery marched back into her apartment. Helen followed and quietly changed into her work clothes, combed her hair and put on some lipstick. Then she knocked on Phil's apartment door. He was watching Thumbs chow down. The cat crunched his food happily. Helen put her arms around Phil. "I'm sorry. Please forgive me. 'Wonderful Tonight' is the perfect wedding song."

"Are you sure?" Phil asked.

"I've never been more sure about anything in my life," she said, and kissed him.

Thumbs patted her leg with his huge paw, demanding fresh water. Helen filled his dish, then said, "It's nine thirty. I need to be at work."

"I'll drive you," Phil said.

"I'll walk," she said. "You give Thumbs some quality time. He'll miss us when we're on our honeymoon."

It was another sultry South Florida summer day. Helen studied the sky, but there was no sign of rain. She opened the salon door to a thrilling sight:

Every stylist's chair had a client. The couches in the waiting area were filled with customers. Ana Luisa was running a customer's credit card through the machine. The phone was ringing. Blow-dryers roared. Carlos dashed around the salon like a hummingbird—fetching towels, robes, glasses of water.

"Look at this," Helen said. "The regular customers are back."

"The celebrities are booking again," Ana Luisa said. "Kim Hammond wants an appointment immediately, and so does LaDonna. *People* magazine wants a story about Miguel Angel's ordeal. *Vogue* is interviewing him Monday."

"Helen!" Miguel Angel said. "I have you to thank for this." He hugged her. "What happened to your forehead?"

"Phoebe got nasty when I confronted her, and she clobbered me. I hit her with an iron bar."

"Good," he said. "I saw her arrest on television. She was naked, the slut."

He fussed with Helen's hair and said, "I should be able to cover that. Are you well enough to work? Maybe you should go home and rest."

"I'm fine," Helen said. "I'm lifting teacups, not breaking rocks."

Miguel Angel turned back to his client, a fortyish woman with light brown hair and an air of authority. "We're doing your color today, Jennifer?"

"Right," Jennifer said.

"Are you getting a cut?"

"That depends on you," Jennifer said. "I don't make that decision."

Under the roar of the blow-dryers, Helen whispered to Ana Luisa, "Did Miguel's hair dryer suck out her brains?"

"Hardly," Ana Luisa said. "She's a partner with a big law firm. You didn't see her when she first started coming here. She had dyed black hair and a short, frizzy perm. Looked like a grandmother. Miguel Angel's remake took fifteen years off her."

Helen brought Jennifer a Diet Coke, and she opened her briefcase to read legal papers. Two hours later, she left the salon looking regal and confident.

The afternoon passed quickly. Helen poured water, sliced lemons and fetched magazines.

At four o'clock, Ana Luisa came over to her. "Margery is on the phone. Your sister says she and her family can stay at a hotel in Boynton Beach tonight or come see you in half an hour."

"Tell Kathy to come to Lauderdale," Helen said. "I'll see her about six thirty."

"You'll leave now," Miguel Angel said. "You won't be in tomorrow, either. You'll spend the day with your sister."

"But—"

"I don't want to see you until Saturday," Miguel

305

Angel said. "Show your face before then, and you're fired. Now leave."

Helen left.

Kathy and Tom's blue minivan was pulling into the Coronado parking lot when Helen arrived. A weary-looking Kathy climbed out of the passenger seat. Tom helped the two children out of the minivan. "Watch it, Tommy," he said. "Be careful of your little sister."

"Helen, are you okay?" Kathy was a little plumper than Helen remembered, and her temples were touched with gray. "What happened to your head?"

"It's just a bump," Helen said.

"Looks like it hurt," Tom said. His blond hair was thinner, and his glasses were thicker. But he still had that sweet smile. Helen liked the way he held Kathy's hand after more than a decade of marriage. Her sister seemed happy, a woman content with her life.

Tom picked up a sleepy Allison. Helen's niece had downy dark curls and silky skin.

"This is Phil," Helen said, as if she was unveiling a prize.

Phil gave his lopsided grin. "Can I help carry something?"

"Those two red suitcases," Tom said.

"You don't mind that we're early?" Kathy said.

"I have tomorrow off," Helen said. "We can spend it by the pool."

306

"I wanna see the ocean," Tommy Junior said. He was a sturdy boy with his father's blond hair and his mother's serious eyes.

"Your daddy can take you," Kathy said. "Your aunt Helen and I will talk."

"And drink wine," Helen said. "Let me show you to your apartment." She unlocked the door to her place and handed Kathy the key. Most of the living room floor was taken up by an inflatable green gator.

"Is that your gator?" Tommy Junior asked.

"No, it's yours," Phil said. "The Little Mermaid sand castle set is for Allison." He set down the suitcases.

"And what do you say?" Kathy prompted.

"Thank you, Uncle Phil," Tommy and Allison chorused.

Margery appeared in the doorway, wearing purple shorts. Her wraparound sandals showed off tangerine-painted toes. "Have you met my land-lady, Margery Flax?" Helen asked.

"I've certainly talked to her," Kathy said. "Nice to finally see you. Thanks for taking care of my sister."

"She needs a full-time keeper," Margery said. "I'll be glad to marry her off. Would you like a drink?"

"Wine for me," Kathy said.

"Beer, please," Tom said.

"I'm hungry," Tommy Junior whined. "When do we eat?"

"In a few minutes," Phil said. "Your hot dogs are on the barbecue grill."

Kathy fixed two plates for Allison and Tommy. The little boy wolfed down his hot dog and asked for another. Allison took one bite and put her head down on the table.

"She's sound asleep," Kathy said.

"We have roll-away beds for the kids," Helen said. "I'll help you set them up."

The two women went back to Helen's apartment. "Phil is definitely a keeper," Kathy said as she unfurled a sheet. "Much more thoughtful than Rob. This is a new beginning. Tom and I are so happy you found Phil."

"Me, too," Helen said.

"Then what's wrong?" Kathy said.

"Nothing." Helen stuffed a pillow into a case.

"That means something. Don't lie to your sister."

"I just feel uneasy, that's all. I was hit on the head yesterday and it still hurts."

"Are you worried Rob will come back and cause trouble?" Kathy asked.

"He hasn't been seen in months," Helen said, plumping another pillow. "So my troubles are gone."

She turned to her sister. "Kathy, I'm afraid I'm making another mistake getting married again. I was crazy about Rob, and that marriage went wrong. What if I'm making another bad choice?"

"You're a different woman now," Kathy said.

"Do you remember how you acted when you married Rob? Mom pushed you into the wedding. I think she wanted Rob for herself."

"She sure loved him more than she did me," Helen said. "Mom will never forgive me for divorcing Rob. She sees all of my flaws, but none of his."

"Mom sees what she wants to see," Kathy said. "She never saw any of Dad's faults."

"Or floozies," Helen said.

"Do they use that word anymore?" Kathy asked, and giggled. "I can say this now, since you've changed. You were the original Bridezilla when you married Rob. Everything about that wedding had to be perfect—the flowers, the dresses, the reception. I begged you for a different style bridesmaid dress. That blue froufrou made me look fat. But you wouldn't listen. You said it was your day and nobody would notice the bridesmaids."

"Oh no." Helen blushed with shame. "It's too late to apologize."

"Marrying Rob was punishment enough," Kathy said. "I tried to warn you about him. I caught Rob kissing your maid of honor before the wedding. You said I was jealous."

"What a bitch I was," Helen said. "Kathy, you were right from the beginning. Rob was never faithful, but I didn't want to believe that. When I finally caught him with our next-door neighbor,

Sandy, it was like I woke up after a long illness. I suddenly saw a lot of things I'd tried hard not to notice."

"A skill learned at our mother's knee," Kathy said. "You're a better person, Helen. You've learned from your mistakes, and from working those jobs where nobody sucks up to you. I like you and so does Tom. This time, listen to your sister: Marrying Phil is the smartest thing you've ever done. There's no reason to feel uneasy about this wedding."

"I guess I'm not used to being happy," Helen said, and hugged her sister.

Chapter 32

Helen spent her last day as a single woman sitting by the pool with her sister, Kathy. They drank white wine, slathered each other with suntan oil and giggled for no reason.

"I can't believe you talked Tom into taking both kids to the beach," Helen said, pouring her sister more wine.

"Oh, I used a little persuasion," Kathy said. "Good thing Tommy and Allison are sound sleepers." She giggled again. "Phil is the real saint, wanting to go along with two screaming kids."

"He is a find," Helen said. "I couldn't see Rob volunteering to take his niece and nephew to the beach. I saw Tommy Junior hauling his inflatable gator out this morning. I'm glad you have a minivan. I don't think it would fit in a sedan."

"Tommy Junior slept with it last night," Kathy said. "I'm afraid he'll want to take it to school."

"Is Sister Philomena still teaching?" Helen asked. "She might think it's a long-lost relative."

"Helen!" Kathy said, and collapsed into more giggles.

When she finally quit, Kathy said, "Listen, Helen, I don't want to spoil the mood, but Mom is getting strange."

"She's always been strange," Helen said.

"No, I mean seriously off the rails. She's more religious than ever—the way old-school Catholics were fifty years ago. She picketed the church fund-raiser movie because she said it was obscene."

"What was the movie?" Helen said.

"*Gone With the Wind.* The Legion of Decency banned it decades ago as morally objectionable."

"I thought the Legion was disbanded in the 1980s."

"It was," Kathy said. "But Mom said moral standards last forever. She also stood up in church and screamed that Bethesda Miller was a sinner who should not take Communion because she was an unmarried mother. Father Martin tried to talk to her about charity, but Mom called him a corrupt compromiser."

"She's married to Lawn Boy Larry," Helen said. "This should be his problem."

"Mom moved out of Larry's house and went back to hers. She says sex without procreation is condemned by the pope. She wants to get some special dispensation to renounce her marriage vows and become a sister."

"Oh, Lord," Helen said. "Can she do that?"

"I don't think any religious order would take Mom. Sisters are different today. They have to love people as well as God. They have to be forgiving and kind. They're not like the horrors in *Sister Mary Ignatius Explains It All for You* anymore. Mom would never pass the psychological tests. Tom and I think we might have to put her away in a home. She's very disruptive at church."

"That's awful," Helen said.

"It's getting worse," Kathy said. "Mom is taking off without telling us. She'll disappear for three days to a week."

"Where's she going?" Helen said.

"She takes trips out of town. Mostly senior bus tours. Last time she went to the casinos in Tunica."

"Mom is gambling?" Helen asked.

"She won thirty-five dollars—and gave it to the church."

"Does she have a gambling problem?" Helen asked.

"No," Kathy said. "She just gets on a bus and disappears for a while. My big fear is she'll go somewhere without telling us and have a heart attack or something."

"How can I help?" Helen asked.

"You can't. But please understand if we have to put her in an institution."

"You'll have more than my understanding," Helen said. "I'll pay half the bills."

Helen hiccupped and realized she'd better quit drinking or she would have a hangover tomorrow. She nearly dropped her wineglass when she heard a high, squeaky voice shriek, "Mommy!"

"That's my name," Kathy said. "Don't wear it out."

Allison came running up in a pink ruffled swim-suit, carrying her Little Mermaid sand castle set. A tired Tommy followed, dragging his gator.

"You got some sun," Helen said.

"We saw a real fish in the ocean," Allison said. "Daddy said it was a snapper, but it didn't snap at me. We saw pelicans and I built me a sand castle and—"

"Easy now," Kathy said. "Don't trip over your tongue."

The kids had had a good time. Now they were tired and cranky. Kathy shooed them inside to shower and change while Uncle Phil broiled ham-burgers for dinner. Allison managed to eat half a burger before she fell asleep at dinner again. Tommy Junior wolfed down two, but looked sleepy.

Tom carried the kids to bed. "They're both asleep," he said. "I left the blinds open so we could check on them."

"Steaks are ready," Phil said. He was wearing a chef's apron and carrying a long-handled fork. Kathy, Tom, Helen and Phil settled in to juicy steaks, roasted potatoes, baked beans and tossed salad.

"Dinner is done to perfection," Tom said. "Sure beats road food."

They sipped their drinks contentedly and listened to the chirping crickets. Tom slapped at a mosquito, and Helen lit a citronella candle. Kathy caught her yawning in the candlelight.

"Time for you to go to bed," she said. "Tomorrow is an important day."

"Can I say good night to my niece and nephew?" Helen asked.

"I hope they're still asleep," Kathy said. "But you can peek at them through the blinds."

Helen looked at the sleeping children curled up in the roll-away beds. Tommy had his arm flung around the inflatable gator. "I can't believe how much Allison looks like you, Kathy," Helen said. "She even has your nose. Tommy Junior looks like a little angel."

"That's because he's asleep," his father said.

"Good night," Helen said. "And thank you both for being here."

"Wouldn't have missed it," Kathy said, and hugged her sister.

"Hey, do I get a hug, too?" Phil asked.

"If you walk me home," Helen said.

He kissed Helen at Margery's door. "This is our last night apart," Helen said. "Tomorrow, we'll be together forever."

The next morning, Helen opened the kitchen door to see her wedding day.

The sky was clear blue with a few cotton-ball clouds. The sun was warm, maybe a little too warm, but the air would be cooler at seven that evening. Helen watched Phil and her brother-in-law set the white rented folding chairs in rows. Long tables draped in white were grouped alongside the pool.

The two men were sweating in the sun, drinking beer and joking. Helen was pleased to see her groom getting along with Tom. Her brother-in-law had never criticized her ex-husband, but Helen knew Tom didn't like Rob. They rarely spoke, much less joked.

Her sister, Kathy, waded in the shallow end of the pool, splashing in the water with Allison, while Tommy Junior pretended to wrestle his inflatable green gator. They waved at Helen.

Margery carried out a basket of plastic forks and knives wrapped in napkins.

"Can't I do something?" Helen asked.

"Stay out of my way," Margery said.

Helen studied the bruise on her forehead in Margery's living room mirror. It was turning an ugly yellow-green. She paced and fretted and tried to read a magazine, and finally fell asleep. At three o'clock, her landlady woke her up. "It's time for you to get ready. I'll drive you to the salon."

"Phil can drive me."

"No, I need him to help set things up," Margery said.

Helen showered, threw on her jeans and a shirt. Margery dropped her off at the salon. "I'll come back for you at six," her landlady said.

"Here comes the bride," Ana Luisa said when she saw Helen. The phone rang and the curvy blond receptionist made a dive for it.

"The MTV dancers want an appointment with Miguel Angel next week," she said.

"The salon is so busy," Helen said. "Do you have time for me when there are paying customers waiting?"

"Let them wait," Ana Luisa said. "They wouldn't be here except for you. They could have made appointments earlier."

Miguel Angel greeted Helen with a kiss and a warm hug, a great compliment from a man who didn't like to be touched by clients.

"Wash Helen's hair, Carlos," he said. "I'll be finished in a minute."

He was blow-drying the hair of a fifty-something woman. "Well, what do you think?" he asked. He handed his client, Elaine Frances, a hand mirror so she could see the back of her hair in the salon mirror. She studied the cut, front and back.

"Perfect. Cheaper than a face-lift," Elaine said. "And no telltale scars. You're the only man for me."

Miguel Angel laughed. Carlos dusted off the chair, and Helen sat down.

"I'm not the only man for you, am I?" Miguel Angel said.

"No, but you're in the top five," Helen said. "Thanks for giving me yesterday off. Kathy and I had a good time."

"I'm glad," he said. "You enjoy your sister. You should spend more time with her."

Miguel Angel combed Helen's wet hair away from her face and began putting on her makeup. First, he carefully covered her face with foundation. "How is the wedding going?" he asked.

"I had a fight Thursday with Phil over something stupid," Helen said.

"Good," he said. "You've got that out of the way. Now you can enjoy your wedding." When Miguel Angel decided her face was evenly covered, he drew those startling dark lines at Helen's jawline, nose and under her cheekbones, the way he did for Honey. Then he began shading shadows with a triangular sponge into her round, rather flat face.

"I'm worried," Helen said.

"Why? You don't think Phil will leave you at the altar? Look up." He lined her eyelids with dark blue.

"No. But I can't get it out of my head that something will go wrong."

"It will," Miguel Angel said. "Keep looking up. No, don't blink." He swore softly in Spanish, then used a Q-tip to remove the smeared eyeliner. "Something always goes wrong at a wedding ceremony. Your best man will forget the ring. A baby will cry. The florist will forget to send a bouquet. But you'll still get married."

"My other marriage was a disaster," Helen said.

"But it's over. You're not that woman anymore. You are older and wiser and you've chosen a better man. Look up." Miguel Angel touched her eyelashes with mascara, then painted her lips raspberry red. He added a dusting of blusher.

"Now you are a blushing bride," he said.

"You had to paint that blush on," she said.

Miguel Angel pulled out his blow-dryer and pretended not to hear as he dried her dark hair in sections, pulling it smooth with his powerful wrists. He was finished in half an hour. She had a shining, shoulder-length mane, sleek and silky. There was no sign of the shaved patch of hair.

He dabbed under her eyes with a makeup sponge. "There," Miguel Angel said. "You look perfect."

Margery suddenly appeared behind him. "You do look damn good," she said. "I can't even see the bruise on your forehead."

Helen could. She felt as if that area was outlined in neon.

"I'll stop by your apartment and put on your veil just before the ceremony," Miguel Angel said. "You're getting married at seven, right?"

"How can you go to my wedding?" Helen asked. "Your salon is full of customers. Isn't that an MTV dancer sitting on your couch? And that brunette is a reality TV star—what's her name?"

"What's-her-name is right," Miguel Angel said. "She'll be forgotten in a month. None of them would be here if you hadn't cleared my name. Last week, I was poison. Now everyone wants me. They can wait."

Helen stood up and swayed slightly.

"What's wrong?" Margery asked. "Have you eaten anything today?"

"Coffee and aspirin," Helen said.

"Nourishing," Margery said. "You're going to eat before you collapse on me."

"But what about my lipstick?" Helen said.

"Here." Miguel Angel handed Helen a small pot of lipstick. "Take this. And eat something, please."

Margery dragged Helen to a nearby sandwich shop, where she picked at a chicken sandwich. After ten minutes, Margery said, "Have you finished torturing that chicken?"

"I can't eat," Helen said.

"Then let's go. You're getting married—for better or worse."

Chapter 33

"Ick!" Helen brushed away a cobweb on her shoulder. "That's a big hairy spider. Why are we taking the Dumpster route to your place?"

"Because I don't want you to see the yard before your wedding," Margery said. "It's a surprise."

"The spider was definitely a surprise," Helen said.

"Quit grumping," Margery said. "It's just a bug. The spider is harmless unless you're a fly."

The back route to Margery's apartment was a narrow walkway lined with items that should have been hauled to the dump ages ago—broken lawn chairs, an old water heater, a car tire and rusted yard tools, all wreathed in spook-house spider-webs.

"I could blindfold you and take you through the front entrance, but that would smear the paint job on your face." Margery unlocked the door to her laundry room, and she and Helen stepped around a laundry basket, an old lamp and a broken bedstead.

"I have to change into my ministerial robe," Margery said. "Put on your wedding dress and then we'll go outside."

"Do we get to use the door, or do I have to crawl out the window?" Helen asked.

"Don't be smart," Margery said. "Phil, Tom and Kathy worked all afternoon getting the yard ready for this wedding. I want you to look properly surprised."

"Were the flowers delivered?" Helen asked.

"Yes, and the wedding cake. The food is on the tables. Phil got the ice for the drinks. Peggy and Elsie are here and so are their escorts. Kathy, Tom and the kids are fine. Phil is changing into his tux. So far, he hasn't come to his senses and fled. Let me run my aging carcass through the shower and then you'll get married."

Helen washed the cobwebs off her arms and ran a washcloth over her legs. Her makeup was miraculously untouched. She took her wedding dress out of the plastic bag. She was surprised by its simple beauty, and glad Margery had bullied her into buying a new dress. A new life needed a fresh start.

She slipped on her dress and sandals and looked at herself in the mirror. Not bad for a forty-one-year-old bride, she thought. Not bad at all. Miguel Angel's makeup job took off at least ten years. She took her veil out of the box and checked it for wrinkles, then carefully refolded it.

Helen knocked on Margery's bedroom door and asked, "Would you zip me up, please?"

"Come in," Margery said.

Helen stopped dead at the sight of her landlady in a Roman collar and purple satin robe.

"Well, what do you think?" Margery asked, and twirled once.

"Incredible," Helen said.

"I think so, too." Margery zipped Helen's dress and latched the hook at the top, then said, "You look lovely."

"Thanks." Helen could feel her eyes tearing.

"Don't you dare cry, Helen, and ruin Miguel Angel's makeup. Go sit in the living room and I'll be right out."

A knock on the kitchen door announced the stylist's entrance. Margery led him into the living room. "You look beautiful," Miguel Angel said to the bride.

"Thanks to your makeup job," Helen said.

"I needed something to work with. How are you?" Miguel Angel asked.

"Nervous," Helen said. "But it will be over soon."

"It's a wedding, not a dental appointment," Margery said.

Miguel Angel dabbed at Helen's face with a makeup sponge and touched up her lipstick with a brush. "Should I put on the veil?" he asked.

"Yes," Helen said. "Though you did such a good job with my hair, it's a shame to cover it."

She opened the box and handed him the veil. He pinned it in place, and finally said, "Perfect. I'll go outside and sit down."

"There are no special covers for these chairs," Helen said.

"I like them better naked," Miguel Angel said, and gave her another hug.

"All ready?" Margery asked. "It's showtime."

Helen opened the kitchen door. The evening sun had turned the Coronado a delicate seashell pink. The light had the surreal clarity seen just before a subtropical sunset.

Helen's nephew, Tommy, was pink with sunburn, and sporting a new pair of khaki shorts and blue knit top. She could see the comb tracks in his damp hair. Tommy sat in a chair outside her apartment, solemnly guarding a pet caddy and a plate of cut-up cooked shrimp. The shrimp were Phil's wedding feast for the six-toed cat. Helen could see Thumbs through the bars of his cage, furiously trying to tear a white bow off his neck with his giant paws.

Tommy began feeding shrimp to the irate cat to distract him. Helen smiled at her nephew. "You're doing a terrific job, cat wrangler."

Tommy grinned and looked like a younger version of his father.

Helen finally saw the backyard. "It's gorgeous. The lights, the candles, the flowers. You ordered extra flowers didn't you?"

"A few," Margery said. "I grew my own bougainvillea."

The aisle was lined with blazing tiki torches. Each torch stand was decorated with a big white satin bow. The wedding bouquets were laid out on the umbrella table.

The long tables were laden with a feast. Helen

saw a roast turkey, a spiral ham, an enormous bowl of Peggy's special Thai chicken salad, brownies and the hors d'oeuvres that Helen had ordered. The two unsliced tomatoes plopped on a plate had to be from Cal. He brought the same thing to every Coronado party.

Sprays of purple bougainvillea and white orchids decorated the tables, and tall white candles in crystal holders cast a soft glow. The tiered wedding cake towered over its own flower-bedecked table, with Phil's groom's cake next to it. Helen could see the guitar had a tiny icing carrot as a pick. It looked like the one in the photo on the Clapton *Unplugged* CD.

A silver tray held a pile of donation cards.

"I love it," Helen said. The food, the flowers, even the candles had personal meaning. Her friends had given her a dream wedding, and it was so much better than her so-called perfect wedding to Rob.

All of the white chairs were filled by guests. Helen recognized some. Tom Senior was wearing a gray suit, and had Allison on his lap. She wore a frilly blue dress and pulled on her father's tie. Next to them were Helen's salon coworkers. Ana Luisa winked at Helen, and the two stylists waved. Carlos smiled, squeezed her hand as she passed, and said softly, "You look beautiful." The cluster of stern-faced men with short hair could only be Phil's cop friends. Others she didn't recognize.

The CD player burst into Clapton's "Wonderful Tonight."

Peggy was first down the aisle, with Pete the parrot on her shoulder. Both Peggy and Pete looked exotic in bright green. Pete eyed Peggy's bouquet with unnatural interest. Peggy was met at the top of the aisle by her dark-haired escort, Daniel. He looked like a male model in that tux, and he had the kind of curly hair that women liked to ruffle. Helen remembered her mother saying, "Handsome is as handsome does" and hoped that Peggy had finally found the love she deserved.

Helen's jaw dropped when she saw Elsie. Her senior bridesmaid wore a pale pink tea-length tent dress and dyed-to-match heels. Her hair was a soft silver tipped with pink. Elsie looked triumphant, as if she'd waited her whole life for this moment. She was escorted by a muscular hunk of beefcake in his midtwenties, with blond hair and a jaw you could use as a T-square. Helen could swear she saw his pecs rippling under the tux.

"Where did you get her escort?" Helen whispered to Margery.

"Quiet," Margery said. "He's rented for the occasion. He gets a bonus if he keeps her happy."

"How happy?" Helen asked.

"That's none of your business," Margery said.

Helen's sister, Kathy, wore orchid silk. She was met by Cal in the rented tux paid for by Phil. Cal looked uncomfortable. Kathy looked supremely happy. She smiled at her sister and winked.

Helen barely noticed. She saw Phil, her Phil, in his tuxedo. His silver-white hair was pulled into a ponytail, and he had a sprig of bougainvillea in his lapel. His shoulders were broad, and Helen thought they would be nice to lean on for the rest of her life. She walked down the aisle on shaky legs and smiled at her husband-to-be.

"You look wonderful tonight," she whispered. "Like James Bond at the casino."

"At Your Majesty's service," Phil whispered back.

"Shut up you two," Margery hissed, "so I can get you married." Her cigarette sent up smoke like incense. Margery crushed it, and glared the wedding guests into silence.

Helen held Phil's hand and stared into his blue eyes. Her marriage to Rob vanished into another dimension. That man had never existed. Now there was only Phil.

"We are gathered here this evening to celebrate the marriage of Helen and Phil," Margery said. "I thank God and anyone else that these two are finally getting married. Let's get the legal part over with. If anyone knows any reason why this couple may not marry, let that person now declare it."

A bent, wrinkled woman with a haystack of dark brown hair slowly stood up in the back row. She was dressed for a funeral, in deep black.

"Stop the wedding!" she screamed.

"I beg your pardon?" Margery said.

The woman clung to the chair back and shrieked, "That woman is getting married under false pretenses. Her name is not Helen Hawthorne."

"And how would you know?" Margery asked.

"Because I'm her mother," the woman said. "The wedding is off."

Epilogue

Is there a lawyer in the house?" Margery asked.

Peggy's strapping escort stepped forward. "I am," Daniel said. "But my specialty is contract law, so I'm not really up on domestic situations."

"Helen here has been going by another name," Margery said. "Can she still marry Phil?"

"I'd have to check the case law," Daniel said. "But as I understand it, you can call yourself anything you want, as long as there's no fraud involved."

The wrinkled old woman charged forward, her shriveled body powered by outrage. Her bird bones were bent and brittle-looking. Her too-thick brown hair was a dark nest. "But there is fraud," she insisted. "That woman is trying to fool God and man. She's still married in God's eyes."

"I'm divorced," Helen said.

"Do you have your decree?" Daniel asked.

"Uh, no," Helen said. "I never wanted to see it—or my ex—again."

"Religion aside, can she marry?" Margery said, dragging the subject back to the present.

"She changed her name to avoid the court ruling," Helen's mother said. "She didn't want to pay Rob what was rightfully his."

"Rob had no right to my money, or to me," Helen said. "My mother is a nutcase."

"Nutcase or not, is she right?" Margery asked Daniel.

"I'd have to research the law," he said. "But right now, I couldn't say if the wedding will be valid."

"Then I can't marry them," Margery said.

Helen could hear the guests murmuring in confusion. Thumbs set up a mournful howl, though that may have had more to do with the end of the shrimp. "It's okay, kitty," Tommy said, and tried to entertain the cat with the bow Thumbs had torn off his neck.

Kathy abandoned her bouquet and put her arms around her mother. "Mom, how did you get here?" she asked gently.

"I took the bus," her mother said.

"Why are you doing this?" Kathy asked. Helen could hear the tears in her sister's voice.

"What God has joined together, let no man put asunder," their mother screeched. "I warned her. I sent her letter after letter, but she didn't listen to me. She never did."

Helen stared in shock at the wrinkled little woman. "Mom?" she asked. "You sent those threatening letters? But you don't live in Ocean City, Maryland."

"Your great-aunt Marie does. She forwarded them from different towns in the area, the way I asked her to."

Aunt Marie? The old woman who talked about her operations when Helen met her one Thanksgiving years ago?

"But why?" Helen said.

"To save your immortal soul," her mother said. "I'd rather see you dead than burning in hell for divorcing your husband." Her mother's eyes were mad. She trembled and gasped for breath. Helen feared she might have a heart attack.

"Sit down, Mother, you're upset," Kathy said.

"Of course I'm upset," her mother said. "My daughter's soul is in peril."

"Grandma?" little Allison said. "Is Grandma sick?"

"I'd better call an ambulance," Margery said, and went inside to dial 911.

The paramedics arrived and carried Helen's mother to the hospital. "I'll go with her," Kathy said.

Phil put his arms around Helen and said, "What do you want to do?"

"I don't know," Helen said. "I feel like I've been turned to stone. I'll go to the hospital later, when I'm not so shocked."

"What do we do in the meantime?" Phil asked.

"Eat and drink, if we can't be merry," Helen said. "Otherwise, this food will go to waste. I'll tell the guests what happened."

"Maybe we could return the tuxes this afternoon and get our money back," Cal said.

Helen could hear Eric Clapton singing his song of hopeless love, "Layla." "You've got me on my knees," Clapton howled.

"Helen, we will get past this. We will marry," Phil said.

Helen slipped out of Phil's arms and sank down in a rented chair. Her fashionably painted face dissolved in her tears. "Do you really mean that?" she asked, trying to smile. "Do you still want to marry me when you'll have a crazy mother-in-law?"

"I'll have a beautiful sister-in-law, a terrific brother-in-law, an adorable niece and a nephew who wrestles alligators and wrangles cats."

Helen managed a half smile.

Phil got down on his knees and took her hand. "Sweetheart, we will get married. I swear it. I'll go to St. Louis, clear your name, and we'll live happily ever after."

Helen looked at the bare spot on her left hand where her wedding ring was meant to be. "You will?" she said.

"I promise, if it's the last thing I do." Phil kissed her.

Center Point Publishing
600 Brooks Road ● PO Box 1
Thorndike ME 04986-0001 USA

(207) 568-3717

US & Canada:
1 800 929-9108
www.centerpointlargeprint.com